MW01232307

DEADLY PAST

CHARLOTTE DEAN MYSTERIES BOOK 4

PHILLIPA NEFRI CLARK

To finding the love of family

CHAPTER ONE

"I HOPE THIS RAIN EASES UP BEFORE I GO HOME." ROSIE stared through the bookshop window at grey skies and a steady downpour. She'd sat there for the last few minutes, her fingers tapping on the arm of her wheelchair.

Charlotte was on her knees dusting shelves near the front of the shop. Books were piled beside her, ready to return to their allocated space. The whole day had been about cleaning and tidying rather than serving non-existent customers. Not that she blamed people wanting to stay home on such a dreary day.

"Don't like your chances. You'll be soaked before you reach the corner so why not take Lewis up on his offer to collect you?"

"Well, he has something on this evening and I would prefer he doesn't worry about me when he needs time to get ready."

From Rosie's demeanour, Charlotte knew she was concerned about whatever her fiancé was doing later on. After returning the books to the shelf, Charlotte stood and stretched. She longed to go for a run or a swim but Kingfisher Falls in the dead of winter wasn't offering much in the way of options to do either. She joined Rosie at the window, waving as Mr Lee strode past with his golden retriever.

"Good thing they both have raincoats!" Rosie said.

"I'm feeling a bit at a loose end with Trev away. How about I be super cheeky and drive you home and invite myself to stay for dinner? I'll order home delivery."

Rosie gazed up at her. "You are stressing about nothing."

"Sorry?"

"Trev is fine. Staying in the city during the trial rather than driving up and down the freeway in this weather day after day was a better option."

"I agree. And I know he is okay. But I'd like some company and if Lewis is busy…"

"We shall have a girl's night in." Rosie grinned. "I have a new bottle of Macedon Ranges gin waiting to open."

"Not one to say no, but I do have to drive home." Charlotte followed Rosie back to the counter.

"Better idea. You grab whatever you need for overnight and stay. Just use Trev's room which is freshly made up. Deal?"

"Deal. What shall I order for dinner?"

"Haven't had Italian for a while."

"Um…last Saturday night at Italia? Two couples. Table near the fireplace?" Such a lovely evening with Trev and Lewis.

"I meant at home. But it was a nice night, wasn't it? Seeing you and my son all lovey dovey makes me happy."

Lowering her head to cover her burning cheeks Charlotte busied herself shutting down the computer she used. Lovey dovey was an exaggeration, but they had held hands a few times during the dinner.

"Do you mind if I run upstairs to get an overnight bag?"

"You'll need to run if you are to avoid being drenched."

Rosie was right. Even between the back door of the book-shop and her landing at the top of the flight of stairs, the rain was heavy enough to soak her hair. She'd move her car to outside the bookshop so getting Rosie from her wheelchair into the passenger seat would be under cover for all but the last bit.

After packing a small overnight bag, she hesitated at the kitchen counter, her hand hovering over a large envelope and her brow furrowed. No harm taking it. She could decide later whether to ask Rosie for her thoughts. The envelope went into the bag.

———

Rosie's car was in the garage so Charlotte pulled as far up the driveway as possible. By the time they got inside the house, both were soaked through but laughing. Rosie was expert at moving between a car and her wheelchair but the rain made everything so slippery she'd nearly ended up on the ground.

"Drunk even before one drink." She unlocked the front door with water dripping down her face, her glasses in a pocket and hair loose from its bun. "I'll head to my bathroom to dry off and let you use the other one. You know where Trev's bedroom is."

Charlotte did. She'd stayed overnight once before, when there'd been a break-in and she'd wanted to remain close to Rosie. Trev still lived hours away at River's End then, but now he'd reclaimed his old bedroom until he found his own place. This week he'd spent as a key witness in a trial from his previous posting. Charlotte had gone down to the court on the first day as a witness as she'd been living in River's End during the events.

A few minutes later, dry and changed into warmer clothing, Charlotte searched for Rosie. She found her in the living room at the small bar, staring at a range of options. Rosie's two cats, Mellow and Mayhem, lifted their heads from food bowls outside the sliding door then returned to their dinner.

3

"Should we start with a gin and tonic, or straight into the cocktails?"

"If we start with cocktails I'll be sunk before dinner." Charlotte flopped onto an armchair. "Which is about an hour away."

As Rosie made drinks, the cats slipped back through the cat door. Mellow jumped onto the arm of Charlotte's chair to say hello but Mayhem didn't bother with as much as a glance in her direction. He stalked to Rosie, meowed once, then took himself off again.

"One day, Mr Mayhem, you will come for a cuddle." Charlotte said as he disappeared in the direction of Rosie's bedroom. "Does he like Lewis? I've not noticed."

"No more than anyone else. Trev is the only one apart from me to get the time of day from him, and then it is usually followed by a growl. But Lewis doesn't take it personally." Rosie handed Charlotte a drink and wheeled to the sofa. In a moment, she'd slid across to make herself more comfortable, lifting the footrest and holding her drink aloft. "Cheers, darling."

"Cheers."

The rain got heavier, if that was even possible, thundering on the roof. Mellow moved onto Charlotte's lap and made herself comfortable.

"You mentioned Lewis was doing something tonight. I hope not out in this?" Charlotte glanced at the window.

"No. He's at home but there is a real estate agent meeting with him." Rosie's lips tightened. "Cecil, you know, from the corner up from the bookshop."

"To talk about selling his house?"

Rosie nodded. "I can't imagine how it feels. He lived there with his lovely wife for so long. All their history is there. A lifetime together."

"I guess only Lewis knows how he feels, and it may bring up some bittersweet memories, but he loves you, Rosie. He proposed because he wants to spend the rest of his life as part

4

of your life. And you both deserve to retire in comfort after all the years of hard work."

The sheen in Rosie's eyes gave away a lot more than she'd said, but she nodded.

"You'll be there to support him if he finds it a bit over-whelming. Houses are filled with memories, aren't they?"

Even bad ones.

She'd put her mother's house on the market last week.

"Charlie, are you thinking about your mother?"

"Yes." She sighed. "Not that it is the same as Lewis'. Mum's house will be bulldozed and replaced with a trendy new one but at least the proceeds mean her future is paid for. Her care is expensive so selling is the best option and besides, nobody would ever live there in such a rundown place." Charlotte took a larger than normal mouthful of her drink to force her feelings about the whole thing back into the mental box she'd made for them.

"I'm sorry, darling. I didn't mean to raise something upsetting."

"Actually, I'm glad you did. There's a lot I've never told you about my past and I thought…well, I hoped, you might let me show you some of the things I have from Mum. I'd value your opinion."

Rosie's face lit up. "I should love to help out. Before or after dinner?"

CHAPTER TWO

EVEN ON SUCH A MISERABLE WET EVENING, HOME DELIVERY from Italia was on time. It was dropped off by Bronnie, who normally waited tables in the lovely little Italian restaurant.

"Nobody wants to come out tonight to eat in, so I'm doing deliveries rather than miss a shift." Bronnie refused the offer to come inside and hurried back to her car beneath an umbrella. Charlotte suggested it was time for a refill so Rosie obliged while she unpacked dinner.

At the table, they ate for a while in utter bliss. Since arriving in Kingfisher Falls, Italia was one of two restaurants on Charlotte's go-to list. The other was India Gate House, owned by the parents of her friend, Harpreet. One of the owners of Italia was Doug Oaks, who along with his wife Esther also owned a ladies boutique and were long-time residents and friends of Rosie. And now of Charlotte.

"They never fail." Rosie speared a strand of pasta. "So delicious."

"Do you know they have a new chef? So Doug can take a step back?"

Rosie's eyebrows raised. "I did not. Who is this person?"

Charlotte grinned. "We should have been consulted. Esther mentioned him. He's new to the region."

"Well, it is high time Doug and Esther did more than work. They've never had a chance to travel and that's something they talk about a lot." Rosie pushed her plate away with a sigh. "Great idea of yours. And speaking of you, what do you want to show me?"

The sudden emptiness in an otherwise-full stomach made Charlotte pause. Her history, childhood, all the difficulties, were things she'd rarely discussed with anyone. But until Rosie and Trev, there'd not been anyone she'd trusted enough to share with. Christie in River's End came close, but Charlotte had left before she was ready to speak of it all. Trev knew a bit and so did Rosie, but even Charlotte didn't know much.

"If you'd rather not…" Rosie put her hand on Charlotte's arm with an encouraging smile.

"I do. Let me get the envelope and we'll have a look."

She collected the envelope from her bag in the bedroom. It was odd being in here knowing this was where Trev lived now. His move home from River's End a few months ago had been occupied with crime solving rather than house-hunting to date.

Back at the table, she opened the envelope and slid the contents out. "I have more at home, but these are the items on my radar."

"And they were your mother's?"

"Yes. Well, they arrived in a box from Lakeview Care, not long after I moved here." Charlotte shook her head. "I was so afraid of what I'd find, I ignored most of the contents. Only the Christmas cards, which raised the question of the mysterious sender."

"Your sister."

"Yes, Zoe. And since discovering I am adopted, it makes things more complicated. I want to find her, but my mother can't or won't help. Short of another trip to Brisbane with specific questions which probably will be ignored, I am at a loss how to proceed."

"And you don't want to go back." Rosie said.

"Never if I can avoid it." Charlotte's recent visit to the place she'd grown up ended with despair and confusion. At least she'd got a few answers but they led to more questions. "I've been through all the letters. But not the baby book or address book and I could use another...perspective."

You mean support.

"You've never looked at your own baby book?"

"Not that I remember. And knowing Angelica...my mother, it will be either empty or covered in comments. There were also paperbacks filled with red editing."

Rosie's eyes lit up. "Was she ever a teacher, or editor?"

About to reply that Angelica flitted from job to job until quitting when Charlotte was old enough to work, a memory flickered to life. Her hand in Dad's, skipping beside him to pick up her mother from work one day. Opening the heavy, glassed front door to a huge room filled with books.

"She worked in a...library."

"You have a shocked expression on your face, darling. Have some more gin."

Charlotte sipped. She would have been young, under eight, because Dad left when she was eight. Mum was wheeling a library cart and humming as she put books where they belonged.

Rosie's phone rang and she went to answer it.

How had Charlotte not remembered this until now? If Angelica was a librarian, her obsession with correcting what she saw as mistakes in books made sense. Sense to a troubled mind. And perhaps this contributed to Charlotte's love of reading.

"Oh my goodness!" Rosie's voice cut through her thoughts. Rosie's worried, high pitched voice. Charlotte pushed herself to her feet and hurried to find her.

"We'll come now. Hold on, I'll tell Charlie," Rosie's face was white. "Charlotte, there's a fire near the bookshop. Lewis heard the fire trucks go past and got a notification."

Charlotte checked her phone. "I have the alert as well. Looks like the corner of the block, not us."

Rosie was listening to Lewis as Charlotte raced for her trench coat and handbag. She returned as Rosie hung up.

"We've been drinking so I can't drive. I'll run down." Charlotte was already making for the front door.

"Lewis is coming to get me so go. I won't be far behind. Be careful!"

Charlotte was on the street in a few seconds and almost slipped as she tore along the pavement. Water gushed across the concrete and she moved to the road for a firmer footing. Rain made visibility poor but she had to get to the bookshop.

She rounded the corner onto the main street and froze. Fire trucks filled the street and smoke plumed despite the downpour. Even from here, several blocks away, the sky had an eery red glow. She thought she saw Lewis drive past in the opposite direction. If the fire took hold, Rosie might lose her business. And Charlotte might lose what was in her apartment above.

Move, Charlie!

At the roundabout, a Country Fire Association vehicle—a branded car—was parked to prevent access to the next block. Cars on either side waited, some with their drivers getting out for a look. Even in the rain.

Charlotte dashed over the road and sprinted along the block before hers. The shops here might be at risk. But as she reached the next road, she slowed, then halted at the edge of the footpath. Smoke billowed through the shattered windows of the corner shop. It was the real estate agency. The firefighters were in action and a police car was in the middle of the road.

She headed to the opposite side where the café was. From here the fire appeared contained to the one shop. Nobody lived above it, thank goodness. Her apartment over the bookshop was the only one along there. All her instincts urged her to find a way to the apartment. Her laptop. Her box of memories. Passport. Secret stash of cash for a rainy day.

Rainy day now!

Her phone rang. Rosie.

"I'm outside the corner café but the road is closed." She answered.

"We know. Are you okay?"

"Yes, and so is the bookshop. It is the corner shop alight. The real estate agency but thank goodness nobody would be in there at night."

There was a long silence and Charlotte headed back toward the roundabout. "Rosie?"

"Darling, the agent Lewis saw tonight was heading back there."

Charlotte did an about turn. "When?"

"Um, how long ago, Lew?"

His voice was muffled in the background.

Rosie relayed the information. "An hour or a bit more. Surely he'll have left."

"Why don't you and Lewis go home and I'll update you as I have news? I'm safe where I am and out of the worst of the rain." And worried sick. What if someone was inside?

"We're heading to my house. But I'm worried about you. All that smoke, darling."

"Looks worse than it is close up. The rain is dampening everything and from the look of things, the fireys have it almost out now. Let me know once you're home, okay?"

"Lewis is staying for a while so once you know the bookshop is safe, please come home."

"I will."

Something was going on. Two of the firefighters were conferring with the police officer. Charlotte recognised him as being from Gisborne, a close by and larger town. There was an intense conversation happening, with gesturing and looks at the blackened shop. She moved closer.

The rain stopped.

Words drifted her way.

Deliberate.

Break in.

Body.

Charlotte gasped. Surely she'd misheard. A body?

Lewis' visitor had returned to the shop after their meeting. It couldn't be them. What possible reason would there be for anyone to be inside a burning building? You'd run. Find a way out.

Unless…no. No more murders.

CHAPTER THREE

TREV UTILISED HIS SIRENS AND LIGHTS ALONG THE CALDER Freeway, his speed in keeping with the poor conditions. When the fire came up on his phone, all he wanted was to be home. He'd been finalising paperwork after the trial wound up and had his suitcase in the patrol car ready to get back to Kingfisher Falls tonight. With all the uncertainty around the length of the trial, he hadn't told his mother or even Charlie he might be back. And he'd planned to tiptoe into the house, not arrive in a panic.

Controlled panic.

He took the turn-off to Kingfisher Falls. He'd had a two-minute conversation with his mother which reassured him she was safe. Charlie hadn't picked up when he rang, but Rosie had been quick to say she was observing from a distance. The latest report from dispatch alarmed him. A body found in the fire.

From the top of the hill the aftermath of the fire was obvious. Dark smoke sat above the town like a scene from a horror movie. Nausea rolled around in his stomach. If someone hadn't called it in, had the fireys not controlled it so fast, the bookshop might have been in flames right now. And Charlotte's apartment above it only had one door in and out.

Time to buy a house, Sibbritt. Think about the future more.

Trev manoeuvred past traffic caught in the closure, going up on the footpath with two wheels to squeeze through. He stopped the patrol car near the one already parked in the middle of the road near the fire. He'd send the officer up past the bookshop to turn back cars heading down from the direction of the lookout.

He climbed out to the suffocating stench of smoke and cold fingers of rain beating on his head, grabbing out wet weather gear. Trev shrugged into it, pulled a hood up and zipped the front. It helped a bit.

"Trev!" Charlotte was under cover outside the corner café and he ran to her. She was soaked to the skin, hair plastered against her skull and eyes wide.

"You must be freezing." He held her in his arms for a moment. Not long enough to warm her or reassure her but at least he knew she was okay. He stepped back, still holding her hands. "Go back to Mum's. Get dried off."

"I can't. If something changes...the wind, or anything," Her lips were trembling.

"Charlie, it'll be okay. I'm going to speak to the guys now and won't be leaving until everything is safe. That includes the bookshop and the apartment."

"There's a body. Someone was in there."

"Nothing's confirmed."

"I heard someone say so. A fireman."

"Even more reason to go home. To Mum. And she'll be worrying enough for both of us about you, so at least be there with her. Please."

"I'm going." Her hands gripped his. "But be safe, Trev." She reached up and touched his lips with hers, then she was sprinting back the other way.

She was scared. He gazed at the gutted shop. This was enough to scare anyone.

————

Rosie insisted Charlotte have a hot shower before debriefing. There was a welcome smell of coffee and something baking as she emerged from the second bathroom, hair wrapped in a towel. She'd dressed in tomorrow's work clothes having nothing left until her other clothes dried, other than her night-wear, and with Lewis in the house and Trev possibly heading back later, she wasn't about to parade around in those.

She stopped as a thought struck her. Lewis looked up from near the oven, where he stood holding oven mitts.

"What is it, dear?" he asked.

"Um…Trev may be home tonight at some point. I'll move my stuff out and sleep on the sofa."

Rosie appeared from the living room with Mellow on her lap. "You will do no such thing. Trev didn't tell us he was home tonight, so he gets the sofa."

"Besides," Lewis added as he peeked into the oven. "He may be there most of the night. Fires are nasty things."

"What are you cooking? All I can smell is coffee and oh!"

Lewis slid out a tray of chocolate chip cookies.

"We thought you'd be cold so coffee sounded like a good idea and cookies go well with coffee."

A few minutes later the three of them sat around the coffee table with steaming cups and a plate stacked high with morsels of deliciousness. Lewis passed napkins and then lifted the plate to offer to Rosie. His hands shook and Charlotte took it from him with a smile.

"Here, let me. You've done the hard bit." She made sure everyone had cookies then took one and sat again. "You're stressing."

He nodded. "I'm very worried. Cecil was going to return to

the agency to finish some work. We'd had a good meeting and he was positive the house will sell quickly and for considerably more than I expected." Lewis reached his hand Rosie's way and she grasped it. "He said he'd drop by tomorrow with some paperwork to sign."

"It is only a rumour that there's a...well, body, in there. There was so much smoke it would be hard to tell." Charlotte sipped some coffee and warmth coursed through her. Poor Trev was still out in the weather.

"I should have arranged another night. This weather is so bad that he shouldn't have been out in it." Lewis shook his head.

Charlotte put her cup down. "This wasn't a car accident. It is a fire. Now, *if* there is a body in the building, nobody knows whose. You blaming yourself for something outside your control is not helpful. Is it?" She was aware of her tone. Doctor Dean. Calm but firm.

Lewis gave her a small smile. "You are correct, of course. All we can do is wait."

"And eat cookies." Rosie bit into one. "Mmm."

Mmm indeed. "Lewis, would you show me how to make these? I'm trying to increase my culinary repertoire." Charlotte resisted another cookie. "So far I've taken some lessons with Doug for Italian dishes and been taught two breakfast menus by Lachie Forest."

This time, Lewis' smile was wide. "Ah. The young entrepreneur. Lachlan has many talents for one so young."

Lachie was almost nine years old. He and Charlotte shared a long running joke about the little pine tree she'd bought from his parents who owned the Christmas Tree Farm. When Abbie, his mum, was in hospital having his little sister, Lachie stayed with Charlotte. And last week he'd spent a few hours helping her in the garden for some pocket money, but then gave her breakfast tips.

"He takes after his Dad," Rosie said. "Darcy can turn his

hand to almost anything and once those seedlings in his green-houses take off, he'll have the rates debt paid in no time. And that at least will get Jonas and Terrance off his back."

Charlotte knew the inheritance of the Christmas Tree Farm came with a massive debt load, but had every confidence in the young couple who'd adapted to make their new lives work. "Is Terrance even back at work? After Kevin's funeral I thought he'd gone to ground."

"I think he is," Rosie frowned. "But the law isn't done with him yet. Too many unanswered questions in his part of the death of poor Violet."

The mood in the room darkened as each seemed to go into their own thoughts about the young woman who'd loved Terrance and been killed for it by his own brother. A brother who'd tried to then harm Violet's sister and Charlotte before plunging over the falls. In Kingfisher Falls, a lot can happen in a short time.

CHAPTER FOUR

THE WELCOME AROMA OF COFFEE BREWING WOKE TREV. Then he noticed the soft fur of a cat against his neck, which was at an odd angle. He forced tired eyelids open enough to see daylight and groaned. The cat hissed and abruptly departed, leaving his skin cold.

"Mayhem, that was uncalled for." Rosie's voice was low and came from the kitchen.

Trev stretched, opened his eyes the rest of the way, and pushed himself upright. The sofa wasn't long enough to accommodate his height but he'd been grateful for anywhere to rest when he'd snuck in a few hours ago.

"Darling, go have a shower and change. I'll make some breakfast." Rosie came out of the kitchen. "What time did you get in?"

"Three, bit later." Trev straightened and groaned again. "Getting old, Mum."

She laughed and wheeled away. "Leave the blankets for me."

He wasn't going to do that so folded them and returned them to the hall cupboard. His clothes were all in his bedroom and the door was closed. He'd help his mother first.

Rosie was cracking eggs into a bowl. "Charlie's in my bedroom dressing. She used my shower so you have access to your room."

"Sweet of her. Of you both. Be right back."

The shower eased the aches in his muscles from being in the rain and cold for so long, and helping move heavy beams to make the building safe. His heart was heavy and he still smelled smoke even when in clean clothes. As the steam cleared from the mirror he stared at his reflection, unsurprised by the exhaustion lining his face. It was from more than being away for days at the court case.

All he wanted was to climb into his bed and put his head under the pillow. Hide from the day ahead and what he'd seen overnight. But he had too much to do.

Charlotte and Rosie were in the kitchen now. He watched them for a moment as they prepared breakfast together and his heart warmed. This was why he did his job. To keep good people safe. Or try to. Charlotte glanced up and her smile was enough to make him want to get down on one knee and propose.

Marry me. Live with me so I can protect you forever.

He opened his arms and she snuggled against him for a moment.

"I'm glad you're back." She pulled back to look at him, her eyes searching. "Breakfast and coffee. Then tell us stuff." Charlotte kissed his chin, which made him smile. She wasn't short, but unless she rose on her toes she couldn't quite reach his lips.

He helped carry cups of steaming coffee to the table which was set for breakfast and already loaded with eggs, bacon, hash browns, mushrooms, and toast. His stomach growled. The last meal he'd had was lunch yesterday and even then it was only a quick sandwich between court sessions.

The three ate in silence for a few minutes. Trev caught Charlotte and his mother a couple of times staring at him as though waiting for answers. He needed food and knew once he began to talk, his breakfast was probably over. So he smiled and finished the delicious meal. When his coffee cup was half empty, he prepared his thoughts.

"Lovely meal. Thank you both."

"Pleasure, dear. We were worried about you being out in the wet last night."

"Part of the job, Mum. There's not a lot to tell." He sipped more coffee.

"The bookstore is okay?" Charlotte asked.

"Yes. The fire was out before getting the chance to spread."

Rosie leaned forward. "So no other shops affected?"

"Just the realtor. Apart from lingering smoke and the shop next door has some water damage." Trev put down his cup and sighed. "I'm sorry to say there was a body discovered inside the shop. Thanks to the quick response by the CFA, the fire hadn't reached the body."

"Was it smoke inhalation? Who was it?"

"Mum, no cause of death until the coroner does their thing. But I doubt it. The victim had a gunshot wound."

Charlotte was quiet. Was her sleuth-mind already ticking over, or like him, had she had enough of violent crime in their town? He hoped for the latter.

"It wasn't...you see, Trev, Lewis saw Cecil last night to put his house on the market and he said Cecil was going back to the real estate agency to do paperwork..." Rosie's voice trailed off and he put his hand over hers.

"Sorry to say it was Cecil. His family have been informed and he'll be formally identified soon. I might talk to Lewis about the visit. Get an idea of timing." He pushed his chair back, ready to stand. "I'm sorry you both had such a shock last night. Sorry I wasn't here sooner."

"Trevor, we were fine, thank you."

He smiled at Charlotte's firm tone.

"I have no doubt. When would you like to go and see if everything is okay?"

She was on her feet in a second. "Now would be a good time."

"You two go on and I'll make my way down in a bit. Actually, let's just close the shop today, Charlie. Seems wrong to trade after what happened. Can you put a sign on the door? I might visit Lewis." Rosie collected plates.

"Happy to wait and drop you over." Trev helped clear the table and followed her and Charlotte, whose hands were also full. "Even though the rain stopped earlier, it isn't the nicest weather out there."

"I'll find out if he's at the shop and decide if I drive down or not. No need to worry about me, but let me know how things are."

Trev had parked the patrol car in the driveway behind Charlotte's car. "Just stay close behind and I'll get you to the bookshop. Not sure if the road is open yet."

The road was open but only on one side, with a fire truck still outside the burnt-out shop and a uniformed officer directing traffic. Trev parked near the bookshop and met Charlotte at her car once she'd gone into her driveway. Her face was tense. Trev took her hand and waited for her to meet his eyes. When she did, there were questions in them.

"I know you are probably formulating who is responsible but this crime is one which makes little sense."

"I'm not...not really." There was a flicker of her lips. "Not yet. But whoever did this either was caught in a robbery by poor Cecil and killed him to keep him quiet, or it was cold blooded and the fire set to cover evidence. Either way, which Kingfisher Falls resident is behind this murder?"

So, you're not sleuthing?

It was hard to avoid grinning but Trev managed. Charlotte couldn't help herself and although she'd landed in some tight spots because of her curiosity, she also saw evidence where nobody else did.

"Let me go do my job for a bit and we'll talk it through later. I need more to go on and you, my sweetheart, need to reassure yourself the shop and apartment are unharmed. Unless you want me to look with you?"

Charlotte pressed her lips together but shook her head.

Trev longed to pull her against him and kiss the worries away but it would need to wait. "Assuming I can get away, would you like to meet for lunch? Maybe the café, where I can also keep an eye on things. And would you let me know how Mum is? Bit concerned about her."

"I will. And yes to lunch. Go be a police person."

"Kiss first."

"Nope. Work first. Then maybe a kiss." She laughed and made for the back of the building.

A cold wind whistled along the driveway and Trev zipped his jacket to the top.

CHAPTER FIVE

MUCH AS TREV'S OFFER OF A KISS TEMPTED HER, Charlotte needed to know the bookshop was in one piece. She had met with a business banker a few days ago to begin the process of financing her purchase of the bookshop from Rosie. And although Rosie was the one who'd initiated the idea, she was also the one avoiding some of Charlotte's recent questions.

It wasn't a surprise.

Rosie struggled with change. It took ages for her to accept she could have a second wonderful relationship in her life after losing her beloved husband years ago. Charlotte wasn't about to push or rush her friend into anything. The bookshop meant a lot to them both and whether she worked there or owned it, there would always be happiness among the shelves.

She unlocked the back door and disarmed the alarm before locking herself in. The shop smelled of acrid smoke. Not unbearable but unpleasant. Later she'd spend some time here with the back door open and some scented candles.

Upstairs, the smell was far worse. Being higher up, the smoke had drifted across from the corner and with the rain last night, settled above the whole block. Charlotte ventured onto the balcony. There was activity below with fire investigators arriving and Trev huddled in conversation with Katrina and Bryce, detectives she was becoming all too familiar with. She liked them both, but would rather see them on a social basis than in their official capacity.

Leaving the sliding door wide, Charlotte went through the apartment and opened every window, then the front door. The temperature dropped inside but as she brewed coffee, the smokiness reduced.

Rosie sent her a message.

At Lew's house. Will let you know when leaving.

She texted back.

Bookshop okay. Have apartment windows open to clear smoke. Having lunch with Trev. Talk soon.

A love heart was the response and Charlotte smiled. Almost since she'd moved to Kingfisher Falls, Rosie had hinted at, suggested, and even insisted Trev was the right man for Charlotte. Sometimes her enthusiasm had been too much for Charlotte, when she didn't even understand her own emotions or accept she could have a future with the gentle, handsome police officer. But everything changed and it was fair to say they were a couple.

Coffee cup warming her hands, she headed to the third bedroom, the one which overlooked hectares of bushland behind the shops. Only recently had the big window been accessible. A large wardrobe covered it for many years and moving it had led Charlotte to the discovery of a shallow grave deep in the forest.

So much happened afterwards. An investigation into long-buried remains. The odd behaviour of the sister of the victim who disappeared as quickly as she arrived in town. And an attempt on Charlotte's life by the killer. During all of this, Charlotte had visited her mother in Brisbane and discovered she was adopted. And had a sister. Somewhere.

She stared over the trees. The morning was grey with low clouds and a bite in the wind. For a long time she'd been spooked by the dark and moody forest, only cutting across one corner to shorten the distance to the top of the waterfalls. She understood why. There'd been such sadness and loss there. And although the place was easy to get lost in, Charlotte no longer feared its depths.

You need a name. Not just forest or bushland or scary place.

Charlotte made another coffee and returned to the window. This parcel of land was a curiosity. Locals assumed it belonged to the council but the recent events in its midst raised questions. Part of it was council land, once owned by a previous resident of Kingfisher Falls. Nobody knew why council owned it or what they intended to use it for because it was overgrown and forgotten.

New information revealed some of the land was privately owned. Kevin and Terrance Murdoch were born and bred local brothers who'd once run a conveyancing firm. At some point they'd made a quiet purchase. With Kevin now deceased, Terrance presumably was the sole owner. And he was a member of the council.

With a sigh, Charlotte closed the window. Staring out at the forest wasn't helping her understand. Trev's time in the city at the trial interrupted his investigation into the Murdoch brothers and with the fire...and poor Cecil, who knew when he'd revisit it. It might not even mean anything. Charlotte had a dim view of the council, based on their actions and sometimes inaction. None of it was a priority now. She had to find out who killed an innocent real estate agent and set fire to his shop.

———

Back downstairs, Charlotte propped open the back door of the bookshop to let air circulate. She'd have liked to have the front open but didn't want to confuse customers, several who'd already peered through the door to see if anyone was there.

She lit several candles along the counter. Rosie had taken

to collecting scented candles after spending time with Harmony Montgomery, the clairvoyant. Charlotte had to admit to loving the subtle scents and even bought one for the apartment. She'd extinguish them before leaving, but for now they filled the bookshop with a combination of citrus, roses, and the sea.

Back in River's End, her friend Christie sold her own line of candles through her beauty spa. She should ask her to send some.

Charlotte stopped in the middle of the bookshop and wrapped her arms around herself. River's End was where she and Trev met. Where she began to deal with her past and seek a new beginning. She missed the pristine ocean beach bookended by rocky cliffs, the sweet town, and many of its residents, including a certain golden retriever named Randall.

Her phone rang and she jumped.

It was Trev. "Still okay for lunch?"

"I'm starving. Not sure why after that breakfast."

"Ten minutes okay for you?" There was talk in the background. "Sorry, make it fifteen. Meet you there."

Then he was gone again. He was so calm about it all. But that was Trev. Cool headed. Kind. Calm. Charlotte stopped reminiscing about the seaside town. She checked the front door was locked out of habit, then blew out the candles. There was a slight movement from the pavement and the hairs rose on the back of her arms, even before she glanced up.

Sid. Ex Leading Senior Constable Sid Browne was once the sole police presence in town. And as corrupt as could be. From the first time they'd met, he'd decided Charlotte was trouble and wanted her out of town, going as far as to make threatening phone calls and put bad reviews on the bookshop's page.

Charlotte stalked to the window where he stared in. He stepped back, as though not expecting anyone inside. She put her hands on her hips and levelled her gaze at him. He knew not to cross her. They'd had enough encounters to size each other up. Only twice had their mutual dislike been set aside. Once when she'd helped him arrest some thieves, and then when he helped her after she'd been put in a dangerous position by someone else.

Sid glared at her, took a cigarette from his pocket, and lit it.

She took her phone out and photographed him, then turned the camera to show him the image. Cigarette hanging out of his mouth, he leaned forward and gave her a thumbs up. Charlotte rolled her eyes and turned her back. Enough of his silly tactics. Whatever he was doing wasn't as important as her lunch date.

After turning on the alarm and locking the back door, Charlotte made her way to the front of the bookshop, relieved to find Sid was gone. There was the feel of rain in the air as she crossed the road. Fire and police vehicles still blocked part of the road and a uniformed officer put on rain jacket from behind his patrol car. There was movement inside the burnt-out shop as investigators sifted through the damaged building. Such a big job for them. She waited as a car was waved through. On the diagonal corner, Sid watched the real estate agency with Terrance Murdoch.

Charlotte carefully took a few photos of them, pretending to be answering the phone when Sid spotted her. She waved at him and he nudged Terrance, gesturing toward her.

For a moment she thought Terrance was about to storm over the intersection. Even from the distance the reddening of his neck and face was obvious and his hands clenched into fists as he stepped forward. Sid grabbed his arm and said something.

Time to find Trevor.

She was already on Terrance's radar. He blamed her for his brother's recent death even though she'd done nothing but attempt to talk Kevin out of making a terrible decision. But Terrance was a man who blamed everyone else when things went wrong. And he was grieving his brother plus facing a lengthy investigation into his part of Kevin's criminal activity, so not the person to stir up. Those two men were up to something.

Something sinister.

CHAPTER SIX

"WHY ARE THOSE TWO OVER THERE?" DETECTIVE BRYCE Davis nodded in the direction of Terrance and Sid. "If I were them, I'd be keeping my collective heads down."

Trev followed Bryce's line of sight. "Happy to go ask them."

"Trust the detective..." Bryce chuckled, his attention now on the other corner.

Before even looking, Trev knew he meant Charlotte. Bryce's nickname for her might have started as sarcasm for her amateur sleuthing, but was now a term of respect with a touch of humour.

Charlotte was on the diagonal corner from Sid and Terrance and using her phone. As a camera. He'd seen her take enough photographs to know, even from this distance, what she was up to. Snapping shots discreetly.

"What are you doing?" he muttered.

"I bet she suspects them of killing Cecil." Bryce said. "My guess is she'll find a way to link them to corrupt real estate deals. Or blackmail. Perhaps the underworld."

"Funny. Now she's waving at them as if they are old

friends. I'm meeting her for lunch so I'll get a look at the camera. We're done for the minute?"

"Go. Once Katrina gets back, we'll head to the station and set up a workspace."

"I'll meet you there."

Trev was pleased to be out in the fresh air. The blackened shell of the shop was thick with the stench of smoke. Office furniture was misshapen from heat or destroyed. The glass of the windows and door were smashed, with shards still underfoot until clean up could begin. The metal filing cabinets were undamaged as well as random items like Cecil's iPad, discovered under his body.

There was no sign of Charlotte. Jonas Carmichael had joined Sid and Terrance. The three of them turned away when they noticed Trev, and walked down the street toward the roundabout. As always with those three, something dodgy was going on.

Charlotte was at a table near a window, scrolling through her phone. She glanced up as Trev approached and smiled. The same beautiful smile that always touched his heart. He kissed her cheek before sitting opposite.

"Thought this was a good table. You can watch what's going on over there." Charlotte put her phone down. "I asked Vinnie to send our coffee once you arrived."

Sounded wonderful. He looked over the menu, certain Charlotte already knew what she wanted. When Vinnie arrived a few minutes later with their coffee, they ordered. After an appreciative long sip of coffee, Trev reached his hand out.

"May I see?"

"Oh. Did you...here." She unlocked the phone and opened the gallery. "Those three are up to something. I got a pic of Jonas from over here when he fronted up."

"Theories?"

"No."

He grinned and her lips flicked up in response.

"Fine. Yes. You can see from the photos they are there for a reason. Look at Jonas' body language." She pointed. "He's afraid. Or nervous. Expecting the worst."

"Maybe he's upset. Might have been friends with Cecil."

"Sure. Anyway, Terrance has this vibe about himself. If I had to put a word to it…" she bit her lip.

"Charlie?"

She bought herself time by drinking some coffee.

Over near the realtors, Katrina drew up and Bryce wandered to her car and got in.

"Satisfaction. Or relief. I need to see these on a bigger screen."

"Why would he be relieved?" Trev always paid attention to her theories, even the ones nobody else would consider. She wasn't right every time but had a knack of seeing events and people in ways most others missed. It was more than her being a psychiatrist. She just knew people.

Charlotte leaned forward, her eyes alight. "*That* is the question! It is obvious he has an agenda, and has had for a long time. Probably about land and if he owns some of the bushland and council owns some of it, and he is here with Jonas who is the incoming mayor…if you believe him, well, it makes sense."

"Join some dots for me, please."

She sighed. "Okay. That land must be worth something. A lot if you believe local newspapers saying the region is gaining popularity for its liveability. Close enough to Melbourne to commute for work, but perfect for raising families. Except it is quite expensive to buy up here, so perhaps the land owners want to build cheap housing."

"Pretty sure they can just apply for permits, Charlie. No need to kill anyone and besides, why would Cecil be a target in all of this?"

"I can't do all your work for you." She grinned as lunch appeared.

Trev kept half an eye on the corner as they ate. The fire

investigators were busy. They had first look at any fire crime scene. Bryce and his attendance were more about security and observation at this point. Cecil's remains were with the coroner and a report expected within a day on his cause of death and other relevant information.

"Sid was hanging around before."

He shot his eyes back to Charlotte, who was looking for something on her phone. She showed him an image. Sid with a cigarette hanging from his mouth and a surly expression. "Was he outside the bookshop?"

"Yup. I had the back door open to let fresh air in and all the lights off. He was having a good look through the front window."

"He must have seen you take this."

"Oh, I showed him the photo. He gave me a thumbs up."

"Charlotte." Trev shook his head. "Why must you stir him up?"

"Shows him I'm neither afraid of him nor about to put up with his nonsense. I know he's up to something with his recent return to watching the bookshop and I won't have it."

Her phone beeped and she huffed at the interruption and then checked her message.

Trev didn't know whether to laugh or be cross. Sid wasn't in a position to use power against her or the bookshop any longer, but he was always on the thin line between criminal behaviour and just being a pest.

She put her phone down, lips pressed together.

"Not Sid, I hope."

"No. It was Mel—she's the lady living next door to Mum's house. She said the *For Sale* sign just went up and thought I'd like to know."

"Which is a good thing, isn't it?"

"Yes. Sooner it sells, the quicker I get to move on."

"So why the frown?" Trev took one of her hands and she curled her fingers around his.

31

"When I was up there and met Mel, she mentioned someone looking for me some time ago and speaking to her husband. She'd forgotten to ask him about it but just did." Her fingers tightened. "I thought perhaps it was my Dad, or Zoe."

"But?"

"It was a woman. She described her to me."

There was an odd expression on Charlotte's face. She knew the person and it bothered her. The fingers gripping his told Trev this was a problem for her.

"Who is she?"

"Either a coincidence or it is Alison. The patient I broke confidence over."

Trev didn't know how to reply. There was a deep pain in her eyes. Her guilt for a mistake with a patient that resulted in distress for the woman involved and Charlotte almost losing her licence. He didn't know the full story, only the snippets she'd shared from time to time, but he did know it was the final straw that led to her leaving Brisbane last year and fleeing to River's End.

Am I selfish to be grateful for this?

Perhaps not the circumstances. But he was grateful to have her in his life.

"Charlie, why would she be looking for you?"

"I'm trying to work it out. I might call Mel a bit later and see if her husband remembers anything else. I don't know how she even found the address of my mother's house. Wrong on a few levels."

"You okay?"

She smiled, but there was some effort. "You need to go, don't you? Maybe Kingfisher Falls needs Bryce and Katrina to move here seeing as they are in your station almost weekly."

"Actually, there is a chance I might get another officer stationed here thanks to the past few months crime activity and increasing workload. But yes, I'd better get back to work. As long as you're okay."

"I'm going to go find your mother and we will both be fine."

He wasn't convinced, but kissed her outside the café and watched as she headed toward Lewis' shop before going the other way to retrieve his patrol car.

33

CHAPTER SEVEN

Lewis's shop was closed and the lights off. Charlotte stood in the doorway to message Rosie. Then, she reread Mel's text. The description fitted Alison. About thirty. Short dark hair. Thin. Intense. But why would she visit Angelica's home? Did she think Angelica was there and wanted to speak with her? Perhaps she wanted to reach out in peace.

No contact would ever happen between them again. Not that it was an issue now with Charlotte living two states away, but she'd agreed to never have contact with Alison again and it suited her. Although she acknowledged her misdiagnosis of the woman, her gut told her there'd been more going on. Charlotte had thought Alison on the brink of harming her own husband and brought the police into it. The subsequent investigation served to expose nothing but an unhappy marriage, and a second opinion on Alison's mental health found depression rather than the personality disorder Charlotte believed was there.

The last time she'd seen Alison, the woman had forced her way into a lift with her and told Charlotte her husband had left and that she would never forgive her. It was hard for Charlotte to sympathise because despite everything, she still stood by her belief Alison had planned to harm her husband and the girl-friend she thought he had.

The phone beeped.

I'm home now. Have you eaten yet?

Yes. Just had lunch with Trev. On my way. Do you need anything?

No. Will put coffee on.

Sounded good. She had to collect the clothes from last night she'd left at Rosie's house anyway.

She passed Esther's ladies boutique expecting it to be closed as so many other shops were, but Esther emerged from the doorway and hurried after her.

"Charlotte! I was hoping to see you."

"Hello. I thought you'd be closed." Charlotte gave her a hug. "Lewis is and the photo shop and us, of course."

"I thought I'd begin doing stocktake seeing as town is so quiet and leave the door open in case. But I was so worried about you. Is everything alright at the bookshop?"

They turned to look at the corner. Traffic was flowing through the intersection again. There were less bystanders and only one fire vehicle in sight.

"Smoky smell and worse upstairs, but no damage at all. The shop between us has some water damage from the fire hoses, but nothing too bad I think."

"Whatever is going on in our little town, Charlotte?" There was sadness in Esther's voice. "Thieves. People dying. Old graves. A fire. When will this crime spree end?"

Charlotte didn't know how to answer. There were connections between some of the crimes. People with agendas. Others with grudges.

"Did Doug tell you he's standing for council?" Esther said.

"No! That is wonderful news. Finally get some sensible representation for the region."

"If he gets in. There's only two positions available this year and four candidates, although Terrance is one as his term is up and I believe he won't get much support, even if he's allowed to run. Not after his appalling past behaviour being exposed."

A shiver ran down Charlotte's spine and she glanced around. Someone was watching her from near the roundabout. A woman.

"I'd better keep counting my stock, Charlie."

"Yes...okay, bye."

Charlotte stared at the woman. She was a fair distance away, completely still and facing Charlotte's direction from behind oversized sunglasses. Her coat was thick and almost to her ankles but barely disguised how thin she was. A scarf hid her hair.

It isn't her. Stop imagining things.

Reaching for her phone, Charlotte took her eyes off the woman for a second and when she looked back, she was gone.

Charlotte sprinted to the end of the block. The woman must have gone into a shop around the corner or she'd have seen her cross the road. One by one she peered into each of the half dozen shops, some of the traders waving to her as she did. But no sign of the mystery woman.

She stopped at the end of the shops, gazing around. Had the woman got into a car? Gone down a side alley? Vanished into thin air? Charlotte's heart pounded. If that woman was who she thought...

The streets were as they always were on a cold afternoon. A few pedestrians and cars and nothing more. Not even a woman from the past who didn't belong here.

———

"You still look wan, darling. Drink your coffee and I'll put the heater on." Rosie found the remote control and clicked it. A moment later, warm air wafted through the living room. "That should help. You must put more clothes on if the cold affects you so."

"I'm fine. Really, it was just the worry from last night." Charlotte wasn't about to recount her silly search for someone who she'd imagined. Even if there had been a woman there, it wasn't Alison and there was a reasonable explanation for her disappearing so fast. Bringing Rosie into her fears wasn't fair to her. Not with all the other things going on. She took a deep breath and then sipped more coffee.

"Lewis is still quite shaken," Rosie said. "He's meeting with Trev and the nice detectives this afternoon to run through what he remembers. Poor love. And poor Cecil."

"I'm sorry he's feeling bad. Would you let him know I'm happy to suggest some resources to offer some comfort…as a friend of course, not a therapist. Only if he wants."

"I will. Thanks. Did Trev say what happens now?"

"Only that the detectives are setting up a base in the station again and once the fire investigators are finished, they will confer. The autopsy is happening today so they'll have a better idea once the pathologist's report arrives."

Rosie nodded, her face serious. "I wonder if Cecil walked in on a robbery. Although why set a fire after killing him?"

"Hide whatever they stole. If it is what happened."

"What do you think?"

Charlotte stood and collected Rosie's empty cup. "I think we need more coffee. There's little point speculating until there are some facts."

"Never stopped us before."

"True." Charlotte went to the kitchen with Rosie following. "As the official girlfriend of the resident police officer, I probably should practice some restraint."

"I think that is a terrible idea, darling. Not you being Trev's girlfriend, which is almost the best thing you could be," she grinned, "but not gathering clues isn't going to solve the crime."

Rather than involving herself in a discussion on what might be better than being Trev's girlfriend, Charlotte made fresh coffee. Her future with him played on her mind enough, let alone discussing possibilities with his mother, much as she adored her.

Trev arrived as they were going back to the living room. "Don't mind me, just need my laptop." He waved and kept going to the small study he shared with Rosie.

"Do you think he needs coffee?" Rosie asked.

"Only if you have takeaway cups because he surely won't drink that stuff at the station."

"I heard that." Laptop bag over his shoulder, Trev wandered in. "And I've applied for some funding to spruce up the station so a coffee machine will be first on the list if its approved." He perched on the arm of Charlotte's chair. "Lewis is meeting me in a few minutes. I'll try to keep the interview brief."

"He's a bit upset, dear. But wants to help."

"Did you speak to Mel yet? About that Alison person?" he touched Charlotte's arm.

Aware that Rosie had turned her attention to her, Charlotte shook her head. "No rush. It is nothing to worry about. Don't you need to leave?"

Trev grinned. "I do." He leaned down and kissed her forehead. "Talk to you a bit later. See you, Mum."

"Bye, Trev."

Rosie didn't take her eyes off Charlotte and the minute the front door closed, her mouth opened. "Who is Alison and why is Trev concerned about her?"

"Nobody and he isn't." Why did he need to mention this in front of his mother, who had just as big an interest in uncovering secrets as Charlotte. "Have you and Lewis discussed a wedding date yet?"

"Don't change the subject." Rosie blushed a pretty shade of pink. "We'll talk about that when we're all together for dinner next. I'm more interested in why you brushed Trev off when he asked about Mel and Alison because you had a look in your eyes. Now, spill your guts."

Would you believe I saw something that wasn't there?

"The lady who lives next door to my mother's house mentioned there was someone looking for me. Ages ago. From the description I got today it was the patient I had in Brisbane, the one I breached confidence over."

Rosie leaned forward. "Oh, I am sorry for pushing. Just tell me to back off if something is personal."

Charlotte laughed.

"I mean it. There's nothing you can't tell me, of course, but I will never take offense if you need to keep something to yourself."

"I do love you." Charlotte kissed Rosie's cheek. "Sorry to laugh, but you are as bad as me when you think you're onto something. Eyes on the puzzle."

"Not sure if you are complimenting me or chiding me."

"Neither. I didn't want you worrying about me. That is all."

Rosie sat back, her forehead creased. "Why would she look for you, this Alison? Aren't you supposed to stay away from her?"

"She was paid a lot of compensation and there were papers signed agreeing to no contact from either side and no public discussion of any of the details of the case, not that it stopped some media coverage."

"I don't want to pry…well, let's be honest, I do. What actually happened between you and Alison?"

Somehow, Rosie's matter of fact interest reassured Charlotte. "I've had two difficult patients. One really bad one, the man who tied me up in the cave in River's End."

"When Trevor saved you?"

Charlotte smiled. "He helped. And he was brave, because he rappelled down the side of a cliff and he isn't a fan of heights."

If Rosie looked any prouder she'd burst. Charlotte wasn't about to tell her he'd arrived after her captor tried to shoot a boat at sea with an antique gun that misfired, injuring himself instead.

"Anyway, I'm not expecting another Bernie. Or I'd hope not. Alison came to me to help with thoughts she was having about her husband. They'd only been married a couple of years but from the beginning she suspected he was seeing someone else. Referred to this mystery woman as 'the girlfriend'. Her husband denied it and a private detective found no evidence. I treated her for a couple of conditions including a certain type of paranoia. Of course, she then thought I was trying to trap her into something and over time began dropping hints she meant to harm her husband. I was sufficiently concerned to inform the appropriate authorities."

"Sounds reasonable."

"Except she wasn't planning anything. Perhaps she was deliberately baiting me to see what might happen but I couldn't prove it and I certainly didn't see it coming. Either way, the fallout was that she lost her marriage and took me to the disciplinary board for breach of confidence and all sorts of other accusations."

Rosie took Charlotte's hand and squeezed.

"I hung on to my licence, barely. My insurance paid out a lump sum of compensation which is another reason I stopped practicing…too hard to find an insurer I can afford now. The place where I practiced made it clear I was no longer welcome. So, I took a suitcase, and left Brisbane."

Aware her heart was racing, Charlotte took a long, slow breath.

"I don't know how you tolerated all that nonsense, but you know, darling? You're here now. Here and safe in Kingfisher Falls and very loved."

CHAPTER EIGHT

LEWIS PUSHED HIS SPECTACLES BACK TO THEIR PROPER place instead of where they'd sat on the end of his nose as he'd stared at his hands.

Trev placed a cup of coffee in front of him. "I apologise in advance for the coffee. Please feel free to ignore its presence."

At last Lewis smiled, although only a glimmer. Trev had known Lewis all his life and was concerned by the sadness on the older man's face. Their interview was part way through and this was the first time Lewis had looked him in the eye.

"I can only imagine how distressing this is."

"Charlotte tells me I am not responsible…but all the same, had Cecil not been at my home to inspect it, he may very well have avoided this terrible tragedy."

"I think you should listen to Charlotte. We are a long way from knowing what happened but there is not one chance you had any bearing on what a killer did. None, Lewis."

Bryce piped up from over at the whiteboard. "On top of that, Charlotte knows stuff, so trust her."

Now, Lewis did smile. "Thank you. I shall try a bit harder."

"Let's get this done, then you and Mum can get back to planning your wedding." Earlier, Lewis had mentioned they were working on a date. "We've gone over the time of Cecil's arrival and departure. Do you recall any phone calls or messages he might have received during his visit?"

"None. His phone was on silent. He used his iPad to write notes and take a few images of the house."

Bryce wandered across to the desk. "You saw his phone?"

"I did. The minute he stepped inside, he took his phone out and changed the setting. He even told me he keeps it on silent mode when he's with a client. Why is that?"

"We've not located his phone at this time. Is there any chance he dropped it at your house?"

"I imagine it is possible, if unlikely. You are welcome to come and have a look around." Lewis said. "We were in every part of the house and even outside for a few minutes but it was wet, so we stayed on the covered porch. It is odd though as it was in the inside top pocket of his jacket and I don't recall him removing it."

Trev glanced at Bryce. Finding Cecil's iPad and wallet but not his phone added to their suspicion he'd been the target all along.

"Is there anything else you recall of the evening, Lewis?" Trev asked. "No matter how small it seems."

Lewis shook his head, then his eyes widened. "Well, this might have no bearing...we were having a cup of tea and talking about my plans to retire. He said he wants to work for another ten years. He does...did, love his job so much." He dropped his head again.

"You went to school with Cecil, I believe?" Trev waited until Lewis glanced up with a slight nod. "And forgive me, but you are both at an age where retirement is fairly common."

With a smile, Lewis nodded again. "Couple of oldies. Not that I feel it most of the time."

Trev grinned back. "You outclimb me on any ladder, that's for sure. What was odd about him saying he intended to work for another decade though?"

"Oh. I forgot the point for a minute. He said something about turning down an offer to buy the building. He's owned it for years and intends to rent it out as retirement income when the time comes."

Bryce took out a notepad. "Did he happen to say who made the offer on the building?"

"Afraid not. Just that it was a generous offer and they'd been annoyed when he turned it down."

Trev finished typing up the interview, printed it and got a signature from Lewis. He saw Lewis out after arranging to drop by and take a look for Cecil's phone. Lewis walked to his car, shoulders drooped, and Trev's heart went out to him.

Back inside, he checked out the whiteboard. Bryce was at the other desk on the phone, to Katrina from the sound of the conversation. At the top of the board was Cecil's name and a photo of the man. A reminder of why they would work hard to uncover the truth. Beneath was the sum of what the police knew so far.

Precious little.

Bryce hung up and joined him, black marker in hand.

"Preliminary report is Cecil was shot at close range. In the back."

He scribbled notes on the whiteboard.

"Did his killer sneak up on him, or did he know them and turn away." Trev pondered aloud. This was shocking news. "Did he die from that?"

"Yeah. Hit his pacemaker so would've been quick at least. With his phone disappearing and the fire, I'm taking an early bet on premeditated murder."

"Unless his phone is at Lewis'. What about his car?"

"Katrina's just searched it. She's meeting me at his house next. What do you know about him?"

Trev returned to his desk as his phone beeped. Message from Charlotte that she was home. "Um, I've always known him but never had much to do with him. Delivered the paper to him as a kid. Mum and Dad bought the house from him after her accident. He sold our other one which wasn't wheelchair friendly. He lived alone. Think his wife died a long time ago and he never remarried. He was a member of the church choir."

"Kids?"

"Not that I remember. I'll check with Mum if you want more personal info. He was one of those people who lived to work. Always either in the office or at an open house. Has a part time receptionist who comes in for a few hours a day. I've already spoken to her but she was pretty shaken so will follow up a bit later."

Bryce collected his keys. "Real estate agents must see and hear a lot. Private stuff when they are inspecting a house. Renters with issues. Let's see what we can get from his iPad first. Any recent interactions we need to take a closer look at. Are you going to Lewis' house?"

"Soon. I'll look at the iPad first if it's cleared for me to use?"

"Go for it."

After Bryce left, Trev stared at his phone. He wasn't comfortable with Charlotte being back in the apartment. There was no logic behind the feeling but he wished she'd stay at Rosie's a bit longer, even if he had to squash himself onto the sofa. He tapped a message back.

Dinner tonight? Italia with Lew and Mum if they'll come?

All of them needed a chance to catch up after he'd been in the city all week. They needed to talk about wedding plans, and the trial he'd attended and even the fire if it helped.

Yes please. Shall I call Rosie?

Trev smiled.

Thanks. Just going to Lewis' house so will ask him.

She sent a smiley face back.

He'd worried earlier that mentioning Alison in front of his

mother might have upset Charlie, but now he sighed in relief that she was fine.

———

"Why, why, why?" Charlotte threw a pillow from her bed onto the floor. She was putting fresh sheets on as part of a cleaning frenzy which hit her the minute she'd got home. Everything smelt of smoke, even her bed. Throwing the pillow was at an imaginary Alison.

Why would the woman go to Angelica's home? Why risk her settlement by contacting Charlotte or her family?

"What family, anyway!" Another pillow joined the first.

Since returning from Brisbane a couple of weeks ago she'd done nothing to find her father or sister. She'd been occupied with the grave in the bushland and then with Trev away, found herself spending her spare time either with Rosie, or hiking around the waterfalls. Although her heart longed to find them, part of her was terrified.

Bed made, she changed her pillowcases and opened the window as far as it would go. This afternoon was a little warmer than yesterday but rain still threatened. At least the smoke haze was gone from outside.

She remembered she'd said she'd call Rosie but wasn't in the mood to speak to anyone so sent a message, bright and happy complete with more of the smiley faces she'd added to Trev's. Dinner was a good idea. Everyone was on edge or upset and being together in a much-loved environment might help the healing.

Room by room she wiped down surfaces and then put the washing machine on with her sheets, towels, and the clothes from the other night. At long last the air in the apartment was fresh again. By this time, Charlotte longed for coffee and stopped to turn on the machine. There was a response from

Rosie, an enthusiastic yes, so Charlotte messaged Trev to let him know.

What a difficult job he had at the moment. Since taking over from Sid a few months ago, Trev had dealt with old murders, missing people, and more crime than he'd probably had in all his years looking after River's End. Yet, he never complained. Just went about his day with a kind and firm approach to those he dealt with. Lewis was in good hands.

Charlotte found herself in the third bedroom, her eyes roaming across the canopy of trees that stretched as far as she could see. Thank goodness the fire hadn't spread to it. The undergrowth was so dense that it didn't bear thinking about the damage a spark in the wrong place would cause.

CHAPTER NINE

Trev met with Katrina and Bryce at the station as night approached. They looked as exhausted as he felt as they gathered around the whiteboard. A long day preceded by an even longer night was taking its toll on them all, and the detectives still had a drive ahead to return to Kyneton, their base station and where both lived.

"Trev, you go first," Katrina said. "Any luck with Cecil's phone?"

"Not at Lewis' house. We both systematically searched the house and nothing turned up."

"And his iPad?"

Trev nodded. "I've copied his calendar, which he kept meticulously from the look of it. He recorded every phone call made and received, appointments, sales, open houses. The lot. It'll take some time to work through it all and I'd like to sit down with his receptionist tomorrow and go over what I need to clarify. Nothing jumps out as odd. No notes about an offer to buy the building."

Bryce crossed his arms. "You'll be busy. Grab another uniform officer if you need some help. Katrina and I went through Cecil's house. With respect and care. He keeps his place uncluttered and clean and the minimum of paperwork, none of which was about the business or alerted us to anything suspicious. He does have a niece who appears to be his only relative and there was a copy of his will leaving everything to her. She's coming in tomorrow to speak to us."

"We're doing a walk through with the fire investigator first thing in the morning." Katrina said. "You are welcome to meet us."

"Thanks. I will." Trev's eyes flicked over the additional information Bryce had added to the whiteboard since his last look. "Who is Neville Anderson?"

"You haven't come across him?" Bryce asked. "New chef at Italia."

"No. Only found out Doug took someone on, the other day. Why is he of interest?"

"Has form. Did jail time for break and enter. One of the local volunteer firefighters knew and mentioned it the other night." Bryce walked to the desk. "Might not mean a thing but we're going to do an interview. Check for an alibi."

This was the last thing Doug needed. He'd taken years to make the decision to hire some help for Italia and whether he knew the man's background or not was a good judge of character.

"Let's hope this Neville guy has nothing to do with it." Trev glanced at his watch. "Anything else? You two must be exhausted."

Katrina smiled. "And I have two kids to collect on the way because Daddy had to work and they've been at a friend's place all day. So, when you and Charlie have a family, don't take some job requiring long absences."

Locking up a few minutes later, Trev replayed her words. If he ever had the privilege of sharing a family with Charlotte, a job needing long absences was the last thing he'd accept. He'd want to be there every day to be even half the dad his own father was. But they'd not talked about a family. Not even about marrying. And nothing meant more to Trev than spending the rest of his life with the woman he loved so much.

———

Knowing Trev was driving Rosie down to dinner, Charlotte walked. It was only around a couple of corners to the plaza, then Italia and its neighbouring restaurant, India Gate House, were at the far end near the park. The evening was cool but clear with the last of the rainclouds vacating the sky a little earlier.

She stopped at the fountain in the middle of the plaza. Thanks to a nasty decision manipulated by Jonas, council had cut off the water supply to the fountain some time ago. In his opinion—which he'd given her at this spot—the traders owed council for a replacement Christmas tree after the one in the roundabout was stolen. He and Terrance had tried to strong-arm the local shop owners into paying for it. It was probably unconstitutional and illegal, but those two men had the rest of the council under their control.

No water. No fountain. If Doug got onto the council board then things would change. Too many agendas there for her liking. But Doug was even-tempered and fair and spoke up about wrong-doing when he saw it.

A cold breeze chilled Charlotte and she huddled into her trench coat and headed for Italia. Not long after she'd moved to Kingfisher Falls, Charlotte discovered the two restaurants on opposite sides of the street. She'd been drawn to one, then the other, by tempting aromas of herbs and spices, one Italian, the other Indian. There were a couple of other restaurants in town but these were the most popular and the ones she frequented.

India Gate House had some of its outside seating around a tall gas heater, too chilly for Charlotte but there were customers being served there. Their server was Harpreet, whose parents owned the place. She ran her own shop most of the time, specialising in framing and photographs, but helped out here when needed.

Charlotte waved to Harpreet, who put down the final plate and hurried to meet her. They kissed cheeks. "I came to see if you were okay but the bookshop was closed. And no answer when I knocked upstairs."

"Oh, I should have dropped in. Sorry, I've been at Rosie's a bit because of the smoke. Going home tonight though. Are you all okay?"

"Too far from the fire to cause damage, but we are so sad about what happened." Harpreet glanced around and whispered. "Who would kill such a nice person?"

"It is awful. I didn't really know him, just said hello a few times in passing, but it is dreadful to think all he did was go to work and...well, you know." Charlotte longed to sit with her friend and see if she had any information about Cecil. Harpreet's family had lived in the town for decades so there might be some snippets of insight.

"I have to go, Charlotte. Rosie and Trev already went into Italia," she grinned. "So, don't keep your man waiting."

"Funny. Catch up for some tea soon?" Charlotte kissed her cheek again and turned. "And say hi to your parents from me."

A moment later she was pushing open the door of Italia. Inviting aromas of garlic and basil and red wine and bread filled her senses and she inhaled to enjoy it all. On one wall an open fireplace crackled and at a window table near it were Rosie and Trev, deep in conversation. Charlotte made it almost all the way over before they noticed her.

Trev stood and kissed her cheek, then pulled a chair out for Charlotte. "We're talking about weddings." There was a sparkle in his eyes.

Whose?

She took off her coat and Bronnie appeared as if from nowhere and whisked it away with a smile.

"Lewis is on his way," Rosie said. "He needs cheering up so this is perfect." She reached for Trev's hand. "Thank you, dear."

"I think tonight is good for us all." Trev said. "Being in Melbourne all week made me appreciate Kingfisher Falls."

The restaurant was filling up with customers. Charlotte's eyes roamed from table to table, recognising many of the patrons either as customers of the bookshop or people she'd met over the last few months. Her gaze stopped on a table at the wall furthest from their own. "Darn." She muttered.

Lewis' arrival saved her explaining her comment and it was a few minutes before she glanced again. Sid and his wife, Marguerite, glared back. As irritating as their presence was, Charlotte struggled to control the urge to wave. Sid brought out the worst in her.

"Ignore them." Trev put his arm around the back of her chair and spoke so the others didn't hear as they chatted. "Us being here must have upset their evening."

"So, I shouldn't send a bottle of wine over?"

He chuckled and the sound of his laughter made her smile.

After ordering dinner, talk turned to the trial Trev had attended for several days. "The jury found Derek guilty of all charges and he'll be sentenced in a couple of weeks."

Lewis leaned forward. "Tell me again…this is the man who tried to sink a boat his ex-fiancé was on?"

"Kind of a long story but yes, he put a hole into it thinking he'd sink it with her now-husband onboard. But she was the one sailing instead and was caught in the middle of a storm. There was a stack of other crimes as well and each one of them will keep him in prison for a long time."

Charlotte let out a long sigh and Trev found her hand beneath the table and squeezed it.

"And you gave evidence?" Rosie asked Charlotte.

"About a couple of the things that went on. I had helped on the beach during the rescue so saw the result of his actions."

"What Charlie means to say is she took over a difficult situation barely knowing anyone involved. She gave everyone a job and was fantastic at calming down understandably distressed people. And saving the life of a beloved dog."

She smiled. "Randall was fine. Just tired. And just because I bossed you around doesn't mean I was in control of anything else. But thanks." Charlotte reached for her glass of wine and sipped.

Rosie beamed. "You two are so sweet. We should have a double wedding."

The wine spurted from Charlotte's mouth and Trev burst into laughter. Lewis offered his napkin which Charlotte accepted with an embarrassed 'thanks'. Rosie looked from one to the other.

"What? It makes sense. One venue. We can be each other's attendants. Share the guests and the reception."

Lewis took Rosie's hand. "Very thoughtful of you, my love, but unless I've missed something, we are the only engaged couple at the table."

"But that will change." Rosie insisted.

The arrival of the main course diverted everyone's attention, but Charlotte couldn't help sneaking a glance at Trev's face. It was amused. Very amused.

CHAPTER TEN

"Did you notice the garden centre has sold?" Rosie sliced into dessert. "This looks delicious."

Charlotte was only half listening to the conversation at her own table as she kept an eye on Sid and Marguerite's. They'd been joined by Jonas, who'd walked in with Terrance. The minute Terrance spotted Charlotte and Trev, he turned and stalked out. But Jonas was still eating dinner with the Brownes and Charlotte wished she could hear their discussion.

"I wonder who bought it? Hopefully, someone who loves plants." Trev said. "Darcy would love a local retailer to sell his seedlings to."

Lewis cleared his throat and Charlotte looked at him. The sadness was back in his face. Earlier, over the main course and with lots of laughter across the table, he'd been more his old self, but now he had the haunted expression of the past day or so.

"It was sold to someone for another purpose, I believe." Lewis said. "An artist, actually, I think a sculptor."

Rosie put down her fork and touched his hand. "How do you know?"

"Cecil...well, he mentioned it. Had been to put the sold sign up." His head dropped.

"How wonderful!" Charlotte wasn't going to let him dwell on the sadness. "What else do you know about the buyer?"

He looked up. "Hm. A woman. Not a local. She's setting up classes for people wanting to learn to sculpt and make pottery and the like. And will have a gallery."

Rosie smiled. "How lovely! I've always wanted to use one of those spinning things and turn clay into something wonderful. I will make sure I'm in her first class so I can make something for our new house."

At last, Lewis brightened. "Now you mention it, pottery sounds quite fun."

"I wonder when it will open." Charlotte attended to her own dessert of gelato, which was melting thanks to letting it sit for so long. "Last time I visited the garden centre it was one big mess. Boxes of unrelated merchandise packed to the ceiling in the shop, the greenhouse in disrepair, and the poor plants...let's not discuss those." She scooped lemon gelato into her mouth.

Trev watched her with a grin. He'd been quiet for most of the past half hour after going over the details of the trial. Since then he'd eaten and listened and nodded and smiled. And eaten some more. Someone needed to make sure the poor man was fed enough. Charlotte almost choked on the icy treat. Since when did an adult man need help with his diet?

"Shall I pat your back if you're going to cough and splutter? Bit insulting to the chef." He put his hand on her back and rubbed between her shoulders. It was nice.

"I'm perfectly fine, thank you, Trevor."

"Excellent. Would hate to have to eat the rest of that because it didn't agree with you."

She passed it over. "Swap. I'm walking home so how about I finish your wine?"

Rosie reached for her phone. "Closer for a photo, both of

you. How about you, Charlie, spoon some gelato into Trev's mouth…what?"

Charlotte never knew whether to laugh or retreat from the teasing. Being part of this family was the best thing ever to happen to her. She flicked her hair dramatically. "There, I shall sip from Trev's glass." She held the pose.

Everyone laughed and heads turned. Including from Sid's table. This time, Charlotte waved. She couldn't help herself. Sid's lips turned up until Marguerite grabbed his arm and said something. What seemed like years ago, but was only months, Charlotte met Marguerite when she was part of the local book club, along with two other women. Glenys was always nice but turned out to be a killer. Octavia was never nice and was killed. And Marguerite? Always rude to Rosie and Charlotte. And still alive.

Doug, in his chef whites, wandered over. "Everything good here?"

Rosie grabbed his hand. "Everything is wonderful. The food was delightful and if anything, even better than usual."

Face serious, Doug raised her hand to kiss. "Then my work here is almost done. Your entire meals were prepared by my new chef."

"Yes, definitely time for you to move on, Doug." Rosie teased. "He is a keeper."

"Is that Neville?" Trev asked. "Neville Anderson?"

Releasing Rosie's hand, Doug turned to Trev. "He's a good man, Trev."

Charlotte looked from Trev to Doug. What on earth?

"Would never presume otherwise. You're a good judge of character." Trev said.

There was an uncomfortable silence as the men stared at each other. Something was wrong and it was obvious this Neville Anderson was the subject of Trev's interest. Was he a suspect of some kind?

"Anyone else planning on running for council?" Doug's eyes were still on Trev. "Could use an ally."

"I did consider it once," said Lewis. "Competition was fierce at the time and I had my hands full elsewhere, so let it go."

"You'd be a valuable member of council, if you'd consider it again," Doug said. "All of your years as a trader, plus the tour bus you used to have...they add up to some serious experience and wisdom about the region."

"Perhaps."

"Give it some thought. I'd better get back to work."

Doug disappeared back through the doors to the kitchen.

"Would it interest you, Lewis?" Trev split the last of the wine between Rosie and Charlotte's glasses. "Might shift the balance of power from Jonas and his followers. Be good for the town."

Lewis pushed his glasses up his nose. "I'm getting too old for that."

"You are not too old!" Rosie leaned against him. "You are perfect."

"In that case, why don't we tell the children the date we've chosen?"

Rosie sat upright with a smile. "Good idea!"

Charlotte reached for Trev's hand beneath the table. This was such a change for him, and his mother. Trev's dad was an amazing man who still featured in their daily conversations. His death several years ago was heart-wrenching for both, and even though Trev was supportive of Rosie moving on, it surely must still be difficult. He squeezed her fingers.

"I've been looking forward to hearing this, Mum."

Lewis put his arm around Rosie. "As long as we can obtain the services of a suitable celebrant and venue, then we plan to marry on the first weekend in spring."

"Oh, that sounds perfect!" A rush of joy filled Charlotte. "If you are looking for a celebrant, Trev and I know someone."

Trev chuckled. "Yes, yes, we do. She married our friends, Christie and Martin, in River's End."

"Send her details across and we'll add her to our list." Rosie glanced at Lewis as if asking a question. He nodded and she turned back. "Charlie, would you do me the great honour of being my bridesmaid?"

Charlotte's mouth dropped open as the recent rush of joy turned to delight. "Me? Are you sure?"

"Darling, I couldn't think of anyone I'd rather be at my side."

Tears prickled at the back of Charlotte's eyes. "Of course, I will. I'm so happy to."

Lewis turned his attention to Trev. "And you, my friend. Will you be my best man?"

Trev's fingers tightened around Charlotte. "I hadn't expected that...but are you sure? There's nobody you'd rather—"

"There is nobody I'd rather have." Lewis reached his right hand over the table and Trev let go of Charlotte to shake it. "You are dear to me and it would mean a lot."

"Then I accept. I'll make sure you get to the church on time." Trev grinned.

———

Trev and Charlotte walked through the plaza, hand in hand. Lewis had insisted he drive Rosie home and Trev wanted to stretch his legs and make sure Charlotte was safely home. His car was parked behind Italia and he'd collect it on his way home.

"Who will escort Rosie down the aisle?" Charlotte said out of nowhere. They'd not spoken since saying goodbye to the others and headed away from the restaurant.

"Good question. Perhaps Mum will be one of those people who escorts herself. She's only traditional part of the time."

They stopped at the fountain. "I hope Doug gets onto council and maybe Lewis as well. This time of year isn't so bad to have the fountain off, but the children love it in the warmer months." Charlotte sounded wistful and Trev wrapped his arms around her.

"Do you mean Charlie loves it in the warmer months?"

"I do. And Jonas isn't getting any love from the local traders for doing this."

"Would you repeat that?" Trev smiled at the confused expression in her eyes. "Just the first bit."

"Okay. I said Jonas isn't...oh. You mean, the very first bit."

"Are you blushing, Doctor Dean?"

She wiggled as if wanting to be free but first, he kissed her forehead. Then, his arms dropped from the warmth of her body and he took her hand again and started walking. "You should practice it. The 'I do' bit."

There was no response and Trev glanced at her. Was that too soon? Too flippant?

"What was that thing between you and Doug earlier?" she asked.

Okay, we'll change the subject.

"Can't talk about it, Charlie. Not yet, anyway."

"Doug's new chef is a suspect. In the fire?"

"Not at all. And that's the end of the conversation about him. Did you notice Terrance come in with Jonas?"

Charlotte looked at him, her face animated. "He saw me first then his shifty eyes moved to you. He tapped Jonas on the shoulder and left."

"Your powers of observation are excellent. What do you deduce from it?"

"Well, he was meant to join Sid and Marguerite for dinner because there were four places. Once Jonas sat at the table, the waiter removed one place. Was it a social dinner, do you think, or a meeting?"

Good question. The reappearance of the disgraced former

police officer in town was curious. Trev understood the Browne's sold their house and moved out of the region, yet here they were again.

"There are some odd connections," Trev said. "Sid, Terrance and Jonas watching the fire investigators at work earlier. Sid looking through the bookshop window again. I'd love to know Sid's motive for returning to Kingfisher Falls and why he's spending time with those two."

"You should ask him."

"I might."

They reached the end of plaza. "Can we go the long way? I'm curious about the garden centre." Charlotte gently pulled on Trev's hand and who was he to turn down the chance to spend more time with her? She seemed to know he'd agree and grinned as she headed for a long alley behind the shops.

"Why are we going along here?"

"Are you scared of the dark, Leading Senior Constable?"

"Nope. Just surprised we're sneaking behind buildings."

"It's a short cut."

"How do you know this is here?"

Her expression was familiar. This alley was involved with something she'd seen, done, or heard and didn't want to share. Which meant she thought he'd disapprove. Not long ago he'd have let it pass.

"Charlotte. No secrets."

She sighed, exhaling misty air as if she'd expected as much. "It was ages ago so it doesn't count. In the scheme of dangerous things, anyway." Charlotte pointed to a narrow space between two buildings back toward the main street. "When the Christmas trees were being stolen, I happened to be taking some photographs of the scene from the roundabout when Sid arrived. I didn't want him knowing I was there so slipped into the alley, there." She gestured. "He couldn't fit through so even if he'd tried, I was quite safe."

"Hold up." Trev strode to the opening and flashed his

phone torch down it. "You hid in there?" He'd struggle to navi-gate it sideways holding his stomach in and then there was the debris and rubbish underfoot. "Let me get this straight. You were taking photographs of the roundabout...after the big tree was stolen?"

She nodded.

"And Sid arrived and rather than deal with him, which I understand, you hid. Not just walked home along the main street?"

"Well...I *might* have taken some video of him violating the crime scene. And he *might* have heard the phone camera beep and looked my way. If so, there's a chance he wasn't happy and therefore it made sense to vacate the scene."

"By squeezing through here to an alley with little light. When you'd been in town...a month?"

"A bit less. So, now you know why I know it is here. Shall we keep going? I'm getting cold." Charlotte rubbed her hands over her arms as if to prove it. Despite her confident words there was something akin to doubt in her eyes.

Trev fought down the need to tell her she'd put herself in danger. She knew it already. Instead, he gave in to the need he'd had since arriving back from Melbourne and kissed her. Properly. And although her lips were as cold as his, she melted against him and set that same fire going he never wanted to end.

CHAPTER ELEVEN

CHARLOTTE'S LIPS STILL TINGLED MINUTES AFTER TREV'S unexpected yet most welcome kiss. She'd missed him these past few days and his return the other night in the middle of a crisis meant more than she'd realised. He might have just teased her about practicing saying, 'I do', but somewhere ahead was their future together.

You need to stop putting up barriers.

They wandered to the end of the alley and turned left. Another couple of blocks along was the garden centre. Or, what was once a garden centre. A dirt carpark was between the road and shop, which was a long building crossing the block. A large sign in the carpark declared this was a prime spot to buy and was partly covered by a 'sold' sign.

"I've not been inside in years." Trev said. "It used to be filled to the brim with every type of plant imaginable. And the best selection of gift ideas which was great for me. Never had to look too far to get Mum something nice."

"Sounds wonderful and not at all familiar. By the time I stepped foot inside, Veronica had let it fall apart. The big greenhouse at the back of the property? Almost empty and with holes in the roof."

They peered through the wide glass windows into a darkened space.

"See that wall to the left? Veronica had boxes piled to the roof filled with the cheap goods she'd purchased in her various attempts to run a business."

Veronica Wheemor was an odd woman with criminal ties who'd moved into town before Charlotte arrived. She'd started several retail businesses, always in close proximity to an established similar shop and with cheap, inferior products. Any chance of her stealing customers failed thanks to her rudeness and lack of regard for the tight-knit community. Not to mention not paying her rent.

"I wonder if the people she owed confiscated them." Trev suggested. "Not a nice woman."

She'd threatened Charlotte with a shovel in the bookshop before being arrested by Katrina. And her boyfriend was a thug. And, if that wasn't enough, she had some strange relationship with Jonas.

"Trev? What was her involvement with Jonas?"

"Um..."

"Not that. And I don't think it was. There was something going on which bonded them but about money. I think."

Trev straightened and looked at Charlotte with a thoughtful expression. "What if it was property that bonded them? It seems to be his thing."

"Interesting observation. I shall take that under advisement." She grinned as he rolled his eyes. "I may need my own whiteboard."

"Are we done here?"

"Can't see any signs of the sculptor, so yes. For now." Charlotte found herself reluctant to leave for some reason. "I have a feeling."

They walked back to the road. "What kind of feeling? I'm a bit scared to ask."

Charlotte giggled. "Nothing sinister. There's just something familiar about sculptors. And I'm not turning into Harmony."

Harmony was a clairvoyant who'd breezed into town and then disappeared without a trace. Rosie adored her. Charlotte didn't believe in such matters...although Harmony somehow knew about her sister, Zoe. A sister she didn't know.

———

After Trev had left to collect his car and do a last patrol around the town, Charlotte sat cross-legged on her bed with her laptop open. The visit to the garden centre was on her mind and she couldn't pinpoint the reason.

She searched for Zoe as she'd done before. Zoe Dean, Queensland. There were women of that name but none which Charlotte thought would be her sister based on age. She expanded the search to the rest of Australia with similar results. It was likely Zoe had changed her surname, either through marriage or not wanting to be associated with Angelica. Leaving the family when Charlotte was so young raised many questions about Zoe's relationship with their mother, and their father.

"And me." She whispered.

Zoe was seventeen, according to Angelica, (check) when she moved out to marry a boy her mother didn't approve of. But their father told Angelica the wedding never happened. Even if Zoe left solely over a man, why not come back to see her baby sister? The regular Christmas cards stopped after eleven years. (check)

A stab of panic struck Charlotte. Had something happened to Zoe? Had she...died?

Almost holding her breath, she searched through each state's records for deaths since Zoe's last Christmas card. Half an hour later, she sighed in relief. At least under her given name, there was no death record.

She bit her bottom lip as the image of the garden centre

encroached in her mind. The 'Sold' sign across the board at the front was what stirred all of this up…but why?

Fingers back on the keyboard she typed 'Zoe Dean sculptor' and pressed the enter key.

Tears filled her eyes and she rubbed them to clear her vision as she clicked on an entry partway down the page.

Zoe Carter Dean. Artist and sculptor.

Charlotte clicked on the website and gasped as gorgeous images of hand carved birds and animals filled the screen. Each was for sale, or sold, and all commanded a high price. She looked at every page, clicking one then another as she sought one photograph. One piece of information to confirm what she knew. And there, at the very bottom of a page about a gallery opening several years ago, was a photograph of a group of people and the caption, 'Guest of honour, Zoe Carter Dean'.

Zooming in on the image made it blur, so Charlotte tried to make out the features of the woman in the centre of the group of four men, which at least made it obvious who Zoe was. Long chestnut hair surrounded a face like Angelica's. A slender body dressed in a long black gown. A serious expression.

The tears welled again and this time Charlotte couldn't push them away. She put the laptop to one side and curled up on the bed as sobs racked her body.

Charlotte didn't know how long she wept for. She'd drifted in and out of sleep for a bit and eventually got to her feet. There were no tears left. Her sister was a talented sculptor and how she'd put the pieces together was a mystery. She needed a therapist who might guide her through hypnosis to find some tiny link in a long-forgotten part of her mind. The mention of a sculptor buying the garden centre had been enough to bring up the shard of a memory.

She left you alone with Angelica.

Numb, Charlotte checked the doors and windows were locked, drank a glass of water, and turned off most of the lights. She left the lamps on and climbed into bed.

CHAPTER TWELVE

An early morning walk cleared most of the negative energy — or at least used up so much physical energy Charlotte had less time to dwell on the emotions of the previous night. The sun wasn't showing itself as she reached the bottom of the falls and stopped, hands on knees, to catch her breath.

She'd carried a pocket flashlight to use on the descent, knowing how treacherous the ground was underfoot. This whole scenic area needed proper attention to fill potholes, repair broken railings and steps, and make the track safe. Tourists were at risk of falling or even getting lost thanks to the poor state of the area, which was dotted with signs for walking tracks and had an information board near the carpark.

Charlotte straightened and gazed up. The sky was clear with a breathtaking display of stars. If the ground wasn't so cold, she'd have lain on the soft grass to stargaze for a while. The waterfall formed a calming backdrop and the last of her stress drained away.

Near the edge of the water was a long-fallen tree trunk and she made herself comfortable on its smooth bark as she'd done numerous times before. For a while she meditated, letting her mind wander to safe places she'd created for the purpose. It was a discipline she needed to follow more than she had lately. When she opened her eyes again, a soft light had replaced the earlier darkness. Birdsong surrounded her and she smiled at the tiny kingfisher watching her from a branch over the pool.

"Hello, you." The azure kingfisher was endangered in this region, although more common in other places. Charlotte counted herself lucky to see one or more at a time on a regular basis, almost always here and in the dawn or dusk. If there was one benefit to the difficult descent, it was to reduce the foot traffic which would disturb the birds. With a flash of blue and gold he was gone, flying low across the pool.

Rather than trek back to the main path and along the street to get home, Charlotte headed to the top of the falls. She'd not walked much in ages and it was amazing to use muscles for more than carrying books around the shop.

It'll hurt later.

It hurt already. Partway up the steps, she stopped for another breather. The sun was above the falls now, casting pale streams of light onto the river on the other side of the pool. The waterfall itself was almost close enough to touch. Clear water cascading…except there was rubbish in the water. Too fast for Charlotte to identify, they fell into the pool and then bobbed up again. She took her phone out and zoomed in with its camera. Beer cans. A dozen or so. She snapped a few images and put the phone away.

Whoever tossed them into the river needed a chat with Trev. Pollution was minimal here in Kingfisher Falls, air, and ground. The alley Trev looked in last night had a fair bit of rubbish along its length but that was rare. The town was proud of how it looked. The worst, in Charlotte's opinion, were people like Sid who tossed their cigarette butts on the ground.

She reached the top and as always, took in the spectacular view below. The river at her side disappearing over the edge with a hint of misty droplets. The pool at the bottom, rippling out from the falls to form a new part of the river. Today it moved slowly but after lots of rain, it could be turbulent.

For a while she followed the river, keeping an eye out for signs of more rubbish. There was no sign of more trash by the time she reached the path home and she turned onto it, ready for a hot shower and a coffee. Or three.

————

"Coffee, dear?" Rosie was at the coffee machine when Trev, in uniform, emerged from his bedroom. Coffee sounded oh-so-good and might wake him up a bit.

"Love one. You're up early, Mum."

"Oh. You're working?"

"Did you need me for something?" He leaned down to kiss her cheek and accepted a cup. "I have to spend some time on the…fire case."

Rosie wheeled past him and he followed her to the living room, dropping onto an armchair once she'd settled on the sofa.

"No, not for me. But you still look exhausted. I know you were out late and I'm pretty sure it wasn't at Charlie's."

"How you deduce that is beyond me, but you're correct." Spending another couple of hours with Charlotte was far preferable than making sure the town was secure, much as he loved his job. "We did take a rather long route back to her apartment, via an alley and the old garden centre, but once we did get her home, she was so tired I simply made sure she was locked in and went to collect the car." He sipped the coffee, relishing the hit of caffeine delivered in such a delicious mouthful.

"We'll circle back to that in a moment, but I know you didn't come in until after midnight."

Trev shook his head. "Sorry, Mum. Last thing I want is to disturb you."

Rosie grinned. "One thing about being a parent is never sleeping until your child is safely home. At least when they live with you. Old habits and all that."

I need to find a house. Poor Mum.

"I'm careful. Always. Last night I drove around town to keep an eye on things. Spoke to a couple of people wandering around, but they had good reason. It felt like the right thing to do, checking the town was safe."

"Yes. And Kingfisher Falls is safer having you here."

Mayhem climbed onto the arm of Trev's chair and stared at him. Trev stared back. The cat wasn't a fan of people but he always came to Trev. "You all good?" Mayhem blinked.

"Now, why were you dragging Charlie through alleys last night?"

Trev laughed. "Are we talking about the same person? Since when could anyone make Charlotte do anything she didn't want to?"

"True."

"Did you know she took a video of Sid back when the tree was stolen from the roundabout? And then she hid from him down a tiny space between two buildings?"

"Maybe. Hard to keep up with her adventures. How is your coffee? I'm going to cook some breakfast if you'd like some."

His mother was as bad as his girlfriend.

"I need to get going, but thanks. If I can cover off everything this morning, then I might see if Charlie wants to visit the Forests. Have a couple of ideas for some landscaping. At the station."

And some wedding ideas for you and Lewis.

The look Rosie shot him said she didn't quite believe him, but she reached for his empty cup. "I'm sure she'd love to visit her little namesake. She hasn't seen Sophie Charlotte for a month or so, thanks to the shenanigans of the town."

A few minutes later, Trev started the patrol car and backed

out of the driveway. Rosie was right if she thought he had another motive to visit the Christmas Tree Farm. Last night, Lewis mentioned he and Rosie had yet to decide on a location for the wedding and reception. They'd decided against a church wedding, having both done those with their first marriages. It seemed they preferred a natural local setting, and although for Trev it would be somewhere around the falls, for his mother there would be some logistic issues. He had an idea in the back of his mind and he needed Charlotte's opinion.

For now, his attention turned to the crime filling his town. This much crime in his small town. How was this happening and why? He had interviews this morning with Cecil's receptionist, and a woman he didn't know. She'd left a message on the line to the police station overnight. Her name wasn't familiar but that was hardly surprising considering how long he'd lived away. Her message was about seeing something the night of the fire. And her phone number, which he'd call once he got to the station. Sally Austin.

The sun wasn't long up when he parked outside the station. As he locked the patrol car, another vehicle drove past slowly enough to get Trev's attention. It was an old station wagon and he couldn't be certain, but he thought he saw Sid behind the wheel. A trail of smoke from the driver's window added to his suspicion. Whatever Sid was up to would need to wait. Trev shook his head as the car rounded a corner and disappeared. He had too much else to worry about and would get to the ex-officer when time permitted.

CHAPTER THIRTEEN

SALLY AUSTIN WAS SOFTLY SPOKEN BUT INTENSE. SHE'D
come in within half an hour of Trev calling and sat on the other
side of his desk, her eyes flicking around the room, rather than
looking at him. The whiteboard was her main focus, which
he'd covered with a sheet before she'd arrived.

"Your phone message indicated you have some information
about the night of the fire at the real estate agency." Trev
prompted. "What would you like to tell me?"

Still not looking at him, Sally took a sudden quick breath.
"Yes. Yes, I saw something. I was taking a walk and a man ran
past me. Yes. Ran past and almost knocked me over."

"Did he bump you? Hurt you?"

"No. But he was close and swerved around me and kept
running. Fast. Running fast."

"Where were you at this point? Which street?"

Sally shrugged. "I moved here a week ago. I don't know
the names."

"That's okay. What was around you? Houses, shops?
Bushland?" Trev said.

"It was around the shops. I had looked through a window.
A clothes shop. Ladies clothes."

"Near the big roundabout?"

"I guess."

Trev typed for a moment or two.

"I didn't know there was a fire," she said. "Thought he must be a runner or something. Jogger. Whatever."

"And which direction did he come from?"

She turned her eyes on him at last. Her expression was cold and Trev's skin crawled. "Behind me. From where the fire was. You know, he was running away from it. Whatever he did."

"You said you've recently moved here. May I have an address?"

"No. You have my phone number and I'm not a suspect so there's no reason to bother me with visits."

Trev lifted his hands from the keyboard as she continued.

"Your job is to find this man and stop him. That is the job of the police. People won't come forward if they are going to be harassed."

Whoa. Settle down.

"I appreciate you coming in to speak about your concerns and can assure you I'm not in the business of harassing people. Not community minded people like yourself. What do you recall about this man? Any description you remember?"

She rolled her eyes. "No point coming here if I didn't. He'd be about my age. Not as tall as you but solid enough. He wore jeans and a hoodie. The hood was up."

"You saw his face though."

"No."

"You mentioned his age being around the same as yours."

"Yes. Actually, yes, I did see his face. Reflected in the window pane. Yes. He had freckles." Sally picked up the handbag she'd dropped at her feet when she arrived. "And on the back of his hoodie was a tree."

Trev's heart sank. "Tree?"

She stood. "A pine tree. So, there you are. All wrapped up.

71

Find the hooded man and you find the killer."

"I have a few more questions, Mrs Austin, if you wouldn't mind—"

"Ms. Ms Austin. What on earth makes you think I'd be married?" The soft tone was replaced with something closer to outrage.

Trev got to his own feet and nodded at her left hand. "Wedding ring. But my apologies for assuming. Before you leave, what time was it? When you saw this man?"

She was heading for the door. "No idea. Mid evening."

"Was anyone with you?"

"Why? Can't a woman walk safely in this town, officer?"

"Not why I was asking." Trev got to the door beside the counter first and opened it. "I'm grateful for your information and if there's another witness, then it also helps."

She went through the door but swung around so fast Trev almost ran into her. "So, you don't believe me. I'm used to that from people like you. Forget I came forward."

With that, she pushed open the door to the street and flung it back but Trev stopped it from slamming. She hurried down the path and onto the pavement, turning to the right without another glance. Oversized coat wrapped around a thin body, Sally Austin bothered Trev on a level he couldn't identify. Why would a newcomer to town lie? He closed the door again, not at all comfortable with the way the interview had gone.

———

His second interview was the opposite. Cecil's receptionist, Mrs McKenzie, offered more help than he needed. That was, in between floods of tears. She'd worked for Cecil for years and couldn't believe he was gone.

"Such a nice man. Always a pleasant word no matter who he spoke to."

Statement complete, she'd got as far as the first door before remembering something. "Cecil was a stickler for keeping appointments. For recording every meeting and he kept notes on the iPad, as you are aware. But his mobile phone was his back-up for if he didn't have the iPad. They didn't sync though and he'd have to transfer the notes over manually."

"And you have no theories on where his phone might be?"

"None. He always had it with him. In case a seller wanted him, or a buyer. Or even a renter. Cecil was available all the time. Anyway, when he turned down the offer to sell the building, it was via a phone call."

"Were you there at the time?"

Mrs McKenzie shook her head. "Not during the call. But I came in with lunch for us both just after. He was a bit out of sorts. Not agitated as such. He never would be. But he mentioned then that the buyer wasn't happy with him and I think it was upsetting for such a sweet person."

After Mrs McKenzie left, Trev returned to the whiteboard and uncovered it. He made some notes.

Cecil's phone may have record of who made offer on building
Priority to locate phone
Potential suspect reported

His hand hovered over the whiteboard. There was no way he was going to write down Darcy Forest as a suspect. Age, build, freckles…and the pine tree logo. Sally Austin could say what she wanted, but if Darcy was the person running along the main street of Kingfisher Falls on a wet night then there'd be a good reason for it. Not one involving a murder.

Trev went back over his unfinished notes from talking with Ms Austin. "You saw him then didn't see his face, then did. Not convincing." Perhaps she was nervous. Or had a police record.

"So you don't believe me. I'm used to that from people like you. Forget I came forward." She'd said earlier.

Might be time to get Charlie to give her opinion on all of this. And it was more than time to visit Darcy.

CHAPTER FOURTEEN

"DOES ROSIE HAVE ANY IDEA WHAT YOU ARE UP TO?" Charlotte grinned at Trev. His message inviting her to drive up to the Christmas Tree Farm with him was welcome. He'd filled her in on his idea of location scouting and she was more than happy to help.

"Pretty sure she suspects me of being up to something." He turned onto the road heading out of town. "Told her I need landscaping ideas for the police station grounds."

"Well, you do."

"Yeah. But more importantly, I remember being up at the farm when Darcy was a kid. Before his mum left and the place was let run down. I was a few years older and there was some function up there. You've been to the house."

"Nope."

Trev shot her a look of disbelief. "You haven't?"

"I'm familiar with the carpark and the pine forest between it and Glenys Lane's old place, and the big shed and sales area. Closest I've got to the house was at the Christmas Eve party but it was still from a distance. Why?"

He smiled. "You'll see. Assuming Darcy and Abbie don't mind us taking a little walk."

"What are you up to?"

"Patience."

Patience wasn't Charlotte's strength. Not unless she had a good reason, but a glance at Trev's amused expression told her she'd have to find some. Fine. "I wanted to talk to you about the river."

"It flows behind the bookshop and throws itself off a cliff then swims to the sea. Eventually."

"Since when did you get so poetic? Did you have some out-of-body experience and ended up in the wrong body? Who are you?" she teased.

"Maybe there's things you haven't found out about me yet."

Of this, Charlotte was certain. There was a depth and heart in him she couldn't wait to get to know.

"I guess there's time now."

His hand reached over to squeeze hers for a second.

"About the river…I was down at the pool this morning and saw our little kingfisher friend again. But on my way up to the top of the falls I noticed rubbish dropping over the edge. Beer cans."

"Into the pool?"

"And floating off to the sea. I should have gone back down and retrieved them."

"No. As much as the pool looks serene, over winter the river can turn nasty very quickly." Trev accelerated as they reached a higher speed zone. "Further north, several smaller rivers combine to join ours and all it takes is some heavy rain up there and that waterfall turns into a mountain of water."

"So, no white-water rafting?"

"Charlotte."

"Joking, Trevor. Just hate the idea of rubbish in the river."

"Me too. Probably youngsters with nothing better to do than drink out in the bushland. I'll take a look around a bit later. But before we get to the Forests, I'd like your opinion on something."

As the road climbed and curved, Trev talked about his interviews. The strange newcomer to town who identified a man resembling Darcy around the time the fire might have been started confused her.

"Do you think she's the sculptor?" Charlotte asked, hoping not. More strange people in town was the last thing anyone needed.

"Should have asked her. Mind you, she wasn't keen to divulge anything about herself so all I have is a phone number."

"Why was she out walking in that awful weather? I was soaked through in seconds getting down to the fire."

After turning into the road to the Christmas Tree Farm, Trev pulled over, leaving the motor idling as he turned to Charlotte. "What is your take on it."

"It wouldn't be the first time someone tried to set Darcy up for a crime."

Last year, when the Christmas trees were being stolen, several locals pointed their fingers at Darcy, claiming he was doing it to get new business. The most vocal of these was Jonas Cartwright, who'd organised a public meeting in the plaza to raise doubts about him.

"Jonas?" Trev's lips tightened.

"Who was hanging around watching the fire investigators. Have you considered finding out where he was that night?"

"He's on my list. Near the top now." He leaned over and kissed Charlotte's lips. "Thanks. Helps talking to you. I'll ask Darcy where he was so I can add it to the notes."

A moment or so later they drove into the large carpark of the Christmas Tree Farm. This property was developed by Darcy's parents, but a decade or so ago, his mother left his father who became a bitter man with no interest in maintaining the once-successful business. After his death, Darcy inherited the farm and with his wife and son, moved from a beachside life to a place he barely recognised. Even the rates were in arrears and all Darcy could do was work every waking hour to bring in enough to offset threats from the council to take his home.

Trev drew into a parking spot closest to the house, which was visible past a low fence and garden. All along the left of the carpark were pine trees, some growing for Christmas sales and others as windbreaks. On the opposite side was a three-sided shed used during the busy festive season, and beyond was Darcy's huge shed filled with his farm equipment and wood-turning tools from his trade as a carpenter.

"Charlotte! Charlotte, you're here!"

Barely out of the car, Charlotte turned just in time to open her arms as a whirlwind of a child threw himself at her. She wrapped Lachie up and squeezed until he giggled and wriggled out of her arms.

He stepped back, sliding the top of a hoodie off his head. "Mum will be so pleased to see you. Oh, hello Leading Cons... I mean Leading Senior Constable Sibbritt. We are honoured by your visit."

Charlotte covered her mouth to stop giggles coming out as Trev solemnly offered his hand to shake. "The honour is mine, Master Forest."

"As soon as you drove in, Mum said to bring you to the kitchen, so let's go."

Lachie tore off again and Trev reached for Charlotte's hand. "See the logo on his hoodie?" he whispered.

"Pine tree. He and Darcy wear them everywhere."

Lachie waited at a gate, which he held open. "Please join us for a cup of tea or coffee. And Mum's delish scones."

They crossed a small area of lawn and climbed a few steps to the wide, timber veranda of a two-storey house. It was an old building which needed some repairs and paint. The floor-boards were new and timber surrounds on the windows and door were unpainted and incomplete. Works in progress.

"Come on!" Lachie almost jumped up and down as he held

the door open. Charlotte stepped through, patting his head like a puppy which made him laugh.

She walked through a small hallway lined with hooks for hanging coats, straight into a huge country style kitchen. Charlotte sniffed the air, her stomach rumbling in response to the delightful aromas wafting from the oven.

Abbie tossed a tea towel onto the side of the sink and hurried to meet them. "Oh, hello!" A hug and kiss later, she gestured to the wooden kitchen table. "Sit. Tea or coffee?"

Over scones with cream and jam, and steaming coffee, Abbey updated Charlotte and Trev on recent events. "Now that Sophie is sleeping through, I'm working a bit to help Darcy get his wholesale nursery known. I've made a website and am getting orders trickling in most days."

"That's wonderful! So, the old greenhouses are all growing plants again?" Charlotte eyed off a third scone and with a laugh, Abbie pushed the plate her way.

"Lots of healthy seedlings from vegetables to flowers. And there's something else we're working on." Abbie poured more coffee for them all. "When Darcy's mother was still here, she occasionally hired out the bottom barn for events."

Trev nodded. "I remember going to one. And was going to ask if the place was still in good repair because…" he glanced at Charlotte, who smiled, knowing now what he was going to say. "Mum and Lewis are getting married and don't have a venue yet."

Lachie appeared in the doorway. "Sophie wants to get up."

Abbie stood. "Why don't I collect Sophie while you finish your coffee? Then we can go for a walk and see the barn."

———

It was perfect. Trev grinned as he stared at the old building. In the style of an American barn, the structure looked sound even if the red paint on the timber was peeled and faded. The double doors were open and inside, the floor was concrete and the ceiling crossed with heavy beams. Daylight streamed through multiple skylights.

"Darcy and I thought we'd do it up and use it for functions again. First though we've been working on the garden, here this way." Abbie headed around the side of the barn.

"You coming or you going to spend the day gazing at Sophie?" he teased Charlotte, who'd been cuddling the baby since Abbie handed her over after leaving the house. Sophie Charlotte Forest was a few months old now and stared solemnly back at Charlotte as if sizing her up.

"I can do both." Charlotte didn't glance at him. There was such love in her face that Trev wanted to kiss her there and then. Best not in case Sophie objected. Instead, he put a hand on her shoulder as they followed Abbie. Lachie had disappeared a while ago.

A wide path led to a lawned area against the side of the barn. On two sides it was protected by neat hedges and garden beds filled with all types of cottage plants. At this time of year not a lot flowered but Trev imagined once spring approached the area would be a riot of colour. The third side was open to a stunning view over the valley.

"Darcy is going to add double doors to this side of the barn so people can walk straight out to the garden. Do you like it?"

"Abbie, this is amazing!" Charlotte wandered to the view. "The town is down there. I had no idea you were so high."

"It is a pretty outlook." Abbie joined Charlotte. "Makes it ideal for special events."

"If council will ever approve it." Darcy appeared from around the corner with Lachie in tow. He and Trev shook hands and he kissed Charlotte's cheek and then Sophie's nose.

"What needs approving? Your parents used to hold events here." Trev leaned against the barn. "Liquor licence an issue?"

"Nah. They claim we're changing the primary use of the land and need all kinds of permits."

"Rubbish. I'm not an expert but am pretty sure you can show prior use and besides, your primary use is still agriculture." Trev frowned. "Is it Jonas being a pain?"

"Who else. And I can't afford a lot to fight it. Might have to wait until the other bills are out of my hair."

Charlotte offered Sophie to Abbie. "Um...she did something."

"Want to help me change her?" Abbie grinned. "I'll show you how."

"I think Trev needs my help for something. But thanks."

"Chicken." Trev said as she reached for his arm.

"I'll help, Mum!" Lachie took off after Abbie and Sophie.

"Got new neighbours, and that's adding to the problem of the permit as they claim it will interfere with their enjoyment of peace and quiet. Or something." Darcy crossed his arms, lips pressed together.

Last Trev heard, Glenys Lane's property was on the market to help pay her legal fees for killing Octavia Morris and years earlier, her own husband. Charlotte had once called the property 'creepy' and he tended to agree. The house itself was in poor repair and its windows shuttered, and out the back was a giant firepit Glenys used to destroy evidence and who knows what else.

"Not a Sally Austin?" Trev asked. She might actually like the place.

"Nope. A Sid and Marguerite Browne. Renting."

Trev let out a long breath. Charlotte's mouth had dropped open, then closed again and their eyes met.

"Yes, so nice to have them living next door. Not. I've made it clear to Lachie he can't go near the boundary fence and isn't to engage with them. I'm pretty easy going but it bothers me having them so close." Darcy stared in the general direction of where their house was behind the trees. "Terrible business, poor Cecil. I remember him from when I was a kid. He told my dad to sell. Offered to put the place on the market."

"Do you remember anything about the night of the fire, Darcy?" Might as well get it over with. "Trying to build a picture of the evening, given I was on my way back from the city."

Darcy gave him a puzzled look. "Can't remember what I don't know, Trev. We were in bed by nine that night. Same as most nights. Didn't even know what happened till the next morning. Was a bit worried about you, Charlie, when we heard."

"Thanks. But we were lucky. The bookshop that is."

"I hope you can get some witnesses, though who'd be out on such a wet night?"

Trev wondered the same after they finished the conversation and he and Charlotte returned to the car. A lot wasn't adding up. Sid and Marguerite living in Glenys' old place. Council being an obstacle to Darcy working toward paying off his debt to them. And someone trying to put Darcy near the scene of the crime. Something bigger than a botched robbery was going on here. He felt it in his gut.

CHAPTER FIFTEEN

"AT LEAST THE RAIN'S HOLDING OFF FOR A BIT." CHARLOTTE tried to start a conversation for the third time since she and Trev took a walk into the bushland. He'd been quiet on the trip home and happy to check out where the beer cans might have come from when she suggested it.

"Hm."

She glanced at his face. Still deep in thought.

"I bought a little raft to try out your theory of going over the falls in winter."

"Funny. I am listening to you." Trev put an arm around her shoulder as they walked. "Sorry to be distracted."

"You're worried about the Forests. So am I."

"Do you feel there's some underlying reason Jonas is out to get Darcy?"

They'd followed the track to the clearing and stopped near the place a young woman had once been buried. Charlotte had stumbled across the grave a few weeks ago, covered in flowers by an unknown—at the time—caretaker. The grave was still marked out with police tape and Trev sighed. "Time for this to go. I'm not sure how to proceed though."

"What do you mean?"

"Still don't have a definitive answer on who owns the land. It may be council, or possibly Terrance Murdoch. Well, at least his brother did, but presumably it will be his once the will is read. We may be trespassing and now the investigation is finished, might have to stay out of the clearing."

Charlotte gazed back the way they'd come, toward her apartment. "So, it is true Terrance owns the land right behind me?"

"Looks like it."

"And the land would then go all the way to behind the real estate agency building?" she turned to Trev. "What if Terrance has plans for the land?"

"Terrance has a number of charges against him which may see him spend a long time behind bars. And if Violet's family file a civil suit against him, this land might change hands."

"Unless..." Charlotte squatted beside the grave, where a few stray asters insisted on attempting to grow despite the cold weather.

"What are you thinking?"

"Not sure. Would council have enough money to buy it?"

Trev offered a hand and Charlotte straightened. They continued toward the river.

"What would council do with it?" he asked.

"Develop it."

"Nah. This little town doesn't want industry here. They'd have a fight on their hands." Trev held a branch up so Charlotte could go ahead. "The thing is, and I'd like to run it past Lewis and Mum for their opinions, I'm not sure Kingfisher Falls Council has anywhere enough money to do much. Look at the state of the trails around the Falls. And some of our footpaths are in poor repair."

"And they wanted traders to foot the bill for a Christmas tree, and removed water access from the fountain."

"If anything, they would probably prefer to sell land rather than buy it."

"How do we force council to answer all these questions, Trev? Can you make them provide the information?"

"Need to talk to Bryce and Katrina. See what they think. This is a bit beyond anything I've dealt with."

Around a bend, the trees gave way to the river. Broad and normally slow moving, it was full and churning at the moment. Sometimes it was so calm and clear, Charlotte would cross with her sandals in her hand, careful of her footing but enjoying the cool water around her calves. Not now though. It looked freezing and grey.

"Let's head toward the bridge at the road. See if we can find anything." Trev grinned. "Not paddling weather."

"Not even close." She took his hand again. "I think the barn at Darcy and Abbie's place would be perfect for a wedding. What if we offered to help them finish the repairs? Painting and stuff."

"I think that's a lovely idea. Would like to help get that permit approved for them but it isn't my area of expertise."

"I'll find out what needs doing. I'm a good investigator."

"You are."

At the end of the bushland, the river flowed under a bridge across the road. From there it weaved around more streets, some Charlotte had never been along. Near the bridge, a dirt track led from the road between a high wire fence.

"What is that?" Charlotte pointed across the river. Instead of thick bushes and trees, an area was cleared. "I don't normally come this way but it looks as though they've been bulldozed."

They crossed the bridge and squeezed between a gap in the fence to get to the other side of the river. Trev grabbed the chain mesh and shook it. "Looks like someone cut this and wired it back up. And there's tracks."

Wide tyre tracks indented the still muddy ground. Bushes were piled high to one side and Charlotte walked around them. "These were pulled out of the ground! Who would do such a thing?" The cleared area was the size of a house block. "And look there." She leaned into the bushes and pulled out a piece of cardboard. "From a slab of beer."

She gazed around and not seeing anything else of interest, joined Trev at the fence. "Can you fingerprint this?" she held it out.

"Charlie..."

"Why not? You just said someone has cut the wire to gain entry, which is trespassing and I saw the beer cans, which is littering and—"

He tilted his head with the expression she knew well. Amusement and patience. Well, she didn't need either.

"Trevor. We need to get to the bottom of this!"

"We will. I'm going to take some photographs and make a report and tomorrow I'll speak to council about it. This is their land so let's see if they are aware of this. Shall we go see if Mum has any ideas about council's liquidity?"

"That's a big word. Are you trying to distract me with a visit to see Rosie?"

"Is it working?"

It was. Charlotte had no ability to stay annoyed with Trev. But she wasn't ready to admit such a thing. "Are you going to take some photos or would you like me to? You know mine are better."

"Be my guest. I'm going to find a bin for this cardboard so you do your thing and I'll be right back." Trev took the beer box and slid back through the wire. "There's one near the corner."

Charlotte took photos with her phone camera of the wire and then the bushes. She wandered around, snapping images of the tyre tracks and a panorama of the whole area. After checking the photos, she slipped the phone away. A movement deeper in the bushland caught her eye and she looked up.

Straight to a woman who stood between two trees. Scarf

around her head, large sunglasses in spite of the late afternoon, she stared at Charlotte.

"Alison?"

No response. Just the unmoving stare. Charlotte's legs froze and nausea bubbled in her stomach. It couldn't be. Wasn't. She reached for her phone. This time she'd keep her eyes on the woman, who was at least fifty metres away. There were lots of low-lying bushes between them but the woman was in a good position for a photograph.

"What do you want?" Charlotte lifted the phone so she could find the camera app and keep the woman in her sight, and as she did, the woman turned and ran. "Wait!"

Charlotte took a photo as she set off after her, skirting around the bushes but not gaining ground. She reached the place the woman had stood and peered into dense forest. "Where are you? I just want to talk." She called.

Nothing. No rustling or crunch of fallen leaves underfoot. Not a flash of movement. And no reply. Had she even been there? Charlotte checked her phone. Her photo was so blurred it was impossible to tell whether there was a person in it, or a tree.

Are you dreaming her up?

"Charlotte! Where are you?"

She wasn't dreaming the anxious tone in Trev's voice. A quick intake of air to steady her pounding heart and she turned back to the cleared area.

"I'm over here."

He ran to meet her, his face filled with concern. "Where did you go? You look as though...did you see something?"

"Um. I think so. Well, not really. Shadows in the trees."

His hands went to her shoulders and he dropped his head closer to her face, searching her eyes. "Did something spook you?"

Someone. A ghost.

86

"Thought I saw someone and went to say hi. But nobody was there. My imagination."

"You're shaking. Sweetie?"

"Let's go see Rosie. It must be gin time and I'm tired of the forest today."

Despite the long look he gave her, Trev dropped his hands and gestured for Charlotte to go first. She wanted to tell him. Let him understand why her hands shook not to mention her heart pound. But how to explain a ghost from the past? Alison wasn't in Kingfisher Falls. She was either seeing things because of her concerns, or there was a random woman who looked a bit like Alison. The fact the woman wouldn't stay still long enough to have a conversation might mean anything. She could be shy. Reclusive.

Time to see your therapist, Charlie. Time for some help.

CHAPTER SIXTEEN

TREV UNLOCKED THE FRONT DOOR AND USHERED Charlotte in with the bottle of wine she'd insisted on buying on the way. They found Rosie at the counter making a floral arrangement.

"Perfect timing! Ooh...nice. Shall we open it now?" Adding one last flower, Rosie smiled at Charlotte. "These are for you, darling."

"Me? Oh, they're lovely." Charlotte kissed Rosie's cheek after handing the wine to Trev. "How did you get such colour and variety at this time of year?"

"There are plenty of winter flowers and you know I love my garden. Next time we have a nice day, we'll go for a walk out the back and I'll show you some that might work in your little yard. Or even in pots on your balcony." Rosie slotted the final stem into a vase. "Remember to take it home. You can return the vase when the flowers are gone."

Trev arrived with three glasses and the wine and set about filling them. "Nice glass of red?"

"As if we'd say no!" Rosie held her hand out and once everyone had a glass, made a toast. "To my beautiful family."

Charlotte's heart—which had finally settled into a normal

beat—filled with warmth. Her place here was accepted in a way she'd never experienced, even long before she'd let Trev into her life. She grinned as she touched her glass to Rosie's and then Trev's. His smile still held a touch of worry. "I'm okay." she mouthed and his face relaxed.

"So, did you go up to see baby Sophie?" Rosie asked. Mellow appeared from another room and launched herself onto Rosie's lap with a meow.

"She's so big now! I was carrying her and couldn't believe how heavy she is." Charlotte said.

"You're not used to babies?"

"Mum, you should have seen how fast Charlotte offloaded poor Sophie when she...well..."

"Filled her nappy?" Rosie laughed.

"I did not offload her! That sounds terrible. I simply let Abbie know." Charlotte wasn't about to explain that she had no idea how to change a baby. And why would she? There'd never been one in her life.

"And did you get some landscaping ideas, Trev?"

"We ended up talking about Darcy and Abbie's new neighbours." Trev diverted from anything that might make Rosie think they'd been looking at a wedding venue. He'd mentioned his mother's suspicion to Charlotte earlier and she'd promised to keep it between them and the Forests for now. "Bit of a shock to find out Sid and Marguerite are renting Glenys' place."

"Oh my. Well, that explains him being his usually annoying self around town but why there of all places?"

"Cheap? It isn't the nicest property." Trev suggested.

"It is creepy and awful." Charlotte added. "But why are they back in Kingfisher Falls? Sid was lucky to avoid being charged with any one of a number of crimes so what would make him want to live here again? Where they aren't respected."

Mayhem stalked into the room and stopped near Trev.

"Hello, cat." After considering Trev for a moment, Mayhem climbed onto the back of an armchair and stared at him. Trev stared back.

"You two are silly." Rosie declared. "Are you staying for dinner, Charlie?"

"Thanks, but no. I have a ton of housework to do and I want to spend a bit of time looking into something."

The look from Trev and Rosie made her laugh.

"Nothing bad. Just want to read up on some of the history of the council here and see if I can find anything interesting. And have an early night."

"What do you want to know about council?" Rosie pushed her empty glass toward Trev and he refilled it. "They are a terrible lot, mainly because most of the councillors won't stand up to Jonas and he has done nothing to build this region. Just tear it down."

Charlotte and Trev exchanged a look. That was exactly what they'd wondered.

"Come on, you two. What is this about?"

Trev filled Rosie in on their speculation about the land, Terrance, and Jonas. She nodded as she sipped and listened.

"If council is having any financial issues, why wouldn't they encourage someone like Darcy to increase local business rather than put up roadblocks?" Charlotte asked.

"Roadblocks?"

"Oh. He is after a permit for something on his property which will help him get out of debt and pay council the arrears from all the years his father didn't pay rates. Instead of helping him get things going, they're making him jump through hoops and he's putting his plans on hold until he's paid off some of their debt." Charlotte shook her head. "Seems a backward step."

"Unless Jonas has an agenda. Wouldn't surprise me if he wants to turn our little town into a ruin so everyone decides to sell up and he can grab all the land. He's a young man with time on his side and based on his shady connections with people like Veronica in the past...Jonas needs watching."

You might have a point.

"Is this about Darcy's greenhouses?" Rosie continued. "Because those buildings have been there for at least thirty years and I think council would have a hard time making him get a permit now."

Charlotte decided this was a comment best not addressed. She'd already said too much and didn't want Rosie working out the Forests might be going into the business of functions again. Much as she longed to sink into an armchair and drink more wine, she pushed herself up. "Sorry. I'm going to go home before it gets too dark, with my beautiful flowers. And I'll open the shop in the morning, Rosie, so take your time."

Trev stood. "I'll walk back with you."

"No need. You still look so tired so do me a favour and take a break. Or cook for your mother." She smiled. "I'll message when I'm home."

He didn't look impressed but said nothing as Charlotte collected her handbag and vase, and kissed Rosie goodnight. He followed her outside where the air was cold and closed the front door behind them both. "You sure? I don't mind the walk."

"Really sure. I'll be home before dark."

Trev touched her cheek and dropped a kiss on her lips. "Be careful, sweetie. Think the rain's heading back."

"I will. Promise."

Before she changed her mind and returned to the warmth of the house, she headed off. At the street she glanced back with a smile. Trev raised a hand and then went inside.

She got as far as the main street before the nerves hit her again. What if the woman was around? Here she was with a vase of flowers which smelt gorgeous but wouldn't be much use in a chase. As she hurried, Charlotte looked as far ahead as she could, jumping at the sight of a woman walking her way.

But it was one of their customers and she summoned a smile and greeting at they passed each other

In a few minutes she was past the roundabout and the first sprinkles of rain began. At the corner she paused to check for traffic. Again, no strange woman watching her. Just cars and she waited for them to pass. One of them was driven by Sid, who sneered at her through his window before turning up past the bookshop.

She followed, relieved when he drove past and over the hill. Nothing was out of place. The bookshop was fine and when she went down the driveway, everything was how it should be. Another minute and she was inside the apartment, door locked and lights on. As she placed the vase on the counter she stared at her hands. They were shaking again.

CHAPTER SEVENTEEN

TREV SPENT THE EVENING WORKING. ROSIE HAD ALREADY prepped an easy dinner and they'd finished the bottle of wine with it. He'd taken a cup of coffee to Rosie after she'd settled onto the sofa with a book to read and the cats vying for the best position on her lap.

He moved into the study, opening his laptop and a large notepad. For an hour or so he dug around in the past of one Jonas Carmichael. It was interesting reading. Graduated top of his private and exclusive boy's school, managing to avoid the scandals it was associated with all too often. There was a mention in one obscure newspaper article about him being the target of a hate campaign after reporting other students for wrongdoing.

"Not our Jonas. Surely?"

What did Trev know about the man? His exposure to him was recent. Jonas was a new resident to the region and their paths hadn't crossed until a year or so ago. Not that he could remember anyway. Mum had a dim view of the man and it probably coloured his own thinking.

She has good judgement.

Trev took a sip from the glass of brandy he'd brought in

with him. He was bone-tired but his brain wouldn't settle and he wanted to push away the riot of worry in his gut. Thinking of Rosie's judgement helped. She'd sized Charlie up within a few minutes of meeting her and decided she was a good fit. In the bookshop and more importantly, in her life. At the time, Charlotte was looking for a reason to leave River's End and Trev didn't want to lose her. Bringing her to meet his mother was a risk. But one that turned out to be the best decision of his life.

His dad had a saying. One that he'd considered many times after he'd driven Charlotte here to visit the bookshop.

Plant a seed, let it grow into whatever it will be. Nurture it, because one day you'll want its shade and shelter.

He'd doubted his own judgement but here he was. In love with a woman who loved him in return. Trev smiled and pushed the remainder of the brandy away. His gut was fine.

Back on the trail of Jonas, Trev made notes as he found information of interest. After school, Jonas attended a prestigious university and gained his law degree, specialising in criminology. This was a surprise. With his background the man could have chosen a career in anything from law to policing.

Or politics.

Which made the move to perhaps the smallest shire in Victoria a curious choice. If he intended to make politics his life, then mayor of Kingfisher Falls Shire was not much of a career move. Something else was going on.

He searched for the time between Jonas taking the bar and now. There was little to find other than a stint at a Melbourne law firm. What was he doing now, apart from drawing a small income from his position on the council? Trev opened the council website and located the page profiling the members of council. What he found puzzled Trev. He went to talk to Rosie.

Mayhem growled at Trev.

"For goodness sake, May, you know darned well Trev lives here so start being nice!" Rosie lifted Mayhem off her lap and placed him beside her where he whipped his tail from side to side as he glared at Trev.

"Right. Well, I didn't intend to upset our friend here, but can I ask you something?" He perched on the arm of the chair opposite.

Rosie turned her book over. "You and Charlotte may choose any date to marry other than the first weekend in spring."

"Oh. Um, thanks, but that wasn't...you're teasing me."

"Only a little."

"I think getting you and Lewis safely married is the first priority."

"And I agree. Now, what did you really want to ask me?" She reached a hand out to Mayhem who tapped at it with a paw as though not ready to forgive her yet.

"Doing some legwork about Jonas. I had no idea he is a lawyer."

"I imagine being away for fifteen years will do that, son. We need an evening with Charlie here, some cocktails, and a whiteboard. Lewis and I will bring you up to speed."

"Actually, that sounds nice."

And it did. The idea of kicking back with his favourite people and getting background information to help him be better at his job was appealing.

"Then let's make a night and do it. And we'll make a few platters of yummy food. However, to answer your questions I do know he is a lawyer. He bought into the small firm which also took over the Murdoch brothers conveyancing company. Why?"

"Anyone else in this firm?"

Rosie nodded. "Accountant."

Trev settled onto the chair itself. "One firm which contains a lawyer, conveyancer, and an accountant. Add that to a council who won't spend money or help the police with information without pressure and it all adds up to —"

"Corruption."

"Mum, you might be right."

Mayhem climbed down from the sofa, stalked to Trev, and jumped onto his lap. Without another glance at Trev, the cat curled up, the tip of his tail flicking.

––––––

Charlotte made her third cup of tea for the evening. She envisioned a long night ahead, perhaps one without sleep thanks to an over-active mind and unsettled imagination. After cleaning the apartment from top to bottom, she'd stood on the balcony with her first cup of tea until the icy air drove her inside. She'd checked and rechecked all doors and windows were closed and locked and had no real idea why. Being up so high, only the door at the top of the steps was of any concern as most people wouldn't try climbing the sheer walls to the windows or balcony.

Earlier, Trev had messaged. She'd forgotten to let him know she was home. Her response was lots of smiley faces and mention of housework, including a selfie with a mop. He'd sent a thumbs up and she'd put her phone back on the counter with a sigh.

She sipped the tea and returned to her laptop which was open on the dining room table. A quick glance through the images showed the extent of the damage to the area over the river. Uprooted bushes, including large banksias which grew throughout the region. A number of gum tree saplings were beneath the pile of bushes. And the ground was so churned up there must have been heavy vehicles on it.

Charlotte clicked on the final image. The camera on her phone was excellent but even it couldn't capture a good picture thanks to her rushed attempt. On the laptop screen it was clear there was a person in the frame. At least she wasn't imagining the woman's existence. There was no hope of identifying her though. A blur of scarf, coat, and sunglasses gave her nothing to work with.

"Who are you?"

If not Alison, then who would do such a thing? Appearing from nowhere, standing far enough away to make recognition difficult, and staring. Perhaps the woman thought she knew Charlotte but was shy.

Her stomach rumbled and she glanced at the time. After ten and she'd not eaten yet. There was leftover soup she'd made a day or so back and as it heated on the stove, she buttered a bread roll. Her little vegetable garden was providing meals here and there now and she couldn't wait for warmer weather to develop more of the beds.

Back at the laptop, she nibbled on the roll as she typed Alison's name into the search bar. Alison Sharnie Tompkins. It returned a dozen or so results which led to articles. Almost all were about the case of the poor woman misdiagnosed and wrongly accused of plotting to harm her own husband. Charlotte's name appeared too often for her liking and some of the incorrect information made her wince. There was nothing after late in the previous year, when Alison's divorce finalised and gained attention the day she left court.

Charlotte ate as she read through a brief account of Alison screaming at her ex-husband outside. He'd refused to comment and climbed into a car driven by a woman. Alison had pounded on the roof of the car and been cautioned by police.

How interesting. This was the Alison she'd treated. She'd seen glimpses of aggression during their sessions. Bursts of fury followed by calmly spoken explanations for her response.

Tired. Upset by her husband. Worried about him being out so late all the time. Afraid he would leave her for the woman she referred to as his 'girlfriend'. Frightened this other woman would harm her.

Alison went as far as to hire a private investigator to follow her husband and it was after hearing there was no evidence of disloyalty that she made threatening comments about him to Charlotte. Looking back, what else could Charlotte have done than report her? Perhaps getting a second opinion first. The problem was how adamant Alison was on only seeing Charlotte.

Soup finished, Charlotte pushed the bowl to one side and searched for a current address for Alison. There was nothing. No phone number, address, or any recent details. "As if you've vanished." Yet, Mel's description of the person looking for Angelica was uncannily similar to Alison.

Was it time to raise this with Trev? Let him use his contacts to make sure the woman was far away? She turned off the laptop and took her bowl to the kitchen. He had so much to deal with right now. A deadly fire, corrupt local council, the ongoing investigation into Terrance Murdoch and even his mother's upcoming wedding. All priorities over her unrealistic fears about a woman who was two states away.

After washing up, checking the door again, and turning off the lights, Charlotte went to the third bedroom. She stood at the window in the dark, staring over the trees to the distant area where she and Trev were earlier. The night was clear, with the moon offering some light. Nothing moved out there. If anything, it was too quiet. If Charlotte kept to the main streets she could walk around to where the bridge was in a matter of minutes.

She got as far as the counter. Phone in one hand, keys in the other, she stopped. It was late. There was something bad going on in Kingfisher Falls. And there was more than one person ready to make her life difficult.

Don't give them a chance.

For once, Charlotte listened to her rational side. She returned the keys to the counter and took her phone to the bedroom. Sleep might be the last thing she wanted, but if she was in bed, she was less likely to change her mind and do something silly.

CHAPTER EIGHTEEN

MONDAY WAS CHARLOTTE'S FAVOURITE DAY OF THE WEEK IN the bookshop. Well, apart from Saturdays, which were all about being busy and catching up with customers and spending time talking to the children who came in just to enjoy the little reading area. Mondays meant ordering books, replenishing shelves, and often creating a new window display.

Much to her surprise, she'd slept well and woken before dawn. A long shower was followed by more time than usual on hair and makeup. Instead of her default ponytail, she used a straightener to curl up the ends of her hair and pulled some back with a pretty butterfly clip.

With time on her side, she headed to the corner café and ordered a takeaway breakfast. As she waited, she answered messages from Trev and Rosie. The latter was confirming Rosie would be a bit late as she was meeting with the florist to discuss potential floral displays for the wedding. From Trev it was a cheery good morning.

She smiled as she replied. Today was a better day. Last night she'd let things get on top of her but a decent sleep had helped. Whatever the week had planned for her, she was ready.

Back in the bookshop, she ate a breakfast burrito as she set up the store. A quick vacuum of the rug in the middle of the store, a tidy of the children's area, and money in the tills, and she was ready to face the day. Broom in hand, she headed for the front door.

And came to an abrupt stop.

She inched back into the relative darkness behind her. Marguerite Browne stood on the footpath, her attention on something further down the road. She hadn't seen Charlotte, so it seemed. Why oh why was she here?

Charlotte needed to sweep outside and unlock the door but unless Marguerite had undergone a personality upgrade…the thought of dealing with the woman turned her stomach. The last few conversations between them were not conversations. More like one sided personal attacks. She checked the time.

Go away, Marguerite!

Grumbling under her breath, Charlotte moved to the front door and clicked the lock open. A car pulled in near Marguerite, who glanced over her shoulder at the bookshop with a sour expression. It wasn't Sid's station wagon, but a late model SUV and the driver wasn't Sid. Not that Charlotte could see more than a silhouette past the dark tinting of the windows but she knew him well enough. As much as she wanted to know who the driver was, it made more sense to avoid a confrontation.

Charlotte stepped out onto the footpath with a bright smile. "Good morning, Mrs Browne!" She didn't bother waiting for a response but turned her attention to the broom. The bookshop window reflected the SUV and Marguerite opening the door.

"Hurry. Get in!" The driver was female and impatient judging from a loud hiss rather than normal voice. The door slammed and the motor roared before the vehicle drove away.

Charlotte watched it leave, even though something about it nagged at her subconscious. Up the hill in the direction of the falls and out of sight in seconds. Hopefully, Marguerite wasn't soliciting more women for the defunct book club. After Octavia was murdered by another member of the club, there was a vote from the remaining members to take a sabbatical. One which saw each member drop away until there was nobody left.

This gave Charlotte an idea. Something positive. She finished sweeping and propped the door open. The weather was perfect this morning.

As with most Mondays, the day began with few customers. The colder months made this more evident than over summer, where people dropped in as they went for early walks. It gave Charlotte a chance to set up the orders in the system and begin her routine of walking the store to create a list.

"I'm here!" Rosie arrived, coffee cups in the holder on the arm of the wheelchair and a small box on her lap. "With goodies."

Charlotte joined her behind the counter and sniffed the air with a small sigh. "Coffee, yum. And what have you got in there?"

"You know I can't resist the delectable offerings from the bakery. Help yourself. There are two of each." Rosie opened the box to reveal six tiny pastries. "I'm talking to the ladies over there about catering the wedding. Well, once we find a venue."

"That would be good! And delicious." Charlotte popped a tiny éclair into her mouth. The cream squished out of the soft pastry to mingle with the slight crunch of chocolate. So small and so much flavour.

A customer wandered in and Charlotte swallowed too quickly and began to cough. Rosie whacked her on the back which made it worse. She waved her arms around in the hope Rosie would stop and had to push her chair away because the message wasn't getting through. Tears filled her eyes and she got to her feet and dashed to the kitchen for water. Once the coughing stopped, she visited the bathroom and wiped around her eyes.

By the time she returned to the counter, the customer was gone and Rosie was about to pick up the last of the pastries.

"Um...you said three each." Charlotte's voice was a croak.

"Didn't you have yours?" Rosie grinned and pushed the box Charlotte's way. "They are beyond tempting. Are you alright now?"

"Just. No more hitting me, thank you." Charlotte sipped her coffee.

"I was saving your life, darling."

"Uh huh."

Rosie reached for the pastry. "I might eat this. Save you from having another attempt at choking." She paused. "Unless you promise to be very, very careful."

Charlotte burst into laughter. She couldn't help herself at Rosie's deep, serious tone. When she stopped laughing, she nodded. "I shall."

"Shall what?"

"Um...be careful not to choke?"

"Fine. But if you do, I shall pat your back again."

Mouth open to respond, Charlotte decided to eat the pastry before Rosie changed her mind.

———

Trev wished his patrol car was closer as a late model SUV whizzed past, hurtling through the roundabout from the direction of the bookshop. He was on foot with several other uniformed officers, going shop to shop in the hope of finding some video footage from the night of the fire. He turned into the photography and framing shop.

"Trevor!" Harpreet was creating a window display. Like Rosie, she had great pride in her shop and presented it so customers were drawn in and felt welcome. She emerged from the window area with a smile. "What brings you by?"

"Would love to say a social call, but we're checking all the shops for any with security footage."

"Oh. From the other night? Poor Cecil." She made her way to the counter with a shake of her head. "Do you know yet... well, if it was deliberate?"

"It was."

"Who would want to hurt him?"

"That's what I'm hoping to find out. I noticed you have cameras under the front awning."

"Yes." Harpreet was on the other side of the long glass counter, her attention on a computer screen. "Give me an idea of the timeframe you want to see and I'll download the footage. It will take a little while, so can I call you to come and collect?"

Trev left the shop hopeful of gleaning some piece of information from Harpreet's cameras. Apart from the cameras at the bookshop and apartment, hers were the best quality in town he'd come across. He'd already transferred the data from the bookshop's system to a speed stick and knew Bryce and Katrina were working through it this morning.

It was disappointing so few businesses in Kingfisher Falls had a security system. With a low crime rate for decades, most sole traders weren't keen to spend money on something they'd never had need for. Low crime rate until the past year or so. After the strange thefts of Christmas trees, a few shops had upped their security. Esther and Doug, for example, at the ladies boutique. Their front window was smashed by the thieves and the couple responded by installing cameras and a decent alarm. Lewis followed suit.

Once he finished this side of the street, Trev wandered to the shell of the real estate agency. The windows were boarded up but the door was open. A couple of fire investigators were deep in conversation in the middle. He kept going. If they needed to speak to him or the detectives, they'd call.

Charlie was outside the bookshop with a long-handled window cleaner, working her way along the front.

"Need a hand?"

She turned with a smile that caught at his heart. There was a pretty clip in her hair with butterflies. The sun created a halo around her and he wanted to wrap her up in his arms and tell her she was an angel.

"What?" Charlotte tilted her head to one side. "Not used to seeing me wash windows?"

"Actually, no. But I was thinking how cute you are."

She blushed and fiddled with the handle.

"Even cuter now."

"Trev. Someone will hear."

"Let them." He took the cleaner from her and leaned it against the window. "I kind of think most people know you and I are an item."

"An item." Her face softened. "I like it."

"So do I." Trev followed his earlier thought and put his arms loosely around her, and when she looked up at him, he kissed her.

"Aw."

Thanks, Mum.

When he lifted his head, he winked at Charlotte. Her colour was still high but her eyes sparkled.

"I should ask you to clean the windows more often if it means a handsome man will sweep you off your feet." Rosie sat in the doorway with an expression of contentment.

"Or at least me." Trev clarified. He released Charlotte and handed her the cleaning tool. "No kissing other handsome men, okay?"

"I'll try to remember." She tried to keep a straight face but the little crinkly lines around her eyes gave away her mirth. "Unless there's an important reason for your visit, I shall return to my work. Can't afford to let my boss catch me not doing my job."

"I think your boss would rather see you kissing her son than washing windows." Rosie mentioned. "Besides, you'll be the boss soon." With that, she spun her wheelchair and returned to the store.

"On that note, I shall go back to my own work. Just couldn't resist coming by." Trev squeezed Charlotte's hand. "Dinner?"

"Would you like to come over and I'll cook?"

Trev's phone rang. Katrina. "I would. Let's talk a bit later."

Charlotte returned to window cleaning as he answered, already striding in the direction of the police station.

CHAPTER NINETEEN

ROSIE TOLD CHARLOTTE TO LEAVE CLOSING UP FOR HER SO she grabbed some shopping bags and headed for the supermarket, unsure what to cook but wanting to make something special for Trev. For a while, she wandered back and forth, considering options, before spying a tub of locally made ricotta cheese. She did a quick search on her phone for a recipe and then collected the ingredients to make a baked ricotta and salad. There were some sweet red apples and she chose a handful. Some cream and pastry finished the basket. Then a bottle of wine.

Back at the apartment she put the wine in the fridge to chill and prepped the little menu. Once Trev arrived, the ricotta dish would go into the oven and when she took that out, an apple tart would go in.

Getting good at this!

She sang as she sliced and rolled and mixed. Today was a good day. Seeing Marguerite was the only downside but at least there'd been no words pass between them and the other woman had more or less ignored her. It did make her curious about the Brownes being back in town though. Something to talk about over dinner.

Charlotte stepped through the sliding door to see if it was too cool to eat outside. Night was almost here and she gazed over the balcony as the street began to quieten.

A large truck rumbled past, slow enough for her to read that it was a removalist truck. She followed its progress to the roundabout and then a left turn. Was this the sculptor setting up shop? And residence, wherever it was they'd moved to. So exciting to see a new business here and one which might draw tourists in.

She shivered. Not warm enough. With a sigh, she went inside. Partway through setting the dining room table there was a knock on the door. Charlotte smoothed her hair as she hurried to open the door.

"I hope you are hungry…oh."

A short, thin man in a suit stood on the landing, a briefcase in one hand and closed umbrella in the other. Charlotte didn't recognise him.

"Hello, sorry, I thought you were someone else."

"Mrs Sibbritt?"

"No. Mrs Sibbritt doesn't live here. May I help?"

He looked Charlotte up and down. "I need to speak with the owner of the building."

"I am happy to pass a message along." Something about him had Charlotte's senses on high alert and she wasn't about to give him Rosie's address. His eyes were cold and not so much as a flicker of a smile softened his grim expression.

"If you wish to wait a few minutes, her son will be here. You can speak with him."

He shook his head. "It is her I wish to speak directly to. May I have her address please?"

"Perhaps you can tell me who you are?"

If she'd thought his eyes cold before, they were icy now.

"Never mind."

He turned and went down the stairs. Charlotte stepped onto the landing. "I'd like to know your name, please."

All she got was silence. She watched him reach the ground and stalk away along the driveway. Tempted to follow, instead she ran inside and to the balcony to peer over. The man was already across the road, standing in the shadows with a mobile phone in his hand.

Charlotte sprinted to the counter for her phone and returned. He was still there, tapping on the screen. She trained her camera on him as he looked up. With a scowl, he spun away and dropped his head. She snapped photos, hoping he might show his face again, but he disappeared down the alley a little further away.

"Damnit!"

Whoever he was, there was a bad aura about him. What was it with strangers and people disappearing when she wanted to photograph them?

"Charlie?"

She jumped, almost dropping the phone.

"I'm here, Trev."

Charlotte met him in the living room. He'd closed the front door and locked it and had a look of worry on his face. "Door was open."

"Oh, sorry. Did you see the man over the road?"

He kissed her cheek and she smiled. Trev smelt so nice. She touched his face to try and reassure him. "I'm okay. There was someone at the door and when they left, I rushed to the balcony and forgot to close it. That's all."

"What man?"

Charlotte showed him the images on her phone as she explained the visit. "He was cagey. Why would he want to talk to Rosie?"

"Dunno. Would you send those to my phone please? He didn't say why he wanted her?"

"Nope. But he wanted to speak with the building owner."

Trev checked his phone as the message came through from Charlotte. "Got them. I'll keep an eye out and send these to the other officers working around town. If someone sees him, we'll have a chat." He strode onto the balcony. "Where was he last?"

"Alley. As you saw, he didn't want to be photographed but I can't really blame him. He doesn't know me or why I'd do that."

"Could be any number of explanations, Charlie. Mum told me a couple of years ago she had a book company representative turn up on her doorstep one Sunday morning. Had no sense of etiquette and was in the area so dropped by with a catalogue."

"How did they have her address?"

"Looked her up online. She opted out of the phone directory after that. But it may be something similar." Trev took Charlotte's hand. "Sorry you had a scare."

No, a scare is a creepy woman staring at me from the trees.

"I'm fine. Would you pour some wine and I'll put our main in to cook?"

————

Over what turned to be a delicious baked ricotta, Trev updated Charlotte on the events of the day since he'd seen her washing windows.

"The whiteboard at the station is filling up at last. No suspects but our understanding is growing of Cecil's last couple of days. Would love to locate his phone."

"There's no way to track it through his service provider or the phone itself?" Charlotte finished the last piece of ricotta, savouring the herb and garlic flavours and hint of chili oil.

"Still hoping to get some news but most likely the battery is flat by now. But even a last location would help."

"Someone took it."

Trev nodded and refilled both their glasses. "I imagine so. The other thing we now know is the fire was lit by a cigarette. Tossed into a pile of shredded paper with some lighter fluid as accelerant. And it was done in an orderly manner, for a fire anyway."

"Set up before Cecil even arrived?" Charlotte picked up her glass. It was horrible to consider the man had returned to his office with no chance of surviving. Why?

"Seems so. Premeditated. And I suspect the killer knew his movements well enough to expect him back at the shop."

The aroma of baking pastry wafted into the dining room.

"I might check the tart, if you don't mind?" No burnt desserts on her watch. Charlotte grinned and pushed her chair back. She collected their plates and headed for the kitchen. The tart was perfect and she slid it onto a rack to cool.

"For someone who complains she can't cook..." Trev had followed with the bottle and glasses. "Loved the ricotta bake, sweetie."

Charlotte's heart glowed. She'd worked hard to improve her culinary skills and discovered a certain joy in creating nice meals. For Trev to enjoy them was a compliment she would take any day. He'd grown up with Rosie's beautiful cooking and at first, she'd been hesitant to try her hand at making up her own dishes.

"Would you like to sit in the living room and finish this bottle?" Trev suggested. "Enough talk of work. Let's find something else to discuss."

"Cool. How about Rosie and Lewis' wedding?"

Trev made a face and Charlotte laughed. "Are you over talking about them?" They sat on the sofa and Trev poured the remainder of the wine into their glasses.

"Never. I'm beyond thrilled Mum found Lewis. If ever there were two people more deserving of a second chance...of course, Thomas and Martha come a close second."

"I miss them. I miss River's End and Elizabeth and Christie. And Randall."

"Then let's make a day and go for a drive."

A rush of happiness lit Charlotte and she grabbed Trev's

hand. "Yes! I would love that so much. Or could we go for a night and that way we can visit everyone! We could stay at Palmerston House and see Elizabeth and Angus!"

"We'll get past this current problem and make a weekend of it. See if Mum minds giving you a Saturday off and I'll get someone to cover for me." Trev's phone rang. He kissed Charlotte's hand and released it. "That's Mum. Hello, we were just talking about you."

He listened, his expression growing serious and his eyes moving to Charlotte's.

Foreboding replaced Charlotte's happiness.

"The house is locked, isn't it? We'll be there in a few minutes."

Trev was on his feet as he hung up and Charlotte climbed to hers. "What's wrong?"

"She's had a visitor. A man with a briefcase and umbrella and an insistence she sell the bookshop to him. Coming?"

CHAPTER TWENTY

"Mum, it's just us." Trev called as he inserted his key into the front door lock. All the way home he'd scoured their surrounds for a sign of this person. First Charlie and now his mother.

"In the kitchen, dear. Making tea."

Trev held the door open for Charlotte to go first then scanned outside in case the man was still loitering. Nothing moved along the street. He locked the door and headed for the kitchen. Charlotte had grabbed the apple tart on the way out, insisting Rosie would need to share it with them. He intended to keep Charlotte close until he'd worked this all out.

"That smells lovely, darling. We'll slice it up in a minute." Rosie looked up as Trev approached. Despite a calm tone of voice, tension strained her expression and she held her arms out.

In an instant, Trev was at her side and squeezing her tight. She was a tough lady and one who didn't scare easily, but distress poured out of her as she held onto him.

"Why don't you both go to the living room and I'll finish making the tea?" Charlotte poured boiling water into a teapot. "I'll reheat the tart."

Back on his feet, Trev gave Charlotte what he hoped was a grateful smile and followed Rosie. She wanted to move onto the sofa and allowed him to help her get comfortable. "Where are the cats, Mum?"

"In my bedroom. Since the time the house was broken into, they get upset with strangers so I shooed them in before opening the front door."

"Should I let them out now?"

"No. Let them stay there for a bit. Until things settle down."

Charlotte carried a tray in and put it down on the coffee table. "You two talk and I'll serve."

Trev sat near Rosie. "Tell me what happened."

Rosie nodded. She was pale and worry filled her eyes. "Well, as I said, there was a knock on the door. You have a key and Lewis always calls if he's coming to visit. I thought it was one of the neighbours, so called out to wait and closed the cats into the bedroom." She accepted a cup of tea from Charlotte with a forced smile. "I opened the door to a stranger. A man in his fifties, I think. Not tall but quite thin. Not much hair. He carried an umbrella which I thought odd as the day has been pleasant enough. And a briefcase."

She paused to sip her tea and Trev exchanged a glance with Charlotte when she passed him a cup. Her eyes gave away her own concerns.

"Before I could say a word, the man asked if I was Mrs Sibbritt, owner of the bookshop and building it resides in. Of course, I said yes, thinking something might be wrong."

"Did he give you his name?"

"No, dear. He said he wished to come inside and I moved my wheelchair a bit so it formed a barrier and asked him what his business was. Not about to let some strange person into my house!"

Charlotte perched on an armchair, her attention on Rosie.

She hadn't poured tea for herself and she gripped her hands together. "What did he say, Rosie?"

"He said he was a business broker who wanted to buy the building! Last thing I expected. I must have looked surprised because he then mentioned a preposterous amount of money as long as I accepted the deal then and there."

"Preposterous?"

"Oh, Trev, he offered at least twice its value. Said he'd make it worth my while to have it vacated and signed over quickly. I asked why. Why did he wish to buy it? And he stared at me with eyes like dead fish and said it was none of my business. Of course, that annoyed me terribly and I said even if it were for sale, I would not consider an offer unless I knew who was buying and why. I mean, what if they wanted to tear it down and put up a high-rise?"

Was this the person who'd wanted to buy Cecil's office? A knot formed in Trev's stomach. "Mum, did he leave a card or anything?"

"Not a thing. I told him the building is not for sale."

"Not to a stranger." Charlotte's voice held a question.

"Not to anyone. Not now." Rosie returned to her tea. She seemed unaware of the confusion on Charlotte's face and Trev himself was confused. The whole reason he'd brought Charlotte to meet her last year was because she was considering selling to someone who'd love the bookshop the way she did. He tried to catch Charlotte's eye to convey his support but she gazed down at her hands.

"Did he leave once you said no?"

Rosie looked straight at Trev, her chin raised. "He leaned down to my eye level and said I was making a dreadful mistake. That he had papers I could sign on the spot to begin the transfer of the property and he would put funds into my account tonight. One last chance. This is what he said, Trev. One last chance or I'd be sorry."

Charlotte gasped.

Primal rage tore into Trev and he struggled to force it away. He needed a clear head. Calm thoughts. But this man had threatened his mother. On his feet, he paced the floor.

"I don't mean to upset you both."

"Rosie, no! You've done nothing wrong and this man…he isn't nice." Charlotte said.

"How do you know, darling?"

Charlotte joined Rosie on the sofa. "He was at the apartment just before Trev arrived. He asked for you and wanted your address which I'd never give him. I asked for his name and his reason for looking for you and he stormed off. I managed a few photos but none of his face. Why didn't I phone you and warn you? I feel awful."

Rosie patted her arm. "No need. You had no way of knowing he'd find me."

Trev stopped in the middle of the room. "So how did he find you, Mum? You don't have a public phone listing any longer."

"Any number of people might have told him. I've been here a long time."

Need to find out who he spoke to.

"I'm going to call Bryce. Let him know. I'll be back." Trev headed for the office. He needed to speak to the detective and get his take on all of this.

———

Charlotte wondered if she'd understood Rosie. She refilled both their tea cups and handed one to her friend before settling again on the armchair. Was Rosie talking about never putting the bookshop on the open market or not even selling to her? A tug of something pulled at her heart. She couldn't identify it. Not while all of this was going on.

"Rosie? Why don't I let the cats out?"

"That's a good idea. They'll be wondering why I haven't

come back." She gazed into her teacup. Since the moment Trev stepped out of the room, Rosie had been quiet. Not met Charlotte's eyes. That awful man had shaken her up.

A moment later she opened Rosie's bedroom door with a soft, "Hey guys, just me."

Mayhem barrelled past her but Mellow stretched and jumped off the bed before wrapping herself around Charlotte's ankles. She leaned down to stroke her fur. Trev was in the study, the door ajar. His voice was angry.

"Yes, I do think this is connected to the fire. We know Cecil was approached to sell by parties unknown and…"

Charlotte straightened, not wanting to eavesdrop. She followed Mellow to the living room. Mayhem was sitting on Rosie's lap facing her, one paw on her shoulder. For such a grumpy cat, he had an uncanny instinct when it came to his owner's emotions. Mellow jumped up beside her and Rosie smiled. At last. "I don't have a spare hand, Mel-mel."

"Here, let me swap the tea for a gin and tonic. I could use one and I'm sure you could too." Charlotte took the teacup and Rosie gathered both cats against her body. After putting the cups and saucers onto the tray, she took it to the kitchen and checked the tart. It was warm again so she took it out of the oven but decided against cutting it until she knew if anyone wanted some.

"Charlie. You okay?" Trev slid his phone into a pocket and then held his arms open.

It took no further invitation for her to snuggle against him. His heart was racing and he held her so tight she almost asked him to loosen his arms. But his muscles relaxed bit by bit and she heard his heartbeat slow.

"I told Rosie I'd make some drinks. Thought it might calm her a bit. And us." She tilted her head up to look at him. "You are stressing."

He kissed her forehead and released her. "I am. And I'll help get the drinks."

Charlotte got the feeling he didn't want her out of his sight and the way he glanced at Rosie reinforced his concerns. Once they all had drinks, he checked the doors were locked. "You'll stay tonight?" he asked Charlotte when he sat again.

"I don't have anything with me."

Rosie managed a small smile. "We'll make do, darling. There're always extra night clothes in my cupboard and you can change at home in the morning. I think you should stay."

"I'll take the sofa." Before anyone could argue the point, she changed the subject. "What did Bryce say, Trev?"

"He's coming down first thing to talk to you both. I sent the photos you took, Charlie, and we'll grab footage from the landing. Having that camera near the door might give us a good image of him." He took a long drink from his glass.

Mellow climbed off Rosie and settled on Trev with a purr.

"I saw a removalist truck earlier. Went in the direction of the garden centre." Time to talk of better things. "I wondered if it is whoever owns the place now."

"We might need to go and say hello, darling." Rosie brightened. "We could take a shop-warming gift."

As long as it isn't warming like a fire.

Charlotte bit her lip, unsure where her mind was leading. Was Cecil murdered and the fire set in order to make the property unsaleable...except to someone who would pull it down anyway? If his refusal resulted in cold-blooded murder, then who was really behind it? The man from earlier was a messenger, surely.

"Trev. There are two shops between the realtor and the bookshop. Has anyone spoken to them about offers to buy?"

Rosie and Trev shot her the same horrified look.

"I know one is empty, but the other one...the hairdresser, well shouldn't they be alerted?"

Trev pulled his phone out. "Mum, do you know how to contact the owner?"

"She's away. After the fire she told me she'd given the staff a week off and she was visiting her daughter in the city. The whole event upset her. But I have her number in my phone, dear."

"I hate to disturb her so late. There's nobody who'd go in after hours?"

"She was quite clear when she spoke to me that everyone had the week off so I can't imagine why. I think you should call though. To be certain. Charlie, my phone is in my handbag still if you don't mind getting it."

Charlotte hurried to the side table in the hallway where Rosie left her handbag each night. She knew the right pocket and slid the phone out. There was a white envelope beside it. One word was on the envelope in Rosie's neat handwriting. Her heart skipped a beat.

Charlotte.

What was in there? After Rosie's strange comment about not selling the bookshop, was it worse than that. Was she letting Charlotte go...was Rosie about to fire her?

CHAPTER TWENTY-ONE

CHARLOTTE GULPED DOWN A SUDDEN SHARD OF ANGUISH IN
her chest. Her breathing accelerated and she took little gasps
to regulate it. Any second now, Trev would come looking for
her. She closed the handbag and leaned against the wall, eyes
closed.

There's no time for this, Charlie.

Everybody was under pressure at the moment. The enve-
lope might be as innocent as an invitation to the wedding.
Except the wedding date wasn't set. Or it might be, what?
Nothing came to mind and Charlotte was left with the choice
of falling into a downward spiral to anxiety or dealing with it.
She chose the latter.

Eyes open again, she straightened her back and returned to
the living room. Whatever was going on with Rosie would be
addressed at the time Rosie wanted to talk. For now, her job
was to support her friend and help find the killer.

"Here you go." She handed the phone over, retrieved her
drink, and sat.

"Are you alright?" Trev asked.

"Of course." Her voice squeaked a bit. "Um...thirsty." To

prove her point, she swallowed a mouthful of gin and tonic a bit too fast.

His expression was suspicious but then he turned to Rosie as she held out the phone. "There's her number."

Trev dialled on his phone and wandered toward the kitchen. "Good evening, Mrs Munro, this is Leading Senior Constable Sibbritt—Rosie's son?" His voice muted with distance.

"Hopefully, she's okay and then we need to find out who owns the empty shop." Rosie said. "I thought it was the last tenants but then somebody mentioned they leased it. I wonder how we find out?"

"Sometimes there's information on when a place last sold. Let me do a search on the address and see." Charlotte tapped a few details into her phone. "Last sold—according to this—about four years ago. It was sold by Cecil but there is no buyer listed." She glanced up. "I would imagine his assistant would know. This might be a clue!"

"Oh, darling. You are a clever girl."

The warmth and approval in Rosie's voice eased Charlotte's earlier concerns. A little, anyway. When this all settled down and the town returned to safety and normality, she'd tell Rosie she'd seen the envelope and let the cards fall as they may.

"Why are you clever? What have you done?" Trev returned. "I recognise that encouragement of Charlie's sleuthing, Mum."

Rosie chose to sip her drink instead of answering, but her eyes twinkled.

"What did Mrs Munro have to say?" Charlotte asked, hoping to divert him.

He grinned as he returned to his seat. "We'll come back to why you are clever. According to Mrs Munro, she was approached a couple of weeks ago to sell her shop."

With a small gasp, Rosie sat forward. "And?"

"She accepted the offer. Says it was generous and allows

her to move closer to her grandchildren. She was waiting to tell the staff until later this month but the fire fast-tracked her decision. Instead, she's paid them all out and begun to pack."

"Well, I never..." Rosie sank back. "Would someone kindly refill this glass?"

Charlotte obliged, refilling hers as well, but Trev shook his head. He probably needed to keep a clearer head. "What I was doing earlier? I did a search on the last sale of the empty shop near us. It was four or so years ago and sold by Cecil. No buyer mentioned. But Trev, if someone has owned it for a while, what if they are behind the murder and fire and the odd man visiting us? Perhaps they wish to own the whole block of shops for some reason. Some bad reason."

"There's merit in your thinking. Tomorrow, I'll raise it with Bryce and Katrina and no doubt we'll have to speak with Mrs McKenzie again. This is helpful. As much as you had a scare, Mum, that man made a mistake coming here."

"Did Mrs Munro tell you the buyer's name?" Rosie asked.

Trev shook his head. "She said she sold through a business broker. She couldn't remember his name but it sounds like our friend from earlier tonight. I've asked her to locate her paperwork and call me tomorrow."

Rosie yawned. "I might relocate to my bed. There's a book I'd like to finish if I don't fall asleep first. Charlie, come and get some nightwear." She reached for her wheelchair and Trev beat her to it and lifted her onto it with no effort. "Nice to have a strong policeman in the house." Rosie kissed him before letting him straighten. "You know where the blankets are for the sofa."

"I do indeed."

Charlotte was on her feet. "I'm happy to make my own bed up once I borrow something to sleep in." She collected the glasses and left them on the counter on her way, then tapped on Rosie's bedroom door. "May I come in?"

"Of course. Watch out for Mayhem because he thinks this

is his bedroom." Rosie appeared from her dressing room with a selection of nightwear. "Use what you want from these. Pretty sure something will fit."

"Thank you. Is there anything you need?"

Every move Rosie made showed her exhaustion but she shook her head. "I'm fine. Once I have a sleep, I'll be okay again. Give me a kiss."

Charlotte obliged and hugged Rosie for good measure. She didn't understand what was going on with her friend but it didn't matter at the moment. Mayhem growled at her from the end of the bed and she stroked Mellow on the way to the door. "Sleep well, Rosie."

"You too, darling. And Charlie?"

At the doorway Charlotte turned.

"You mean the world to me, darling. And no matter what happens, never forget that. Okay?"

"Okay." Charlotte didn't understand but the love in Rosie's eyes was true. And that was enough for now.

———

Trev covered the apple tart with foil and slid it into the fridge. Tonight had not turned out the way he'd expected and he was sorry Charlotte's lovely dinner was interrupted. That man. He placed both hands on the counter and dropped his head. What if he'd hurt Mum? Or Charlie? And the fire. Cecil.

So many problems.

Warm arms encircled his waist and he turned to put his own around Charlotte. Holding her tight meant she was safe. And along with his mother, nothing was more important. If anything happened to them…

"Take a long slow breath." Charlotte's voice was a bit muffled against his chest but he did what she said. "All the way to the bottom of your stomach. Imagine it as a super power. The thing that will make everything work out right. Then let it out as slowly as possible." He knew how to meditate and regulate his breathing and all the good ways of managing stress, but the way she spoke in what he called her 'Doctor Dean' voice added an element of authenticity to what he was doing. "And again."

For a few minutes he repeated her instructions until the knot in his gut unwound and a sense of control replaced it. Then, he dropped a kiss on her head. "Thanks. I'm fine now."

She grinned as she stepped away. "Believe whatever you want. Coffee?"

"Please. I'll make my bed up on the sofa."

"Hey, no, I'm the interloper. And I fit better on it than you do. So, let me do this." Charlotte tilted her head. "You need a decent sleep if you're to catch bad guys tomorrow."

She had a point. "Are you sure?"

"Good. Now, let's have a coffee."

They returned to the living room with their coffees, turning off most of the lights and leaving on a lamp near the sofa. Charlotte curled her feet under her and blew the steam away from the cup.

Outside, the wind chimes responded to a growing breeze with long, low notes. Rain pattered on the roof.

"Kind of comforting, the rain at night." Charlotte's words were quiet. "Soothing to fall to sleep with it in the background, unless it is part of a storm."

"I quite like storms. Sometimes in River's End I'd go for a run at night, alongside the river and onto the beach. One time a storm caught me by surprise and I sheltered near the stone steps. Watched the lightning as it hit the ocean. Impressive."

There was a faraway look in Charlotte's eyes. Perhaps it was the lamp light, or was she thinking of the place she'd called home for almost a year?

"Did you know there's a little cave there in the cliff?" he asked.

She turned her eyes onto him.

"Nothing big, in fact you could fit two people in there. Thomas once told me when he and Martha were courting—as he called it—they'd take picnics there to avoid the scrutiny of her family."

"How sad to have parents who don't approve of your choice of partner." Charlotte said.

"I've never experienced that, thank goodness. Did you?" Almost as he said it, Trev wished he hadn't. Charlotte's father was out of the picture and her mother institutionalised. "You don't need to answer—"

"Trevor. You can ask me anything. Anytime. Sometimes I might not know. Or not know how to answer, but I promise I'll try." She shifted to make herself more comfortable. "I never brought anyone home. Never. Too risky to let any potential boyfriend meet my mother and be scared off for life." Charlotte bit her bottom lip and he put his hand out. After a moment, she took it, gripping his fingers with hers. "I never really had a boyfriend. And I know it sounds silly because I'm too old to have one, but sometimes...sometimes I think of you as my boyfriend."

Had he ever loved her more than at this minute?

"Charlie. I am your boyfriend and you are my girlfriend and I don't care what age we are. It means we are together and love each other. So, go right ahead and think it as much as you wish, but only for a while longer."

Her lips parted as if in surprise.

He lifted her hand and kissed it. "One of these days we're going to change the status. I like the sound of fiancé. And then husband. As long as you like the idea."

"Um. I, er..."

"As you were saying, the sound of rain is soothing at night."

The moment passed and they finished their coffees. Trev knew Charlotte sneaked a few glances his way but he'd said too much and didn't want to push her.

"Well, you need to go and sleep and I need to make my bed." As though nothing unusual had occurred, Charlotte got to her feet and took his empty cup. "Wake me when you get up, okay?"

He hadn't realised how tired he was until he straightened. "I'll give you a hand."

"No. You go to bed and rest." She raised herself up to kiss his lips. "Goodnight."

"Goodnight, Charlie."

Almost at the doorway he heard her say, "And I do like the idea. A lot."

CHAPTER TWENTY-TWO

TUESDAY. WAKING BEFORE DAWN, CHARLOTTE PACKED UP the blankets as quietly as she could and changed back into her clothes from yesterday. The house was silent and dark as she slipped out through the front door, closing it with a click which she hoped wouldn't disturb Rosie or Trev. She left a note on the counter to let Rosie know she'd open the bookshop and not to hurry in.

The rain was gone leaving the air fresh and with a slight scent of spring. It was too early for it yet, but jonquils insisted otherwise, popping their yellow centred white flowers through garden beds to deliver a lingering perfume.

As daylight approached, she took the road to the old garden centre. It wouldn't hurt to go past and see if there was any movement there. She had little in the way of nice things to decorate the apartment and buying direct from an artist was an exciting prospect. And if she was honest with herself, it might make her feel a little closer to Zoe. One day she'd find the courage to contact her, at least, try to. Perhaps one sculptor might even know another.

The place was deserted but through the window, shadowed statues and open packing boxes loomed in an eery display.

There were new windows along the front and to Charlotte, they looked thicker, perhaps reinforced. Such valuable items should be behind grills, particularly with the current crime spree. She pushed her nose against the glass to see better, admiring a tall sculpture of a bird in flight. There was a familiarity about it. Something she'd seen before.

A small red light behind it alerted her to a security camera and when she looked around outside, there were more. Time to get moving and not draw the suspicion of a new resident and fellow trader.

There was little traffic this early and fewer pedestrians. One person went past with their dog and a cheery 'good morning'. Charlotte stopped near the damaged realtor shop. Wrapped in police tape and its windows boarded, it was grim compared to the previous bright display of houses listed for sale she'd passed so often.

Down the side road the street lights stopped not far past the building. Like the bookshop, this backed onto the bushland and had a small carpark at the rear. Further was the bridge where the river flowed through town. And beyond the bridge, around the spot she and Trev were in the other day, a truck was backing out of the fenced area. Charlotte didn't even think for a second. She ran toward it.

The truck was carrying some kind of digging machinery and took a long time to get onto the road. It stayed there as its driver jumped out and returned to the fence.

By now, Charlotte was near the bridge and some sense finally made her stop running and duck into the bushes. There, she turned on her phone, which she'd forgotten was off overnight.

"Come on, come on." She urged as it went through its waking sequence.

The driver was rattling chain fencing and any minute now, he'd be back in his truck and gone. She had to get some photos.

Hoping for a better vantage, she scurried over the road and hid behind a tree in someone's front garden, making a silent apology for trespassing. The phone lit up and she tapped the camera app and peered around the trunk.

Straight into the torso of the driver.

Charlotte squealed and stepped back, somehow hanging onto the phone.

"What the heck you playin at?" Hands on hips, the man was middle aged with a big stomach. He sneered at her with a mouth filled with broken teeth and breath to knock out a dinosaur.

She straightened to her full height and lifted her chin. "What are *you* playing at? Damaging the bushland like that? Digging up bushes and trees and breaking into a fenced off area?"

"What are ya? Some greenie? I'm doing my job. And you don't get to take photographs of me doing it."

"I didn't. I was about to phone my boyfriend. You might have heard of him? Leading Senior Constable Trevor Sibbritt."

The man turned and waddled to his truck.

Charlotte took some photos of his retreating back as she followed.

Do you never learn?

"Who hired you and what job are you doing?" she caught up as he flung the door open to the cab of the truck.

"None of your damned business." He hauled himself in with a grunt and slammed the door shut. The window was open and he stuck his head out. "I'd be real careful sneaking around like that. Never know when a truck might not see you. Use you as a speed hump."

"Are you threatening me?" she lifted the camera and took a photo of him.

"You work it out."

With that, he roared the motor and swung the truck her way so she had to jump aside. She was at no risk given its bulk and slow response, but she got plenty of images of it as it trundled away.

Her heart was racing and she knew Trev would be beside himself, but what else could she have done?

Now she was here, she might as well see what he'd been up to. The fence was in poor condition as though it was opened one time too many. There was enough daylight to see what the man and his machinery had done. Charlotte curled her hands into fists to stop herself crying at the destruction.

CHAPTER TWENTY-THREE

"I think it must be connected. The fire, that nasty man, all the damage being done to the bushland...even the empty beer cans floating down the river." Charlotte dropped onto the stool beside Rosie and picked up her coffee. Since Rosie arrived an hour ago, they'd spoken of little else than Charlotte's walk home.

"You must talk to Trev about it, darling."

"I know. But he's busy this morning so what is the point of—"

"Of what, Charlotte? What do you need to talk to me about?"

Charlotte's coffee spilled as she jumped. She grabbed a handful of tissues to mop it up, thankful she had an excuse not to look at Trev just yet.

"Is that doorbell not working again?" Rosie asked. "I've had it fixed twice and cannot have people wander in here without us knowing. Even you."

"Why? Because I so often overhear you two discussing something about a case or speculating on who is a criminal?"

His voice sounded only half joking and Charlotte tossed the tissues away and planted a smile on her face as she looked up.

Trev was staring at her and her heart dropped. He had asked her more than once not to put herself into danger. But he didn't look upset. It was more exasperation than anything.

"Hi."

Great opening line.

"Care to share?"

"Sure. I'll show you some photos I took earlier." Charlotte found the first one on her phone and handed it to Trev, then took a long sip of the remaining coffee.

He leaned against the counter, scrolling through the images. After the last one, he pocketed the phone and headed for the back door. "Mum, Charlotte needs a ten-minute break if that's okay."

Rosie's mouth opened and closed again. She busied herself with her computer as Charlotte dragged herself after him.

Trev was holding the back door open for her to go through. She slipped past, almost feeling the tension from him. He closed the door and strode to the far end of the yard where he turned and waited with a look of expectation.

"Are you going to yell at me?"

"I don't yell at people, Charlotte. Particularly not people I love. Please come here."

She crossed the distance with one hand extended. "May I have my phone?"

"Not yet. I want a better look at these soon. And if I keep it, then you might not be so inclined to go where you shouldn't."

"I...um, fine. And I was waiting until you finished with the detectives to show the photos to you." Her arm dropped to her side.

"Rather than sending them to me as soon as you were safely home? Charlotte, what possessed you to take on a stranger with no back up? You've seen firsthand how risky it is to be alone with people who are criminals." He pointed up at the window of the third bedroom. "From there you once saw

131

suspicious activity and investigated on your own. And when I say investigated, I mean nose around where you shouldn't be. You are not a police officer or other authorised person. Not trained to follow leads or equipped to deal with the kind of danger you've been in."

"But, I—"

"Haven't finished speaking. Every time you step foot after a potential criminal, or take a photograph, you run the risk of getting the wrong kind of attention." He ran a hand through his hair. "If you were anyone else I'd..."

What? Arrest me? Read me the riot act, oh wait, you are.

"Charlie?"

"Yes, Trevor?"

A flicker of a smile touched his lips. "You may speak now."

"Nothing to say."

He took the camera out and returned to the photographs. "Good thinking getting the truck licence number. Do you have your key to the back gate?"

"Inside, I do."

"Can Mum manage without you for a bit? I'm going to go look at where you took these."

"And I can come with you?" she wasn't waiting for an answer and flew back into the bookshop.

Rosie looked up, startled, as she emerged from the back of the shop at speed. "Oh, is everything okay? Did my son upset you?"

"Need my keys." Charlotte swooped on them from the counter. "No, he didn't upset me but he isn't impressed with me either. Can you manage for a little bit? He wants me to show him where I took the photos."

"Go. Gives you time to apologise."

Charlotte stopped dead and turned. "Sorry?"

"Yes, like that. Darling, you can't be an amateur sleuth and not expect to occasionally be caught out by the police. A little contrition goes a long way."

"What, as in, make him think I'm changing my ways?"

"I raised a smart son, so he isn't that easy to trick. You'll figure it out." Rosie smiled and waved her away. "Shoo. Go and placate the policeman."

With a shake of her head, Charlotte hurried to meet Trev, who was at the back gate still on her phone. She unlocked it and pushed the gate ajar. "Rosie says she'd be fine for a little bit."

Trev gestured for Charlotte to go through first and then pulled the gate closed behind himself. "Did she suggest we use the time to plan a wedding or similar?"

"No, she didn't suggest that."

Charlotte fell into step with Trev and they followed the wide track behind the shops. "I've sent the photos to my phone." He said.

"So, may I have my phone back?"

"Nope."

He held his hand out and she took it with a bit of a huff. He must have heard because his fingers tightened around hers. They kept on the track past the shops, veering in the direction of the river. Trees closed around them and the track narrowed until it was wide enough for a vehicle but not much more. Once they reached the road, they turned and crossed the bridge and on the other side, Trev stopped them both.

"Run me through what happened. What made you come down this road?"

It only took a moment for Charlotte to go over the earlier events. "I was certain he'd not seen me but he must have when I hid behind the tree over there." She pointed at the garden up the road. "Had no idea he'd followed me until I peered around to take a photo."

"Which is my point. Criminals are good at looking out for themselves. If you run into the wrong one under bad circumstances...am I getting through to you at all?"

"I'm not trying to get into trouble."

"Maybe I need to get Bryce involved. Because he won't hesitate to yell at you."

She smiled. She couldn't help it. "True. But you once said you would be harder on me than him and if that's the case, why would Bryce worry me?"

Trev put his hands on her shoulders and leaned down so she had to look at his eyes. "You think I'm not being serious? Charlotte, your wellbeing means everything to me and I need you to understand the risks. That man this morning was twice your size and up to no good. You can't bluff yourself out of everything."

She thought she could, for the most part.

"I'm sorry, Trev."

He blinked. "You are?"

Not sure she was, it still felt the right thing to say. "I'm really not trying to worry you and I will think before I do anything like this again."

"No. You won't do anything like this again. If something is suspicious enough to ring your sleuthing alarm, then it is time to phone me."

"You were asleep."

"It doesn't matter."

"But what if it is the middle of the night?"

"Charlotte."

"Okay, okay. I'll call you no matter what the time."

It was a long moment before he released her with something like a grunt. He probably didn't believe her and she wasn't sure she believed herself. She was fast and fit and could have outrun the driver if need be.

Trev wandered to the fence, hooked his fingers through the wire and stared at the pile of young trees and bushes. Charlotte caught up. "Isn't it awful? This is double the size from last time."

"I'm going to go to the station and run the plates. Time to have a chat to whoever has interests here." Trev offered Charlotte her phone. "Bryce and Katrina need to speak with you about the man at your door. After work is fine."

"Thanks." She took the phone before he changed his mind. "I'll come over as soon as I close the shop. Shall I bring the footage?"

"Actually, Mum is coming by around lunchtime if she can bring it," he checked his watch. "You'd better get going so she can head to the station soon. Stay out of trouble, please."

"I will. I'll even take the street back to avoid finding clues in the bushland. And I'm just teasing you." She lifted herself up to kiss him. "I'll be good."

CHAPTER TWENTY-FOUR

"GOOD? ARE YOU KIDDING ME? HAPPY TO HAVE THAT CHAT with her." Bryce shook his head. "One of these days she'll get in too deep."

Trev grinned. He'd shaken his own head more than once on his way to the station after Charlotte's throw-away comment. She might try to follow his rules but her heart led her head when it came to putting wrongs right.

"Both of you are going about this the wrong way." Head in paperwork at the other desk, Katrina didn't bother to glance up. "The more you tell her to stay away from trouble, the greater the chance she won't."

"Any suggestions?" Trev asked.

"On keeping Charlotte safe?"

"And out of police business." Bryce commented.

Katrina pushed her chair back and stood to stretch. "Give her something to do. She's a valuable asset with her sharp mind and training. And she has instincts about people better than almost anyone I know."

It was true. She had an uncanny way of seeing through a person and although Charlotte might not have the police training to back up her suspicions, she almost always got it right.

"At the moment, my biggest concern is ensuring my family and the bookshop are safe. If Cecil was murdered because he refused to sell his shop, and now Mum refused to sell..."

"We're going to find the killer." Katrina picked up her empty coffee cup. "Let's refill these and take a look at Charlotte's photos."

By the time Rosie arrived to make her statement, their coffee was cold. The search for the driver had raised some unexpected information and they'd discussed at length the best way to use these new facts.

"No sharing this yet." Bryce noted aloud, presumably for Trev's benefit, who rolled his eyes. He wasn't about to tell Charlotte about it, knowing her probable response would be to run to the council office and cause a scene. Although, if he had to arrest her, she would be out of harm's way for a while.

"Earth to Trevor." Katrina led Rosie in with a grin. "Just at Trev's desk is fine, Mrs Sibbritt."

"How many times do I need to remind you my name is Rosie. Please." Rosie smiled and found a spot at the desk. "This is a much nicer place to visit since Sid left. Cleaned up quite well."

"Smells better too." Bryce added as he pushed his chair over and took Trev's place behind the computer. "Trev is making coffee if you'd like one."

There were times Bryce took advantage of his position as a detective. Or at least, he expected the uniformed officers to be at his call more than Katrina ever did. It didn't bother Trev who kept his energy for the important things in life.

"Coffee it is for four."

"Actually, dear, not me. I'll get one on the way back. Unless you've installed a new machine?" she asked hopefully.

"I wish." Bryce tapped on the keyboard. "Thanks for

coming in today. We'll keep this as brief as possible to let you get on with your day."

"No hurry. Not often I get to see my son in action."

"What, making coffee, Mum?" he replied from the far end of the station. "You see it all the time."

"Would you go through the events of last night for me? I'll ask questions as we go." Bryce prompted.

Rosie began to talk and when Trev brought the coffee over for Bryce, her hands were gripping each other. His own responded by curling into fists. When he got hold of that man...

"Trev? A word outside?" Katrina was at the back door.

He collected her cup and his and followed. She was sending a text and he held her coffee until she sent it.

"Thanks, this one is getting drunk no matter what happens!" she took the cup with a smile. "Bryce will look after your mother."

"I know. And she'll tell him off if he doesn't. It's just..."

"Did I ever tell you why I changed my mind about living in the city?" she asked. Since he'd met her back in their academy days, Katrina was intent on staying in the inner suburbs of Melbourne, where she'd grown up and where her parents still lived.

"I thought it was to give your kids a country upbringing?"

"There was a case I worked on a while back. Series of break and enters which were violent. We arrested two men but they made bail and one of them came looking for me."

A shiver went up Trev's spine. An officer's worst fear.

"He made contact with my eldest at his school. Spoke to him over the fence during lunch. Told him..." her voice cracked and she took a sip of coffee before continuing. "...told him he was coming to get me. Trev, imagine what that did to a little boy."

"Did he harm him. Or you?"

"No. We were able to track him down thanks to a quick

response by the school and he is behind bars, but it made us—
my husband and me—rethink our lives. There's nowhere
completely safe but when you have kids, everything changes."

"And you move up here and have had one murder after
another to deal with."

Katrina laughed. "My point, as long as it took to get to it, is
that family matters. I get that you are stressing about Rosie
and about Charlotte. We're going to find this man, you, me,
and Bryce. And in the interim, we believe you'll get a call
today confirming the appointment of a constable here.
Permanently."

This was good news. The region was too big in population
for him to manage the way he had with River's End. There, it
was the distance keeping him busy. Here, it was the crime.

"Once Bryce finishes the interview, he and I will pay
council a visit. Time to speak to a town planner and one or two
people who like hiding in their offices." Katrina said.

"What shall I do? Happy to track down the truck driver."
More than happy to have a few words with him about intim-
idation.

"No. You can do some boring research into our friend from
last night. We'll take a look at the footage from the apartment
first and plan out the day. Okay?" she tossed the dregs of her
cup onto the grass.

Research was one thing he enjoyed. And when it led to
finding a man who might hold the key to Cecil's murder, he'd
relish every minute of it.

———

Charlotte was using the time without Rosie to search what
requirements there were for a permit to run functions at the
Christmas Tree Farm. She started on the website of the local
council, grimacing at the image of Jonas on the front page.
One foot on a shovel on the side of a road she recognised as

coming into town, he held a thumb up. Behind him, a new sign for the town rested against a nearby tree.

"Yeah, you are so community minded. New sign but still no water for the fountain."

There were pages of information, which she ended up forwarding to her laptop. From a quick skim, the prior use of the land for the same purpose would help with the application. There was also a liquor licence to apply for, assuming they'd serve alcohol in the function centre.

She clicked out of the website and deleted the history to avoid questions from Rosie she'd rather not answer yet. Darcy and Abbie needed to talk to a lawyer. Possibly a conveyancer. The only one she knew was Terrance, who was retired. But he'd sold his firm.

Charlotte searched on the computer and sat back with her mouth open. The firm still existed with a sole conveyancer. No longer just a conveyancing firm, its website boasted an accountant and a lawyer. Jonas Carmichael. Closing her mouth, she clicked on his details. Specialising in real estate titles, transfers, and financing.

"You sneaky little man." She breathed.

"I'm not little." Sid leaned both arms on the counter.

Flustered by his silent appearance, Charlotte deleted the history again and then stood. "What do you want?"

"Oh, not happy to see me? Thought we were friends now."

"What do you want."

"See, I reckon you and this bookshop needs a hand." He waved a hand around. "With that terrible incident on the corner, it occurred to me I could use my expertise to offer my services."

Air, sight, and sound pollution? Driving customers away?

"What do you know about the fire?"

"Same as you. There was a fire. Poor old Cecil was caught in it. Hate to see that happen here."

Charlotte stared at him. Even when he'd been a police officer, Sid Browne hadn't cared about his appearance. The first time they'd met he'd worn little more than a singlet and pants. Today he was even worse. His jacket was filthy as if dragged through the mud. Underneath it, a tear in his shirt gave an unwelcome glimpse of grey chest hair. Stubble covered his chin and neck and his fingers with their dirty nails were as yellow as she'd ever seen them.

"Was that a threat, Sid?"

He scoffed, which turned into a racking cough. Charlotte stepped back from the counter and made a mental note to clean the place after he left. Which was going to be any minute now.

"Third time, what do you want?"

"Told you. Offering my services to protect you. Keep an eye on the building and make sure no criminal firelighters have fun here. You'll pay me, of course. Quite well. But I'll do the right thing by you."

It took every bit of self-control Charlotte had not to laugh aloud at this preposterous suggestion. He'd done nothing but harass her and Rosie for months. She tilted her head and smiled in a way she hoped was sweet.

"We already have that under control but thank you."

He blinked and didn't move from the counter.

"Really, as…generous as your offer is…we are fine. So, goodbye."

Sid shrugged and thudded to the doorway where he stopped and glanced over his shoulder. "Bad choice, missy."

Then he was gone and Charlotte dropped onto the stool and dialled Trev.

CHAPTER TWENTY-FIVE

"You should arrest him right now!" Rosie wheeled her chair so fast Trev was jogging to keep up. She didn't seem at all fazed by the effort but he was almost out of breath. "Terrible, awful man and why is he even back in Kingfisher Falls?"

"Don't...know. Mum, slow a bit."

She did and he dropped to a fast walk with some relief.

Should have grabbed the patrol car.

Charlotte's call came as he was seeing his mother out of the station and she'd taken off, giving him no time to do more than text Katrina to say he'd be back soon.

"Thanks. Listen, Charlie's okay. There was no need to hurry off like this."

"Rubbish. We need to see for ourselves. Sid Browne has been gunning for our girl since she arrived and I won't have it. I just won't!" Rosie was forced to stop at the roundabout as cars went through. "Did she sound upset?"

"Yes. No. She was angry."

"Well, so am I."

The traffic passed and they crossed. His phone beeped a message. Katrina, with a few question marks in a row. He tapped awkwardly as he walked. *Sid was at bookshop. Checking on Charlie.*

"You almost ran into the light post, dear. Shouldn't text and walk you know. Whatever is Charlie doing?"

They'd reached the corner and again, waited for traffic to clear. Charlotte stood on the edge of the footpath, hands on hips, staring back at the bookshop. Once they reached the other side, she glanced over. Her face softened but Trev had seen the strain around her eyes. She was almost rigid in how she held herself and the first thing he did when they were close enough was open his arms. She didn't hesitate.

"Darling, we were so worried. Where is that awful man?" Rosie took hold of Charlotte's hand and with a small sigh, she stepped back from Trev to answer.

"Long gone. He was on foot so who knows. But you didn't both need to rush here."

"We were outside when you called. Why are you out here?" Rosie still had Charlotte's hand.

"The door chime isn't working. I tried to fix it but think it needs a new battery. Anyway, I came outside to test it and noticed this." She pointed at the camera above the door. "I don't think that paint got there on its own."

The lens was covered in something off-white. Paint, perhaps.

"The ladder is still in the storeroom?" Trev asked.

"Shall I get it?" Charlotte was gone before he could answer.

Rosie circled to get a better view. "Why. And who."

"Bored kids. We can check the footage."

"Trev, this must have happened overnight. I remember looking at the monitors before I left yesterday and seeing Mr Lee walk past with his dog. Have to admit I've not checked today." Rosie moved aside as Charlotte returned, struggling a bit with the ladder.

"Thanks, Charlie." Trev took the ladder and opened it.

"Have you noticed anything odd with the monitor display inside?"

She shook her head. "Haven't looked today. Only thing we did was download the footage from last night. Here, I'll hold this side."

Supressing a smile, Trev climbed the ladder. He'd never had anyone hold a ladder for him, not since the days he'd help his father do repairs or build a garden structure. At the camera, any impulse to smile disappeared. It was paint from a spray can. "We'll get that cleaned up a bit later. Pity I won't get prints off it though."

Back on the ground, he packed the ladder up. "Do you want me to look at the door chime?"

"No, I'll run over and get a battery soon." Charlotte followed him to the storeroom. "Do you think that man did it?"

"Which one? We're getting a list of men to investigate." Ladder away, Trev closed the storeroom door. Rosie was with a customer. "I know you'll give Mum a rundown later, so let's go over it now in the kitchen, away from the customer."

"I'm more angry than anything." Charlotte began as they entered the kitchen, her eyes on the monitor. It was obvious the one over the door was covered in paint. A little bit of the image came through but it was blurry. "First that he snuck up on me. I was busy looking for...well, I was busy on the computer and he kind of materialised."

"What were you looking for?"

"Oh. Mainly information to help Darcy and Abbie."

"Mainly?" What was she up to?

"Trevor. The point is Sid appeared at the counter and told me he was offering his expert services to keep an eye on the bookshop."

"Huh?"

Charlotte raised an eyebrow. "Exactly!"

"And you'd want this...why?"

"According to Sid, it might stop the same thing happening to us as it did to Cecil."

Over the years Trev had dealt with Sid a number of times. Their interactions were never pleasant and led Trev to be wary of the other man, whose unethical behaviour bordered on criminal. The day Sid Browne handed in his badge—before he could be fired—was a day of satisfaction. But now he was back and Trev's gut screamed it was about revenge.

"Do you remember his words. As close as you can."

"I have an excellent memory."

Charlotte recounted the visit. It wasn't quite a threat. But Sid's interest in the fire was a worry. Was he just trying to cash in on the terrible situation?

"When I said no, he said it was a bad choice. Actually, he said, bad choice, missy."

"Did you feel threatened?"

"Nope. But I rarely have by him. He carries on and is full of his own importance, but when he's had the chance to harm me, he hasn't. In fact, he's helped me. In the past, I might have enjoyed him as a patient. Lots going on in there."

"But not now?"

For a moment, Charlotte looked away. Her shoulders were rigid again and her hands gripped each other. Instead of drawing her into his arms, he waited. Whatever was wrong, she'd talk to him when ready. This was different from the issues with Sid and Jonas and the intruder last night. She took a deep breath and turned her gaze on him. It was steady.

"Not now. I think I'll be paying for past mistakes for a long time, one way or another."

About to ask her what she meant, Trev heard Rosie call goodbye to her customer. He dropped a quick kiss on Charlotte's lips. "It'll be okay, sweetie. And I'm here when you need to talk."

"Oh, there you two are. Come on, I need to know everything!"

———

There was the strangest sensation in Charlotte's heart. An unfamiliar...comfort. But why? She drilled down mentally, seeking the feeling as an observer. It began when Trev told her he was there for her, without having pushed her for an answer. He'd picked up on the chaos in her emotions and instead of attempting to solve her problems or make her feel better, he'd simply acknowledged he knew she was confronted by something and did nothing more than offer his support.

What greater gift could there be?

Charlotte had no idea yet how to explain seeing the woman she thought was Alison. Her subconscious was on overdrive. Clouding her judgement. Interfering with her rational thoughts. Trev's quiet support was a safety net. He'd be there for her. Nobody else ever had. Not her parents. Not even her sister. It didn't matter how much she longed to find Zoe, there was something stopping her. Questions she might not like the answer to. Why would Zoe have left her alone with a mother she knew was not capable of caring for her baby sister?

"Darling? You've not had lunch yet."

"I'm not hungry."

This wasn't true. She was hungry, but her stomach was churning too much to eat.

"Well, would you like a break anyway?"

Rosie had worry lines on her forehead.

"Why don't I go get us both a coffee and maybe some pastries?" Charlotte offered. "I wouldn't mind stretching my legs and perhaps those tasty morsels will tempt me."

The lines disappeared as Rosie smiled. "Perfect. Take as long as you want."

After dropping into the corner café to place the coffee order, Charlotte went to the bakery. It was busy and as she waited, she glanced outside. Straight to the woman she thought was Alison. Across the road, she wore the same long coat and

146

sunglasses. Her hair was under a scarf. This time, rather than try to take a photograph or give chase, Charlotte tried something new.

She turned her back on the window.

It hurt. Every instinct fought against her will to stay strong. Not turn around. Wait in line. In the end, she took her phone out, opened the camera app in selfie mode, and held it up to see behind herself.

The street was empty.

Charlotte spun back to be certain but the woman was gone.

Imagination, Charlie!

If ever there was a time to see her new therapist, it was now. She'd had one visit and quite liked the almost-retired man who took his time taking notes about her childhood. When she got back to the bookshop she'd phone for an appointment and he could help her work through this obsession with a woman who was two states away.

An SUV sped past. The same one Marguerite climbed into the other day. Charlotte took a photo. Might as well. Nothing else to see here.

CHAPTER TWENTY-SIX

AGAINST ROSIE'S WISHES, CHARLOTTE DRAGGED THE ladder out again and cleaned the camera lens. Her boss was busy with customers so had little to say after her initial 'no, darling, leave it for Trev'.

Well, she wasn't leaving anything for Trev or any other man to do, not when she was capable of climbing up and doing it herself. After Christmas, this ladder had spent a bit of time upstairs as she'd repainted the balcony and done small repairs. Awkward it might be, but impossible it wasn't.

The paint was well and truly dried and it took several attempts before the glass was gleaming again. While she was up there, Charlotte swept old cobwebs away, leaving one which was occupied. As long as the little resident stayed out here, they could remain friends.

"Are you ever coming down off this thing?" Rosie was at the bottom of the ladder, her hand on its side. "I don't want you to fall."

"I won't. Promise." Charlotte wiped the lens one last time and descended. "See? I've got good balance and no fear of heights."

"Fear is important, darling. It stops us doing dangerous things."

"Unless we choose to push our boundaries. We can't live in a bubble, Rosie."

Rosie headed inside. "I know. But I pushed myself too far and look where that got me."

Charlotte, think before speaking!

She packed up the ladder and followed Rosie, who'd gone behind the counter. "That was insensitive of me. I am so sorry—"

"No, no don't apologise. I might regret the choice I made that day diving. It was about me pushing a boundary and now my reality is I can't dive anymore. Or walk. But I have a full and wonderful life and am about to get married!" Rosie's eyes glistened and Charlotte leaned the ladder against the counter to go to her.

"Yes you are! And Lewis is the luckiest man alive to have you in his life." Charlotte leaned down to kiss Rosie's cheek before handing her a box of tissues. "And I'm lucky to have you in mine."

Rosie dabbed her eyes. "I feel the same about you, darling. Since that day Trev brought you to meet me, I've adored you. It was meant to be, you coming to live here and work with me. And spend more time with my handsome son."

Charlotte laughed and returned to the ladder. "I'm going to put this away again."

When she came back out, Esther was talking to Rosie.

"Hello, Charlotte. We were just discussing the newest place in town. The arts centre, although I'm not sure what it really is called."

"But you saw a signwriter there earlier?" Rosie asked.

"Yes. And the woman who owns it was hard at work when I drove past. Apart from the signwriter, there was a truck unloading shelves, and it looked as though Jonas just drove into the carpark."

"Jonas. Oh no, the poor woman. We need to put together a welcome package, Charlie, and take it around."

"Once she can draw a breath. From the sound of it, she has her hands full."

Esther nodded. "And she still has to move into her house, according to Mrs McKenzie. She's waiting on the removalist truck to arrive so is sleeping on the floor, poor love. Wanted to make sure her art works arrived safely first."

"What does she look like?"

"Our new trader?" Esther asked.

"Yes. Um…in case I bump into her in the supermarket."

"I didn't really get a good look, I'm afraid. She wore a long coat and hat which is sensible given the weather we're having."

Charlotte left Esther and Rosie talking and went to the bathroom. Once the door was closed, she leaned against it, eyes shut. Was the woman she kept seeing the owner of the arts centre? Not Alison at all but another person who resembled her. Or was it Alison? Didn't add up. Alison was a paralegal which was one reason she'd been so quick to try and sue Charlotte. There'd never been talk of an artistic side and the collection Charlotte had seen the other night was from an accomplished sculptor.

She opened her eyes and turned on the light so she could wash her face. The best way to settle her mind was to visit the new owner. At the worst it was Alison and knowing it would let Charlotte work on ways to manage being in the same town. Most likely though it was an innocent stranger who looked a bit like a woman who haunted her.

Esther was gone when Charlotte came out with two coffees. "I was going to see if Esther wanted a cup but noticed her leaving." she said. "Which shows the front camera is back to normal."

"I wonder who painted it. Nothing showed up when we looked, apart from the sudden blur as the paint went all over it.

And who is even out wandering the streets at two in the morning?"

"Hopefully just some bored person looking for mischief. I'll keep an ear out tonight."

Rosie gave Charlotte one of those looks when she was about to insist on something. And it would be about Charlotte's safety. Or the like.

"Darling, I wonder if you should move in with me for a little bit. Trev can come and stay here and you can have his room. He won't mind at all and then if anyone tries to do anything silly, he'll be down those stairs in seconds."

"You are so sweet for worrying about me but no. The apartment is a safe place and my haven. I love sitting out on the balcony even when it is cold and nobody can climb up there because of the curved canopies over the shop. Same with the walls because there are no footholds and the door is secure."

"As your landlady, I might need to insist!" Rosie smiled but there was a mild threat behind the humour.

"About being my landlady, Rosie, when would you like to talk about —"

"Oh, look at the time!" Rosie backed out of her spot. "I forgot I had to send a late order in so give me a few minutes and I'll run up a list." With that, she disappeared to the furthest corner of the shop.

What's going on, Rosie?

The tug at her heart was back. Not the nice one from when Trev was here earlier, but the one that hurt when Rosie had said the building would never be for sale. Her mind was about to hit overdrive and a rush of panic swept over Charlotte.

"Rosie, are you okay to close today?"

"Yes, darling. Do you want to go early?"

Charlotte located Rosie near the thrillers. "I wouldn't mind going to the falls. All this stress is getting to me a bit and a walk would help."

"You go. Just promise you'll be careful and come home before dark."

"Yes, Mum." Charlotte grinned, relieved at the idea of taking action.

Rosie raised her eyebrows then smiled back. "Good girl. You already know my rightful name. Now all we need is Trev to hurry up and make it official."

"Rosie Sibbritt!"

"Mum to you, young lady. Now, go and see if you can spot your little kingfisher friend."

CHAPTER TWENTY-SEVEN

IT WAS NO WALK THAT CHARLOTTE TOOK, BUT A RUN. SHE'D gone upstairs, changed into running gear, and with water, her phone and keys headed out again. There was a couple of hours daylight left, although the pool itself would be cast into darkness first with its ring of cliffs and trees.

Running was good. She wasn't a runner as such, but in times of stress she used it as a way to disperse unwanted negative energy. In the past she'd barely controlled the need to run, sometimes taking off with no sense of direction. In fact, the first time she'd gone to the falls, it was after a melt-down. It was late at night and she'd had the unfortunate experience of encountering Sid on her way home.

Once she reached the lookout, Charlotte stopped. Her muscles screamed about their lack of regular use and her lungs burned. She took her time to rest and recover, sipping water and bringing her breathing under control. It was a pleasant late afternoon although on the cold side. Even though they were closer to spring, Rosie had warned her of even colder days ahead.

What was going on with Rosie? Charlotte took the path to the pool at a brisk walk. In a matter of days she'd gone from encouraging Charlotte to start the finance process to buy the apartment and bookshop, to stating she had no intention of selling.

Was marrying Lewis bringing up old feelings about the bookshop and Rosie's time there with her first husband? Their marriage was one of a kind and Graeme's untimely death affected Rosie on many levels. Her hesitation in allowing Lewis to make the natural progression from friend to suitor had been tied up in feelings of disloyalty to the man she'd loved for decades, the father of her beloved son. Charlotte had helped her sort those feelings and knew she was happy to marry Lewis.

But was it too upsetting to give up the one constant in her life — the bookshop she'd built from the ground up?

Charlotte sighed then smiled as a long puff of white air left her lips. Down here in the midst of the old trees it was a lot cooler than the lookout. She reached the bottom and stepped onto the soft grass near the pool. This was better.

At the water's edge, she relaxed her shoulders and held her arms out to each side as far as they'd go, fingers extended. Nice. She rotated her torso in gentle moves to iron out little kinks. There was more tension in her body than she'd noticed.

The water in the normally calm pool was high and restless under the waterfall which pounded down with unusual force.

There was no sign of the kingfisher but the kangaroos she'd come to know hopped out of the bush to take turns drinking. She always stayed still in their presence, aware of one big male eyeing her every time they met. As much as she longed to stroke the velvet fur of the bolder youngsters who often came within a few feet, she knew better. Kangaroos were capable fighters and wouldn't hesitate to force her into the water if she was viewed as a threat.

As she'd expected, dusk settled quickly, accompanied by an icy chill. When the mob left, she followed at a safe distance until on the path to the top of the waterfall.

At the base, before she began the steep ascent, the roar of rushing water and plume of mist it caused were irresistible to observe. A last shard of sunlight cut through the particles in the air and Charlotte took her phone out. This was a much better use of her camera than trying to capture images of ghosts.

She put the phone away, rather proud of the pictures she'd taken. There might be one good enough to get Harpreet to enlarge and frame. The vantage point was amazing, right against the cliff alongside the waterfall. A narrow outcrop formed a ledge to the fall itself but it was too dark to see if it went behind the cascade. How wonderful if it did. On another day, a fine one with less water barrelling down, she'd explore.

The climb was as bad as she remembered. Broken steps, missing rails, holes where the ground should be. Another reason to support Doug in his campaign to join council.

Out of breath at the top, Charlotte perched on a large rock close to the river. Water bottlenecked then gushed over the edge. Trev once mentioned many smaller waterways met up with this one further north and with the amount of recent rain, it created a writhing, churning river forced into a narrow channel once it left the pool.

Her phone beeped a message from Rosie.

Are you home yet?

She grinned and replied.

Almost there.

Before Rosie sent Trev to check, she'd better get home. Evening was minutes away and the bushland was no place to wander around in the dark.

———

Trev sat in the patrol car outside home for a few minutes. This afternoon he'd gone backwards, at least as far as finding any answers about Cecil. What he did have was a disappointing result from the detectives. They'd got information but it wasn't what he wanted to hear and the two women in his life wouldn't like it either. There was no sign of Charlotte's car so if she was here, she'd walked. If she wasn't?

He tapped on his phone.

I'm outside Mum's. Are you inside or at the apartment? Need to talk about something.

She was probably as tired of the uncertainty as he was. Strange men turning up at her door. Sid stopping short of threatening her. Mum acting weird about the bookshop. He'd not discussed this with either of them and wouldn't unless invited. His mother was as loving toward Charlie as ever so it wasn't due to some issue between them.

Trev checked his phone. Charlotte normally replied to messages in seconds but nothing yet.

Rosie opened the front door and waved. He climbed out and leaned his arms on the top of the patrol car. "Stay inside, Mum. Too cold out here."

"Then come inside, dear. Seems logical."

"I'm waiting to hear from Charlotte. I have a bit of information and would rather tell it once to you both than repeat myself. Assume she's not in there with you?"

"Charlotte went for a run."

"A run. Charlotte doesn't do running. At least, she always told me that."

"She does now. Needed to de-stress a bit and headed off to the falls a while ago. In daylight, so don't give me that look. I got a message about half an hour ago saying she was almost home."

Which meant she was only thinking about going home.

"I might go find her. See if she's back yet."

"Phone her."

"I will on the way. You don't mind me bringing her back for a bit?"

"Silly question. Go get her. We'll order in." Rosie closed the front door as Trev slid behind the wheel. He dialled and let the call go to Bluetooth as he turned the car.

"You've reached Charlotte. Please leave a message and I'll get back to you."

Beep.

"Hi Charlie. I'm heading to the apartment, if you are free to come up to Mum's for a little bit? Have some news. Anyway, I'll be there soon."

If she'd been running, she might be in the shower. Or gone shopping.

Or be up to no good out in the bushland.

"Call me." He muttered to himself.

Although it was early, the streets were almost deserted. A heavy mist descended on the town, creating a spooky aura around the streetlights and casting shadows in odd places. More like the middle of the night.

Almost at the roundabout, Sid drove through in his station wagon, smoke wafting through the open window. He was driving in the direction of the old garden centre and something made Trev follow him at a discreet distance.

Sid pulled into the carpark of the garden centre. There was new signage across the façade. *Kingfisher Falls Gallery & Creative Hub.* Nice. Trev slowed and found a parking spot close enough to watch Sid but hopefully not be seen. The carpark was empty apart from Sid's car and although there were new lights over the entrance and windows, the inside of the building was in darkness.

Out of his car, Sid prowled around the frontage. He peered in, cupping his hands either side of his face which was pressed against the glass.

Trev nosed the patrol car forward until he was within a quick sprint. There, he parked and turned the motor off. Sid took out tobacco and a paper and rolled another cigarette and lit it, puffing away as he strolled along the frontage. The front door opened and a figure stepped out. The new owner?

It was a woman in a long coat and a scarf around her neck. Her hair was short and dark but he was too far away to pick up her features or estimate her age. She spoke to Sid, who walked back to her. Her arms were wrapped around her and her body language alarmed Trev. She was either afraid or freezing but with Sid so close, Trev figured the first option. He climbed out of the patrol car.

Before he got much further, Sid said something and the woman hurried inside, closing the door behind herself. He laughed and tossed his smoking butt onto the ground.

"You have three seconds to pick that up." Trev strode over the road. "I will write you up for littering. Three, two—"

"Yeah, yeah, yeah." Sid bent down with a groan and grabbed the butt. He straightened with further complaints. "Forgot where I was."

"Unless you thought you were at home, that isn't even the beginning of an excuse." Trev reached him. "What is your business here?"

With a staged look of confusion, Sid shrugged.

"What was your business with the woman?"

"You been tailing me?"

"Answer the question."

"Curious. Saw the fancy sign and wanted a look. See if there's anything I can come back and buy for my Marguerite. Didn't know anyone was inside."

Trev didn't believe him for a minute.

"What did you say to her?"

"Who? Oh, her…" Sid stared at the door. "She wanted to know who I was so I introduced myself. Then she invited me to bring Marguerite to shop another day." He turned back with a sneer. "You got nothing on me, whelp."

Give me some time.

"Back in your car, Sid. Weather's about to turn nasty so take it easy on that dirt road of yours."

Once Sid drove off, Trev tapped on the door of the building. There was a sound inside. A shuffle of feet, but no response. Poor woman probably had enough for one night. He wrote his mobile number on the back of his card and slid it under the door. He'd drop by in daylight to introduce himself.

There was still no message from Charlotte. Back in the patrol car, Trev made a U-turn and went to find her.

CHAPTER TWENTY-EIGHT

"CHARLOTTE, YOUR PHONE BEEPED." HARPREET WAS BEHIND the counter in her shop, tapping on a keyboard.

"How is your hearing so good?" Charlotte had left her phone and keys on a counter near the door when Harpreet invited her in half an hour ago. They'd both been at the supermarket and when Charlotte showed her the images from the waterfall, Harpreet told her it was time for a drink while she had a better look.

"You forget. I still work at the restaurant some nights and have to hone my hearing in over the music and my parents shouting at each other." She giggled. "Don't tell them I said that. It is more they call loudly to each other."

Charlotte laughed. She'd eaten at India Gate House a lot and always to a backdrop of kitchen noise. Harpreet's parents were amazing cooks but they did get loud on occasion. She checked the phone, dismayed at missed calls and messages. "Harpreet, I'm just popping outside to call Trev back."

She dialled as she went outside, shivering as the cool air went straight through her running clothes. She'd not been home yet, going to the supermarket to find something for dinner. Had Rosie told Trev she was out late and now he was worrying about her?

Before the call connected, she hung up. The patrol car was coming around the roundabout and she waved as it neared. Trev parked and was out in a couple of seconds.

"Everything okay?" he asked.

"Everything's fine. I've just been in with Harpreet and didn't have the phone close."

"Ah."

"Ah? What's wrong? Do you want to come in out of the cold?"

He shook his head. He hadn't even smiled yet and the worry lines around his eyes were almost permanent these days. She had a silly urge to reach up and smooth them away.

"I've got some news for you and Mum. Just hoped to tell you together as I could use both your opinions. And Mum wanted to order in if you'd like dinner with us. Once you're finished here of course."

What kind of news?

"I'll only be a minute but I have some shopping to drop home." She held her hand out and he took it, his own hand much warmer than hers. "I'll let Harpreet know and then I'll run home quickly."

"You look cold, sweetie. Feel cold."

"I am. Need my coat. Shall I meet you at Rosie's?"

"Give me your keys and the shopping and I'll drop them at the apartment and wait for you. If you don't mind."

Of course, she didn't. A moment later she'd grabbed her one bag of groceries and keys and he was driving off.

"I'm going to have to go, Harpreet." Charlotte leaned on the counter to look over her friend's shoulder. "Oh, that is stunning!" Harpreet had one of the photos enlarged on her screen. "This will look nice as a print."

"Better yet, as a canvas. Leave it with me and I'll come up with some options. Go be with your man."

"He just needs to tell me something, and Rosie. Probably about that man from last night." Charlotte had updated Harpreet on the events of the previous evening as a warning to be extra careful. "I'll see you tomorrow?"

Harpreet gave Charlotte a kiss on the cheek as she opened the door for her. "We'll have our drink another time. Be careful out there."

Outside again, the mistiness was remarkable. Thank goodness it was such a short walk home. At the corner she waited for a truck to pass, jogging on the spot to warm up. She recognised the driver. The same man from this morning. He waved as if they were best friends and she watched the taillights until the white air enveloped them. She needed to follow him.

"Charlotte."

Trev was on the balcony.

"Bother. I mean, coming!" she raised her voice for the final word only and jogged to the apartment.

———

The drive to Rosie's was in silence. Trev hadn't mentioned the incident on the corner but Charlotte knew him well enough to expect a comment at some point. She'd wavered a little too long there staring after the truck and if anyone knew her thought process it was him.

He pulled into Rosie's driveway and turned the motor off.

The house was pretty under the blanket of mist. "Looks like a cloud fell from the sky." Charlotte said as they headed to the front door.

"Means we have some bad weather ahead." Rosie opened the door. "Might look picturesque but mark my words, in the next day or so we'll get a deluge. Perhaps a gale blowing. And even snow."

"Snow!" Charlotte followed Rosie inside. "How wonderful!"

"How freezing!" Rosie replied. "And where have you been all this time, young lady?"

Charlotte giggled.

Trev had closed and locked the front door and headed for his bedroom. "Just going to change and she was fine, Mum."

"I'll be the judge of that. Charlie, would you like to order some dinner for us? Lewis is joining us in a few minutes and I promised him I'd have four cocktail glasses ready for something special he wants to make."

"Sure thing. What do you fancy tonight?"

"Pizza. Something meaty, please."

Charlotte tapped on her phone. "What about Lewis?"

"Falls special."

Should she wait to ask Trev what he wanted? The shower turned on. Nope. Not holding dinner ordering for him. He could have the seafood and she'd get vegetarian and if he wanted, they could share. And garlic bread. Yum. Her stomach rumbled.

Dinner ordered, Charlotte caught up with Rosie in the dining room. "I thought this was a good place tonight. We can talk over dinner and make some plans."

"About before…I was heading home when I got your first message but realised I'd got nothing in the fridge for dinner. At the supermarket I bumped into Harpreet—"

"Oh, how is she?"

"She's well. Anyway, I showed her some photos I took, here, I'll show you," Charlotte searched her phone. "and we ended up at her shop looking at them on her screen."

Charlotte handed the phone over. Rosie scrolled through. "Ooh!" She zoomed in on some. "These are stunning! I'd forgotten how the colours change depending on the time of day and weather. I do miss visiting."

"Then we must find a way to get you down there. Council has got to listen to complaints about repairing and improving the path."

"Still won't get me to where you took those images." Rosie handed the phone back with a smile which pulled at Charlotte's heart. Part reminiscing and loads of regret. "There's a ledge that, if you are very careful, leads behind the waterfall."

"I saw it today! I wondered how far it went."

"You do need to pick your timing, so not after heavy rain but you can walk along it and then just when you begin to get spray all over you, the rocks widen a bit and by hugging the wall you can slide behind the downpour. Right in the middle, it actually opens up into a shallow cave with enough room for a picnic."

Oh. To sit on a picnic blanket with a bottle of wine, crusty bread, and a seafood salad. Perhaps strawberries and cream. All behind a cascade.

"Mum, how do you know this?" Trev wandered in wearing jeans and open necked shirt.

Charlotte stared at him. So handsome. Yet so unaware of his good looks. Or of his kindness. And the aura of strength and quiet confidence was a potent mix.

Trev grinned at her and her skin heated up. Way to go, being caught checking out the local law enforcement. But somehow, she didn't really mind and she smiled back. After all, this was the man she loved.

"Never you mind how I know. Arrange a nice picnic and take your darling girl on a romantic date there when there's a nice day." Rosie headed out of the dining room. "Lew is here."

"I ordered you a seafood pizza but you can share my veggie one if you like." Charlotte said.

"As long as it wasn't Hawaiian, I'll eat just about anything."

"You don't like pineapple on your pizza? I never knew that."

Trev grinned. "One of my darkest secrets, Charlie." He put his arms around her. "I wonder what else I should reveal?"

She snuggled against him. He smelt good and she closed her eyes. "Hm. What is your favourite colour?"

"Not a dark secret. I love orange."

"Okay. Then, do you prefer dogs or cats?"

Charlotte felt his chin rest on the top of her head lightly. It was comfortable. Heart-warming.

"Depends on the cat. But if I could only pick one or the other it would be a dog. Kind of fell in love with Randall in River's End. What about you?"

"Same."

"We can always get a dog and a cat." Trev said.

Oh.

"Any more questions?"

"Mountains or sea?" Charlotte was still thinking about them living together and having their own pets.

"Sea. Much as I love this town, the sea is in my blood."

Charlotte leaned back to look at him. "You miss River's End."

"I do miss it. Love the beach and the cliffs. But if I lived there again, I'd miss being here." He laughed shortly. "Can't win."

She slipped her arms around his neck and lifted herself onto her toes. "Then we must visit there often."

"We must." Trev kissed her nose. "And that sounds like Mum and Lewis. Time to have a talk about things."

He released her as they came in and Charlotte wished things were different. More time to visit River's End together. Time to get to know each other more. And less crime and worry in this little town of theirs.

CHAPTER TWENTY-NINE

Trev wanted nothing more than to jump in the car with Charlie and drive to River's End. Talking about his home of so many years sparked a longing for friends there and with his relationship with Charlotte growing, he knew he'd see everything in a whole new light.

The reality of now was less appealing. Lewis fussed around the bar shaking some concoction as Charlotte and Rosie teased him. He was about to drop a metaphorical bombshell on them and went over how he'd do so in his head. Again.

We've discovered why the truck keeps going to the parcel of land the other side of the river. Now, there's a few reasons...

Sure. Play it cool and logical.

"There you go, Trevor. My own alcohol-free version of a pina colada." Lewis placed a cocktail glass before Trev with a smile. "I'm practicing for when Rosie and I visit Hawaii."

"Except we won't spare the rum!" Rosie grinned and held her glass aloft. "To family!"

Toasts complete, everyone finally sat at the table and Trev was more than aware of three curious sets of eyes on him. Cool and logical.

"Council has plans for the land on the other side of the

river. Want to build what they call eco-townhouses. Reckon they are one meeting away from approval and are keeping it low profile to avoid objections."

Good use of being cool and logical, Trev.

Charlotte and Rosie exchanged a look. Lewis raised both eyebrows. Nobody spoke.

Trev continued. "Hadn't meant to blurt it out like that, sorry. The reality is, they have the right to clear those trees to do a proper survey. They've also classed it as overdue maintenance."

"Overdue what?" Rosie's tone warned Trev how unimpressed she was and he risked a glance at Charlotte.

She was chewing her bottom lip. A sure sign of her inner turmoil from past experience. After a minute, she looked at him through troubled eyes. He reached for her hand and she let him take it.

"Charlie, Mum, Lewis...this is a worry. They're not breaking any laws but—"

"All those poor trees!" Charlotte burst out. "Saplings. Old growth. What about the birds and wildlife?"

"Darling, there wouldn't be much of anything living in the ones so close to the road. Not with all the lovely denser forest to build their homes in, but you are right to worry. If homes go into there, what will the impact be? It is right on the river."

Lewis nodded. "Think of the pollution seeping into it even while they build. Let alone once homeowners move in. Cars, chemicals, waste. What is an eco-townhouse anyway?"

"I asked the same question." Trev said. "According to the plans, this is a set of ten two-floor residences. All will be built to fit in with the landscape and have all the bells and whistles of modern eco-friendly add ons. But these days, new homes are built with things such as solar panels and rainwater tanks already."

"More traffic up that quiet street. I'm not against new

homes, not at all. But Kingfisher Falls doesn't have the infrastructure to handle much growth at a time." Rosie said.

"Have to agree. I've lived here a long time and there are plenty of areas being underfunded and overlooked. Roads, schools."

"And the area around the falls, Lewis. It is extremely dangerous in places and there is no way for anyone other than the most able-bodied to enjoy the beautiful place." Charlotte played with the stem of her drink. "Money needs to be spent there to ensure it is safe for visitors and locals alike."

Trev agreed but it wasn't as easy as that. Never was with bureaucracy. "The other thing that Bryce and Katrina discovered was even more disturbing."

All eyes turned to him.

"There is a plan under consideration for a shopping centre. A mall."

"A mall!" If Rosie could have leapt from her wheelchair, she would have then and there. "Kingfisher Falls is a small town. A village. Not a mini version of towns such as Sunbury, not that there is anything wrong with it but not here. Not here!"

Lewis moved his chair closer to Rosie and put his arm around her shoulders. "We'll stop it happening, love."

"How, Lew? If Jonas and his cronies want this to happen, how do we have a chance to prevent him?" Tears formed in Rosie's eyes and her voice came out as a whisper. "He has all the power."

Trev's heart contracted. "No, he doesn't. I know it feels that way but he is one person. Yes, he has the ear of some other members of council, but there are processes to follow. And plenty of opportunities to raise objections. But knowing this is valuable information."

"How so, Trev?" Lewis asked.

Charlotte answered instead. "Clues. Is the developer trying to take short-cuts? Somebody is buying up buildings so it makes sense to believe that is where they want to build the mall. No change of use for the land."

"But what about the shops not for sale?" Rosie looked from Charlotte to Trev. "Will they try to build around them?"

Trev reached for Charlotte's hand under the table and squeezed it. Her eyes met his with a question and he hoped she got his silent message. Don't scare Mum.

"I would imagine not, Mum. The visit you had the other night is probably the first approach you'll get to sell. We are tracking down the man who was here and he'll be spoken to and warned against contacting you again."

"Thank you, dear. I didn't like him at all and the building is not going to be made available for those people."

Charlotte squeezed his hand back and nodded slightly. She understood.

The doorbell rang.

"I'll go." Trev stood. "Imagine that is dinner arriving."

"Let me give you a hand. Any chance of another yummy pretend cocktail, Lewis?" Charlotte leapt up and followed Trev.

Once they were out of earshot, she caught up. "You think the fire was a direct response to Cecil refusing to sell. And whoever is behind the development won't stop until they get all the shops along that block."

"Charlie—"

"And Jonas is short on time because he might lose the election which is why he's resorted to violence."

Trev stopped just inside the front door. "Let me get dinner. But yes."

Her eyes widened and she disappeared to the kitchen.

When he joined her, she'd taken out napkins and seasoning. He placed the boxes on the counter and then his arms around Charlotte. "Thanks for not saying that in front of Mum. She's upset enough."

"I wouldn't. What are we going to do about Jonas?"

Trev grinned. "*We* aren't going to do anything. The detectives are back first thing and we'll go over all the new info and hopefully some more news from requests we've sent out today. But what you can do for me is be watchful." He felt the smile leave his face. "Stay alert for unusual activity. Keep an eye on Mum. Anything out of the ordinary you call me. Just like you did after Sid hassled you the other day. Can you do that?"

She wiggled out of his arms to pick up the pizza boxes. "Easy. Perfect job for me, actually. Spying on people." Charlotte winked and walked away.

"Hey! I did not say spying on people."

"You'd never say such a thing but I knew what you meant. Aren't you hungry?"

He was. Starving, in fact. Hopefully, Charlotte was teasing him. But he had a nagging feeling she was quite serious.

———

As much as she enjoyed stirring Trev, Charlotte wished she'd chosen her words better. For the rest of the evening she felt his eyes on her. Solemn. As though he was thinking of how to rein her in. She wasn't about to put herself in danger. And Rosie was first on her priority list of people to watch over.

The mood in the dining room was sombre. Rosie looked exhausted and almost as soon as the last of the boxes were cleared, she said she might have an early night. Lewis offered to drive Charlotte home and she jumped at the opportunity.

As Lewis and Rosie said rather long and private goodbyes, Charlotte cleaned up the glasses. In the kitchen, Trev dried up as she washed, then took her hands, kissing her fingers. "I'm happy to take you home."

"Thank you. But I think Rosie needs you around and Lewis will make sure I'm back safely."

And you don't get to remind me of what I'm not allowed to do on the trip back.

"Text me when you are locked in the apartment?"

"Promise. But Trev, I'm not at risk. Am I? I mean, if anything, Rosie needs a guard."

His lips tightened.

"Sorry, don't mean to upset you." Charlotte did what he had and drew his hands to her lips. "We need to talk about all of this another time because I think there's more going on than we realise. Jonas isn't…well, he's not a good person."

He sighed. "Agree. Every time there's a crime or something not right in town it leads to Jonas Carmichael but he is just too good at weaselling himself out of any charges."

Charlotte wanted to discuss this more. At length. Over a bottle of wine to take the edge off the panic and worry and gut-wrenching belief Jonas would come gunning for anyone who got in his way. She reconsidered getting a lift with Lewis.

"Ready, my dear?" Lewis, trailed by Rosie, appeared. "Or do you need a moment?"

After squeezing Trev's hands, Charlotte released them with a smile. "All ready to go."

On the way to the front door, Trev whispered, "Breakfast tomorrow? We can talk."

Sounded perfect. She whispered back. "I have eggs and mushrooms. Be there early!"

"Are you two setting up a date?" Rosie pushed the front door open. "You could just stay here, darling, then have breakfast all together tomorrow."

Charlotte kissed Rosie's cheek. "Thank you. Kind of longing for my own bed."

"Hm. Know the feeling. Will you text me once you are home?"

"Of course. And you sleep well."

In Lewis' car, Charlotte glanced over at him. "Thanks for this."

"Pleasure. I think at the moment we need to stay close to

each other. If we must be alone, then we need to watch out for each other in other ways."

"But what about you, Lewis?"

"Me? I can open my garage remotely and drive straight in. Then unlock the internal door and I'm in the house. And I'm quite safe, my dear. Nobody is going to come after me because my shop isn't in the area of interest. Rosie's is... and that bothers me."

Me too.

"Are you going to Hawaii for your honeymoon?" Time for a nicer subject.

"Oh, goodness, no. Rosie is teasing but one day we shall visit it. When we both retire and wish to travel, that is one place we've never been to. Have you been?"

"No. I have to admit I've not left Australia. Work always came first and I've had my...mother to, um, keep an eye on."

"I imagine it is a bit more than that. Rosie has mentioned your poor mother has some health issues and you've dedicated much of your time to helping her." Lewis turned onto the main street and silence fell between them.

Once again the night was misty and cold. Few people were out and the supermarket and takeaway shops were all closed. Ahead, at the roundabout, a person waited in the middle of the slightly raised circle. Where once the Christmas tree stood was now an empty space with a few plants dotted around the edges. Another council failure.

Lewis slowed as he entered the roundabout, his attention on the road. Charlotte's eyes were drawn to the person. What an odd place to stand, particularly late in the evening.

The person stared back.

Charlotte's heart skipped a beat.

It's you.

Long coat. Scarf wrapped around her head. Oversized sunglasses—as if she needed them at night. She turned as the car passed to stare at Charlotte.

"Lewis..." she looked over her shoulder as they exited the roundabout.

"Hm?"

The woman stepped off the roundabout and ran across the road in the direction of the old garden centre, disappearing in seconds.

"What did you wish to ask, my dear? And what are you looking at?" He glanced over.

Charlotte faced forward again, clenching her hands into fists on her lap. "Sorry, nothing. I thought I saw someone I knew."

"Shall we turn around and investigate?"

She forced a laugh. "I think investigating anything is against Trevor's rules. His long list of rules I need to follow."

They reached the bookshop and Lewis parked near the driveway. "I'm sure he has your best interests at heart. I'll walk in with you and no arguing." A smile touched his lips and he climbed out.

"I appreciate it. Just let me check the camera." Charlotte peered up. The light was on and there was no sign of paint. She checked the front door. Secure. A newspaper was under the door and an envelope. Short of unlocking the door it would have to wait for morning. Everything else appeared normal and undisturbed so she joined Lewis at the edge of the building.

"All good?"

"Yes, thank you."

The driveway lights flicked on and at the bottom of the steps, Charlotte insisted Lewis let her run up without having to traipse up and down. "All safe here, and I'll lock the door." She waved.

"Goodnight, Charlotte. Sleep well." Lewis disappeared from her sight and she locked the door behind herself and sprinted to the balcony. From there, she watched him until he was back in his car and driving away. For a moment she stayed at the railing, gazing back at the roundabout. All was quiet. But she hadn't imagined seeing the woman. If it wasn't Alison, it was someone playing some bizarre game of their own.

She locked the sliding door on her way inside. The night air had chilled her and a long hot shower was overdue.

CHAPTER THIRTY

WEDNESDAY. SLEEPING WAS NEXT TO IMPOSSIBLE. Charlotte tossed and turned for a while and gave up, sliding out of bed to go and make tea. While the kettle boiled, she stared at her reflection in the living room window. Wrapped in a long, cuddly dressing gown, hair in two plaits after the shower, she looked young and a little bit lost.

"I don't feel young."

The whistle of the kettle sent her to the kitchen. It was true. The worries about the fire, and Rosie, and whoever this woman was who looked like Alison — all weighed on her.

Tea in hand, she curled her feet under herself on the sofa. Only one lamp was on. The apartment was warm enough and the cup offered comfort on a primal level as the scent of the tea teased her senses.

She needed to practice yoga again. The kind more about the mind than the body. Perhaps Rosie would join her. They both needed something to balance out the incredible stress of the past few weeks. It wasn't just the current situation which played on her mind, but the events around finding the shallow grave in the bushland and seeing a man plunge to his death over the falls. With the rapid turn of events, she'd not dealt with those minutes out in the dark with Harmony that night, let alone the sadness of finding the grave.

The tea helped. The simple act of sipping and savouring the delicious blend soothed her jumbled emotions. The appearance in town of Alison, or whoever she was, had to have a logical explanation. One she intended to find. The woman was real. And real people were rarely able to hide for too long. Between Charlotte's not-too-shabby sleuthing skills, and some friendly local police, it was a matter of when, not if, the woman was identified.

Then what, Charlie?

She let her mind wander to an amusing scenario of the two detectives and Trev following Charlotte as she closed in on the mysterious woman. A chase on foot through the streets of Kingfisher Falls. Cornering the coated woman and finally, insisting she remove those oversized sunglasses.

Who would it be? Was Alison in Kingfisher Falls or was this a pure coincidence. Or...Charlotte sat up straight. Sid had told her many times he knew all about her past and would make sure everyone else did. He'd threatened her personally and anonymously until she'd stood up to him and like many cowards, he'd backed off. But that was before he'd lost his job and moved away.

Being back here, living in the awful cottage belonging to Glenys Lane who was now awaiting trial, roaming the streets, and peering into the bookshop—or coming in—there had to be something to his odd behaviour.

Charlotte put her empty cup down. Had Sid contacted Alison? Told her where Charlotte lived? Why on earth would he bother though. Unless he wanted to blackmail Charlotte, there was nothing in it for him. No, this was her mind in over-drive. Tired.

Not too tired to read. A good book and another cup of tea were in order.

The tap on the door was perfectly timed. Charlotte hurried from the kitchen. "Password?"

"Um. Croissants."

She flung the door open. "I hope you have some, otherwise, if you are just teasing me, you'll need to find breakfast somewhere…oh."

Trev held out a box. "Enough for our breakfast and some for you later. Is that a good enough bribe?"

Charlotte considered him. He was in uniform and looked as though he'd slept well for the first time in ages. The old sparkle was back in his eyes. She stepped back.

"On this occasion I shall accept the bribe. Please come in."

"Not too early?" he closed the door.

"I've been up for a while." Charlotte headed to the kitchen. She'd barely slept, unable to put the image of the woman in the centre of the roundabout out of her mind. "Coffee?"

"Please. Or shall I brew while you cook?" He eyed off the neat row of eggs and sliced mushrooms. "Is that chili and basil I spy?"

"It is and yes, you're welcome to do the coffee. I might toss the croissants in the oven for a minute as well." Charlotte reached the oven dial at the same time Trev did and their hands bumped. "Oops."

They laughed. It felt nice. Right. Sharing a kitchen with Trev was a good thing.

For as long as it took to cook and serve their meals, the kitchen was a place of laughter and teasing. If this was a hint of what a life with Trev might be like, Charlotte was all for it.

Breakfast was delicious. They sat on the stools at the kitchen counter eating and talking about ordinary things. The chance of snow. Best time of year to hike to the top of Mount Macedon. Whether white or cream was a better colour to paint the living room. Charlotte had never had a breakfast like this one. A small piece of her heart would remember this for a long time.

Dishes done and more coffee poured, Charlotte and Trev moved to the balcony. It was just warm enough to sit out there and watch as the last of the mist lifted under insistent sunshine. The day was beginning in earnest and as the whiteness evaporated, so did the cocoon of pretence that everything was normal.

Charlotte heard herself sigh.

Trev reached over and touched her cheek. "I know. And I promise you this, sweetie. We'll find whoever killed Cecil. They'll be prosecuted and Kingfisher Falls will return to being the serene, safe town it always was."

"Until I arrived!"

"No. All you did was refuse to let crimes happen without proper attention. Sid was bordering on criminal neglect...if not activity, for years so it was timing. That is all."

"Thank you for saying so. Sometimes I feel as though trouble follows me wherever I go." She managed a small smile. "And not all of my own making."

He grinned and picked up his coffee to sip as though avoiding a reply. Fair enough. No doubt he had every reason to believe she landed herself into most situations. But she couldn't bear letting go of something when it was wrong. Not until she'd changed it to a right.

"Last night, we couldn't talk freely because Rosie was upset enough. Do you really think Jonas is behind what's happening?"

"It would be nice to think so because he is a known quantity. We know he has criminal associates. His background hints at someone with the skills to navigate the law." Trev said.

"Not just because he is a lawyer though. Surely there's more going on with him because I see someone who is filled with ambition and prepared to throw anyone else under the metaphorical bus to achieve his goals." Charlotte had given him a lot of thought. "I know you weren't here just before Christmas, but he tried to pin the tree thefts on Darcy to deflect suspicion from those young thugs. And it all came back to his strange relationship with Veronica, who was dating one of them."

Coffee finished, Trev pushed the cup to one side and nodded. "It makes me wonder who put that woman, Sally Austin, up to her report of someone a lot like Darcy near the fire. The other thing which plays on my mind is the reappearance of Sid in town. I followed him last night before coming to find you."

"Followed where?"

"To the old garden centre."

Charlotte sat forward, cupping the remains of her coffee between her hands.

"He stopped in the carpark and went for a good look through the windows. Had a smoke and looked as if he was settling in for the night."

"What happened?"

"A woman came through the front door. Imagine it is the new owner. Anyway, they had a short discussion and I made my way across from the car. Got the impression she might be afraid of him."

"What does she look like?" Charlotte held her breath.

Trev blinked at her. "Look like? Why?"

"Um…"

"Charlotte? What aren't you telling me?"

That I'm seeing ghosts. Jumping at shadows. Imagining a woman into existence.

She forced a smile. "I'm really curious. I didn't tell you, but my sister is apparently a sculptor as well and I am wondering if this new lady might know her."

"Which doesn't answer why you need her description." His eyes teased her. "Unless you are planning on plying her with

179

new clothes as a tribute in order to lower her defences until she tells you about Zoe."

It did sound silly. She needed to take more care of what she said. Charlotte pushed the remaining coffee to one side and leaned back. "That was my evil plan!"

"Right. Back to the story...she closed the door on Sid and he tossed his cigarette butt onto the ground, giving me the opportunity to warn him about littering. He claims he was looking for a gift for his wife."

Trev's phone beeped and he checked the message. "Sorry, Charlie. Katrina and Bryce have an interview with someone which has been pushed forward." He stood and collected their cups.

"Jonas?" Maybe they'd let her sit in on the interview.

"No. He is later today after avoiding me up until the time Katrina suggested to him they would be happy to talk at the council offices."

Charlotte followed Trev inside and once he was ready to leave, gave him a kiss. "Thanks for coming over. I like having breakfast with you."

"Then we need to make it happen more often."

His phone beeped again and he rolled his eyes. "Sorry. Better go."

He ran down the steps with Charlotte watching from the landing, and at the bottom, called up. "I didn't answer your question. The new trader? Couldn't see much of her because she wore a long coat but she had short dark hair. Hope that helps you come up with a tribute. Or bribe."

Despite a sudden weakness in her legs, Charlotte kept her response light. "I don't make bribes, only accept them and only from you."

Trev waved and was gone but Charlotte stayed holding the railing. Long coat. Short, dark hair. It had to be Alison.

CHAPTER THIRTY-ONE

TREV SPENT LITTLE TIME LISTENING TO THE INTERVIEW WITH Cecil's niece. The second message earlier was from Mrs Munro, the owner until recently of the hairdressing salon. She wasn't able to locate her paperwork for the sale yet as it was in her house in Kingfisher Falls and she wanted to stay with her daughter in the city a while longer. So, as the detectives did the interview, he began searching for the man from the other night.

The video footage from the landing at Charlie's apartment provided one good image of him. This, Trev sent off to a friend in the computer forensics area of the department with a request of improving the quality.

Knowing this might take a while, he built a profile of the man based on the interviews, and casual conversations, about him with Charlotte and Rosie.

Cecil's niece left and Bryce pulled up a chair at Trev's desk. "Anything?"

"Waiting on an improved image to run through the system. Setting up a profile now. What about the niece?"

Bryce looked at the ceiling. "Man. So many tears and I don't think for one minute she actually cared about the poor old man. Hadn't talked to him in years. Only relative and had no idea he'd leave her everything. I expect her first phone call will be to a lawyer to expedite the reading of the will."

"Did she kill him?"

"Nah. Doubt she even knew he still lived here."

Katrina returned from seeing the niece out. "One less suspect." She went to the whiteboard and wiped off all mention of the woman. "We need to find this killer, gentlemen."

"Thought we might just sit around and talk about football."

With a small shake of her head, Katrina grabbed her chair and pulled it over to Trev's desk. She ignored Bryce. He seemed unconcerned and was probably used to getting no response from his regular attempts to stir her. But Trev knew Katrina and there was a tightness around her lips he recognised as stress.

"Trev, we have Neville Anderson coming in shortly. Would like you to observe, but not as if you are involved. Watch for anything we might miss, would you?"

"Sure, Katrina. Doug told me the other night that Neville is a good man. Kinda trust his instincts."

"That may be the case, but this is a murder we're investigating. Need a bit more than instincts."

She was right, of course. Katrina didn't know Doug the way he did, and who really knew anyone, anyhow?

Katrina continued. "Depending upon the outcome of this interview, there's a few pressing matters we need to get sorted into some kind of priority list. I know Jonas is finally gracing us with his presence later. What do we expect from him?"

"I reckon he'll find a way to make Darcy look involved." Trev said, leaning back and putting his hands behind his head. "Curious whether he knows this Sally Austin. And where he was the night of the fire."

"Doubt he'd get his hands dirty." Bryce said.

"Agree. But it wouldn't hurt to put some pressure on him. Rattle his cage a bit." Trev was all for stirring the man up to see what fell out. "Wonder if he knows anything about a certain missing phone."

"Pity we'd need a warrant to look for it and until he gives us due cause…" Katrina checked the time. "Mr Anderson should be here in a minute. Keep half an eye on the interview."

The buzzer at the front door went off and Trev got to his feet. "My cue to go and collect him then."

———

There was nothing odd or notable about Neville Anderson. A softly spoken man in his early forties, he was open about the crime that sent him to prison and just as open about the homelessness in his teens which drove him to make bad choices out of desperation. In prison he learned to cook and was able to go into a program on release to become a chef.

"Still hard for a decade to get employers to trust me," he said. "Took whatever jobs nobody else wanted and when Doug reached out to me, I couldn't believe it. Best man I've ever met. I'll never do wrong by him."

Trev believed him. People can change and when they're given a second chance, some turn it into a lifelong repayment of the good done to them. There was a sincerity about the man which appealed to Trev. Perhaps one day they'd talk under different circumstances and become friends. The interview took less time than the one with Cecil's niece, and both detectives agreed with Trev's thoughts. His name was crossed off the whiteboard.

Before Jonas' interview, there was a discussion about how to best manage a man who not only knew the law, but wouldn't hesitate to use it against them. By the time he rang the buzzer, Trev had turned the whiteboard from view again and each had their job to do.

Jonas walked in with his usual swagger and a wide smile.

"Detectives. Trevor. I'm yours for half an hour and then, off to open the new childcare centre."

Bryce gestured to the chair he'd placed in the centre of the room. "Please. We'll get through as fast as you can answer our questions."

As they'd done once before, each officer took a seat facing Jonas in a row backing onto the whiteboard. Katrina took the centre chair as lead. Once Jonas sat, she wasted no time.

"Mr Carmichael, thanks for attending today. We are investigating the recent murder of Cecil—"

"Murder?" Jonas interrupted. "The poor old fellow got caught in the fire!"

"After he was shot at close range from behind." Katrina continued. "The fire was deliberately lit and a person, or persons, either waited inside for him, or were let into the agency after hours for a meeting with him."

"Where were you that night, Mr Carmichael?" Bryce said. He sat casually, one ankle over a knee, arms loosely folded.

"Me? I didn't hurt Cecil."

Nobody spoke and the silence dragged on until Jonas cleared his throat. He reached into a pocket for his phone. "Fine. Let me check my calendar. Right. Began with a council meeting which ran until eight. Then dinner with Terrance. Finished up when we got the fire alert on our phones. After making sure everyone was okay, I headed home to bed."

Trevor wanted to point out that being with Terrance didn't come close to being a credible alibi, but his designated job was taking notes so he kept quiet.

"Where did you meet Terrance for dinner?" Katrina asked, taking the interview back.

"His house. But we got home delivery."

"From?"

"From? Oh, um think it was the Indian place. Maybe pizza. Was days ago. Do you remember what you ate days ago?" He flashed a fake smile at Katrina, whose expression didn't change. Sucking up to Katrina was the downfall of many suspects.

"Perhaps you can ask Terrance."

"Sure. I'll make a note." He tapped on his phone.

"The day after the fire, you were seen in the vicinity with Terrance and with Sid Browne. How did that come about?"

Jonas shrugged. "Wanted to offer help from council. They were on the opposite corner and I stopped for a moment to see if they were doing okay."

Bryce uncrossed his arms with a confused gesture. "Why wouldn't they? Be doing okay."

"Big shock. A fire in town and talk of a body inside. Upsets everyone."

"You said you wanted to offer help from council. Who to?" Katrina pressed on.

"Fire fighters. See if they needed any supplies. Water. Stuff like that. Look, I'm not sure what this has to do with the fire."

"Who did you speak to?"

"What? I dunno. One of the fire crew."

Trev finally spoke. "I observed you leave with Terrance and Sid. You didn't speak to anyone apart from them, not at least until you reached the roundabout."

A twitch in Jonas' forehead accompanied a nasty tone. "You observed? Or your girlfriend, little miss nosy."

Bryce stood and wandered to his desk, which was closer to Jonas, then perched on it. "That is inappropriate. There's more than one person here who saw you that morning. What is your relationship to Terrance Murdoch?"

"I'm his lawyer."

"You're not a defence lawyer though." Katrina said. "You manage contracts for land acquisition. Finance contracts and the like."

"Been checking up on me? What of it?"

"Tell us about the land behind the realtors. It merges into

council land and your own town planner doesn't even seem to understand where the line is."

It was interesting watching the façade of forced friendliness change to barely controlled anger in a few seconds. Jonas' face reddened and he leaned forward. "The town planner is an idiot. Should have retired years ago. It is quite simple, officers. Terrance and the estate of the late Kevin Murdoch own a small parcel of land which abuts council owned land. Some of the latter is about to be sold for development to bring much needed funds to our small council. Where that line is has no bearing on the fire or Cecil's death."

"Tell us about a business broker visiting the owners of the shops along that part of the road. A gentleman who offers large sums of money for a quick exchange of contracts."

The twitch worked overtime. "No idea who you mean. I have an appointment to attend soon so is there anything else?"

"Do you have a theory on who is behind the fire and murder?" Katrina said.

Jonas seemed to brighten up. "In my opinion, he had access to a lot of personal information. Being in people's homes all the time, he'd see and hear things which someone might not want repeated. Might have upset someone"

"Such as?" Bryce was staring at Jonas.

"He was up at the Forests not too long ago to see if they wanted to sell."

"And how would you know that?" Katrina said.

"Heard it from a neighbour. Cecil dropped by to see if the Forests wanted to sell. He's offered before and knows there are developers interested in land up this way for lifestyle blocks."

Where is this going, Carmichael?

A sliver of dread hit Trev's gut. Ever since the strange interview with Sally Austin, he'd expected something to come along and back her claim of seeing Darcy near the fire.

Everyone waited for Jonas to continue and he did, his eyes darting between Katrina and Bryce. "Apparently, he overheard

Abbie tell Darcy if he didn't get them out of debt, she was leaving him. Decided not to knock on the door after that little gem but apparently Darcy followed him out to the carpark. Warned him not to repeat what he heard."

"Right. Which neighbour?"

"Not my place to say."

Bryce had obviously had enough because he was on his feet again and stood over Jonas. "You started this and we can't accept hearsay. Which neighbour?"

With a shrug, Jonas checked his watch and got to his feet. "Fine. It was Marguerite. Cecil went there next because he's managing the property for Glenys Lane and he had to view some appliance needing fixing." He turned his back on Bryce and addressed Katrina. "You want motive? Go ask Darcy Forest where he was that night. I'm done with questions so anything else, send me an email with them."

He stalked out and nobody bothered to accompany him. Bryce's hands were clenched and Trev understood the feeling. His phone rang and he glanced at the others. "It's Darcy."

Katrina and Bryce joined him as he answered and put the call on speaker. "Darcy, I'm here with the detectives and the call is on speaker, if that's okay."

Darcy paused and then, when he spoke, his voice was alarmed as the words tumbled out. "Something's wrong. There's so much…money…bank account. Trev, you gotta help me. Someone's setting me up."

CHAPTER THIRTY-TWO

CHARLOTTE HAD NO IDEA IT WAS LUNCHTIME UNTIL ROSIE reminded her. "I'm worried about you, darling. You seem a bit jumpy, particularly when a customer comes in."

"I do? Um, just used to the doorbell. I'll go and buy those batteries and then it will solve one problem."

"How many problems do you have?" Rosie gazed at her over her glasses. "Current crime issues in the town aside, what's up?"

There was no way to answer that just yet. If she began to talk about Alison, she'd cry. And probably panic and run off somewhere. Then there was the worry of whether Rosie had changed her mind about selling the business to Charlotte. Not the time to raise it.

"I had a nice breakfast with Trev." Best to redirect Rosie when she had a certain look in her eyes. One which usually led to Charlotte telling her whatever she wanted to know. "He brought croissants, which were lovely."

"I meant to ask if you did have breakfast with him! Did you cook?"

"I did. And it was edible. Well, quite decent I think."

Rosie beamed. "Good girl. I know you believe you can't

cook but everything I've ever tasted from you has been delicious. Now, go have some lunch please, and if you don't mind getting those batteries on the way back?"

Charlotte wasn't hungry but collected a coffee from Vinnie and wandered down the plaza. She sat on the side of the fountain in the sunshine. Shoppers hurried from place to place and for the first time today, a sense of calm settled on her. This was a reminder of normal life in Kingfisher Falls. Without the crime and fear. Without Alison.

Stop, stop and think with your head, not your feelings.

Since the moment Trev described the woman at the garden centre-creative hub, Charlotte's emotions had spun dangerously close to out of control. Somehow she'd found a stillness deep inside. A place to force the messy pain and dread until she could give them proper attention. Well, now was as good a time as any. She closed her eyes for a moment to clear her mind. Open again, she focused on the coffee cup.

It made no sense for Alison to come here. She had a big financial settlement and legal agreement not to contact Charlotte. To break this would send them both into court to revisit the whole arrangement. Even if Alison wanted to mess up Charlotte's life, the risk was huge.

So, what was the alternative? Another woman. Someone else who resembled Alison enough to trick Charlotte. After visiting her mother and being back in the old house, her sense of reality might have been affected. Her logic. This woman was simply a new local going about her business and Charlotte's imagination was adding the elements making her look like Alison. And with Trev's description sort-of matching who she'd seen, a new local who may be a bit lost and unsure of her surroundings. She drew a long breath and shook her head. It wasn't Alison.

Esther approached with a smile, her arms filled with a covered food platter. "Just the person I hoped to see!" She stopped nearby, straightening the load and Charlotte stood.

"I'm on my way to the new creative hub with this lovely platter. Hoping our newest trader might enjoy a little taste of Italia."

"What a lovely idea. But why did you hope to see me?"

"Thought you might like to come and say hello. Rosie told me you are on your lunch break before I ran down here. So, like to join me?"

She's not Alison.

Despite her stomach tightening, Charlotte nodded. An opportunity to put this particular fear to rest and Esther would be with her.

They headed toward the alley to cut across to the other road. "Have you met her yet? The new owner?" Charlotte asked. She tossed the remnants of now-cold coffee into a bin they passed.

"Not yet! From what I hear, she's been working every hour day and night to transform the old place. There's been tradespeople left, right and centre for the past few days. I can't imagine how difficult it was packing up art and statues and the like."

"My sister is a sculptor." The words came out before Charlotte could filter them.

Esther glanced at her in surprise. "Your sister is? How wonderful! What kind of things does she sculpt?"

Good question. "Not too certain but I've seen pictures of some. Birds. For one thing." Why did some flicker of a memory tap at her?

"You haven't actually seen her work though?"

"Long story. But she left the family when I was too little to remember her and I only recently found out she existed."

With a soft, "Oh, Charlie." Esther came to a stop. Her eyes were filled with sympathy and Charlotte felt tears prickle in the back of her own. "Have you been able to contact her? I mean, you said you've seen some pictures of her work so…"

"Not yet. It's complicated. Would you like me to carry this

for a bit?" Charlotte's phone rang. "Oh, it's Trev. Sorry, just a min."

They began walking as Charlotte answered.

"Are you at the shop?" he said.

"No. I'm just at lunch. Why? You sound worried."

"Any chance I can collect you—assuming Mum can spare you for a little while. Darcy just had some bizarre news and he's beside himself. Want to run up to see him and wouldn't mind your expertise."

"Yes, yes of course. I'm not far from the station if you're there?"

"Thanks, sweetie. See you soon."

Charlotte put the phone away. "Trev needs a hand with something urgently. Would you mind if I don't come with you?"

"I heard him mention young Darcy. You go. But let me know what's happening, please?"

"If I can, of course. And say hello to the new owner for me."

Charlotte phoned Rosie as she sped up her pace. After filling her in, Charlotte sprinted the remaining distance. For Trev to need her help, Darcy must be upset. And something told her Jonas was behind it.

———

"Where are the detective's going...or are they coming as well?" Charlotte glanced over her shoulder as Katrina and Bryce pulled onto the road behind them.

"They're off to have a chat with Marguerite."

Charlotte spun her head around to look at him. "Why? What did she do to Darcy?"

Trev chuckled. "Calm down, please. Don't need two people to pacify."

"Sorry. Fill me in."

All humour left his face. "Jonas came in for his interview which I'll tell you more about later. Before he left, he made some comments about Darcy and Abbie and…Cecil. Said Cecil was at the farm on a regular sales call but didn't knock when he arrived as the Forests were arguing about money. Sounded bad. Then Darcy followed him to the carpark and warned him not to repeat what he heard."

"What!"

"I know. Says Cecil told this all to Marguerite who was his next stop. So, in a roundabout way, he's making it sound as though—"

"Poor Darcy. He wouldn't harm anyone, let alone an older man who was so sweet. And I doubt if those two argue anyway."

"Can't ever tell what goes on behind closed doors, but I tend to agree."

"And Darcy found out he said this?"

Trev turned onto the road leading from town. "No. And you need to keep that to yourself for now please. Jonas told us to ask Darcy where he was that night—"

"Which you already have!"

"Charlie, let me finish. No sooner had Jonas gone and I get a call from Darcy. All upset. Shocked really. Finally made some sense about looking at his bank account and finding a large sum of money in there. One he knows nothing about."

She had no words. Charlotte sat back in her seat. She'd always known Jonas had something against Darcy but now, was the young man going to be able to prove he had nothing to do with the fire?

CHAPTER THIRTY-THREE

CHARLOTTE WATCHED THROUGH THE SIDE MIRROR AS THE detectives turned into the narrow driveway of Glenys Lane's old property. She was both sorry for them for having to visit the horrible place and at the same time wishing she could listen in. She'd gone there once when Glenys still lived there. The broken-down tiny cottage was bad enough, but around the back was a blackened firepit hidden behind the yard. She remembered all too well the acrid smell of smoke.

Trev took the next driveway to the Christmas Tree Farm. The carpark was deserted and he parked close to the house.

"You okay with this?" he took her hand and squeezed. "If it gets too much, just excuse yourself."

"I think I'll be fine. Helping Darcy is my first concern."

The truth was that Charlotte was beyond furious at Jonas and whoever else was behind this. Trev hadn't elaborated on how the detectives viewed this information. They didn't know the Forests the way she did.

They didn't make it to the gate before Darcy hurried from the house. His normally cheerful face was pale and drawn. His eyes were ringed with redness. Charlotte's heart went out to him. If he'd wept over this, how helpless must he feel? The first thing she did was hug him as tightly as she could. He leaned his head on her shoulder, his body tense, and his heart pounding against her.

"We're here for you." She whispered. "We believe in you."

With a sharp intake of air, he stepped back.

Trev patted him on the shoulder. "Would you prefer to talk out here so Lachie doesn't overhear?"

"Family's away, thank goodness. Abbie took the kids to visit her parents for a couple of days because she's missing them a lot. Come on, I can manage to make us some coffee."

He led the way inside. Once in the kitchen, he looked around as if unable to remember what he was doing. Charlotte took over. "I'll do coffee and you two sit here at the table where I can listen. Go on."

Kettle on, she found cups and instant coffee, listening as Trev offered some small talk. She was a bit unsure why she was here. Trev had a calm and solid manner which let people easily trust him. He could have done this alone.

Trev glanced up at her and his eyes gave away the depth of his concern. But when she smiled, his own lips turned up at the corners for an instant.

I know why I'm here.

Warmth filled her heart. He needed her support.

"Here you go." She placed cups in front of both men and went back for hers. A moment later she was seated opposite Darcy. "Even if you don't want to drink it, put your hands around the cup, Darcy. It'll warm you a bit."

He did so and his shoulders dropped a little.

"Okay, mate, I know you've had a shock, but do you feel up to talking me through what you found?" Trev took out his notepad.

Darcy nodded. "I must have sounded like I was on something before. Sorry. Just couldn't believe it and after the phone call…"

Trev and Charlotte exchanged a puzzled look.

"Phone call? Who?"

"Dunno, Trev. A woman who didn't tell me her name. Said some weird stuff that made no sense at all. But anyway, this afternoon I was doing accounts. Trying to make the income stretch further than it can." He glanced at Charlotte. "Though we're getting a bit in from Abbie's website sales. She's such a clever woman."

Charlotte smiled, hoping he understood she agreed. He didn't sound like a man who was having arguments with his wife.

"Wanted to pay a couple of bills so checked the balance of the account and I almost fell off my chair. I had to look twice. Three times. There's a deposit went in a day or so ago for almost one hundred thousand dollars."

A shiver went up Charlotte's spine.

"I called the bank. They couldn't tell me who deposited it. I have to go to a branch and put in a query. Who has that kind of money, Trev? And who would just give it to me?" His hands shook around his cup until the coffee was at risk of spilling.

Charlotte moved to a chair closer. "Darcy? This isn't of your doing. It could be a bank error. A deposit meant for someone else. You don't have all the facts yet."

"But what if it is for me? That kind of money…it would change our lives. Pay off all the debts that came with this place." He closed his eyes. "Dad left me in a terrible position. I should have sold it off. Given up." When he opened his eyes, they were tear-filled.

"You are not a man who gives up. Are you? This beautiful property is perfect for you and your family but yes, it came with some debt. Which you and Abbie are doing a great job of addressing. Turning it around."

Darcy's lips tightened but he was listening.

"Let's deal with the facts and find out what's going on. Okay? We can take some action."

He nodded.

"Tell us about the phone call." Trev spoke quietly. "Everything you remember. When did it happen?"

There was a mobile phone on the table and Darcy reached for it. "I can tell you the details, but not the number." He tapped on it. "Yesterday at eight twenty-two. Anonymous number."

"A woman, you said. What did she say?"

After putting the phone down, Darcy stared at his cup. "It was odd. Cryptic. She started by asking if I'd paid yet. I asked paid what. Then she said for the sins of my mother. I admit, I was shocked. I don't even see my mum anymore."

Trev frowned. "The sins of your mother? What does that even mean?"

"Sounds religious. Like, old school religious. All I can think is she meant Mum leaving my dad for another man. But how and why would I pay for that?"

Charlotte's mind worked overtime. The 'other man' was once married to Octavia Morris, who'd been murdered earlier this year. She'd never got over losing him and hated the Forest family and their property with a vengeance. Marguerite was her closest friend so was it possible the Brownes had taken it upon themselves to continue the harassment?

"This is just a routine question, Darcy. When did you last see Cecil, and under what circumstances?" Trev's tone was serious and Darcy's brow furrowed.

"Got me thinking now. Must have been a month or so back." he brightened. "Yep, it was before that whole mess with Kevin Murdoch because Cecil mentioned him to me. About him and Terrance being keen to buy my land and would pay top dollar if I was interested."

"And were you interested?"

"Gosh no. And never to those two. My dad would turn in his grave if I let the place be turned into some development and besides, they're not nice people."

Good judge of character.

"Where did you talk to Cecil?" Trev asked.

"Here. Abbie made him a cup of tea and he had a chocolate chip cookie she'd made earlier. Lachie was scoffing them and Cecil was so good with him." He dropped his head. "Can't believe he's gone."

"I know. Any ideas where he was going next?"

"Next door." Darcy lifted his head again with a grimace. "Sid and Marguerite had just moved in and had issues with the oven or something."

Jonas was clever to take a real situation and twist it. Added enough doubt that anyone who wasn't paying close attention might miss the details. Not Trev though.

"I'd like to get someone to look at the phone, see if there's a way to track the caller." Trev said.

"Sure. But can it wait until Abbie's home? This is the only phone on the property until then."

"Of course. When are you going to the bank?"

Darcy ran a hand through his hair. "Best if I go now. How could anyone deposit so much money in one go? And how did they know my account details?"

As he closed the notepad, Trev looked preoccupied. Charlotte addressed the second question.

"Maybe have a think about who you'd have given it to in the past. How do people pay you for things like the seedlings? Or tree deliveries?"

"Duh. Abbie has our bank account details on the website for direct deposits. How did I forget? Okay, not a mystery then."

"Darcy, I'm not an expert on fraud but I'm certain in Australia any deposits over ten thousand dollars requires paperwork. To avoid money laundering and the like. So, ask at the bank to see someone who can sit with you and go through the details. Not a teller. And phone me if you get stuck." Trev stood. "Can you catch up with me once you're back? Give me a call first as I'm not sure if I'll be at the station. Might need you in for a statement."

Charlotte gave Darcy another hug before they left. "Anytime you need to chat, call me. I can't act in an official capacity, but I can help my friends."

A few minutes later, the patrol car nosed out of the driveway.

"He is in shock, Trev. Maybe I should offer to go to the bank with him."

"Doing something positive is the best thing for him now. It helped a lot having you there but apart from the comfort side of things, do you have any observations?"

"Lots."

Trev grinned but stayed quiet.

"This is a set up. But unless they can prove Darcy was near the fire that night, how will they make it stick?" Charlotte puzzled over it. "Surely whoever is behind this isn't just hoping the police will ignore Abbie as an alibi?"

"The word of a spouse isn't necessarily enough to protect a suspect. Not if there's evidence to the contrary. But a bank deposit and hearsay aren't solid evidence."

They reached the end of the dirt road and turned toward town. An SUV approached, sun visor down and the sun reflecting off the windscreen making it impossible to see who was driving. Charlotte turned to watch as it took the road they'd just exited.

"Marguerite got into a car like that the other day. She was outside the bookshop and it collected her."

Trev shot her a glance. "See the driver?"

"Nope. Why?"

"Sped through town the other day when I was on foot. Took a photo of the plates and promptly forgot to check them. If Katrina and Bryce are still up there, hopefully they'll get a look, assuming the driver is visiting or staying with the Brownes."

"Relative?"

"No idea. Maybe Mum will know. Speaking of which, better get you back to work before she fires you."

He was joking, but Charlotte's stomach knotted. What was in the envelope in Rosie's handbag, addressed to her? For that matter, what was in the envelope under the bookshop door last night?

CHAPTER THIRTY-FOUR

FROM THE MOMENT SHE GOT BACK TO WORK THE BOOKSHOP was busy with customers until almost closing time. As soon as one left, more arrived, which made Rosie smile and kept Charlotte restocking shelves.

A drizzling rain began late in the afternoon and as quickly as the rush began, it stopped again.

"Is that the result of your new marketing plan, darling?" Rosie returned from the kitchen with two bottles of water and handed one to Charlotte. "I remember you saying something about Facebook ads."

"Well, I did put a couple up the other night but even so! Mind you, I made it all about spring reads and what have we sold the most of? The display I made of spring reads."

"And gardening books. I must have sold a dozen of them! Perhaps we should do some cross-promotion with Darcy and Abbie."

Charlotte agreed. Now was possibly not the best time though.

"Okay, what is wrong? You keep getting a pensive look on your face so is this something to do with where you and Trev went?"

"Yes. And you need to keep this to yourself if I say what's going on, otherwise Trev will know I've discussed it."

"Sit down and tell me. And when he tells me later, I'll act surprised." She offered a smile.

"Make sure you do." Charlotte tried to look stern and they both laughed. After an appreciative gulp of water, she put the lid on the bottle. "Somebody put a lot of money into the Forests' bank account. And Jonas has made certain suggestions to the police that Darcy had reason to harm Cecil."

"Oh! Oh, I never!" Rosie's face went bright red and her hands waved around. "In what universe would Darcy hurt a fly?"

"Hey...calm down. Deep breath. Nobody believes Jonas but Darcy was terribly upset to find the money there and called Trev. I went along for support. There're some really odd things happening and somebody has thought this all through. Jonas, I imagine, unless someone else is pulling the strings."

"Well, if I get my hands on that man —"

"Here. Water. Drink some. I'm every bit as angry but getting worked up won't help Darcy. Or your blood pressure."

Rosie drank a lot of water and finally put the bottle down, her face returning to its normal shade. "I'm calm. More or less. What can we do to help?"

Charlotte shook her head. "Not much. Trev was meeting with the detectives to compare notes and Darcy will go and see them once he's got more information from the bank. Apparently, Abbie took the kids to see her parents for a few days so at least she isn't being exposed to this. Not yet."

"Hopefully, Jonas and his band of criminal friends will be arrested before she gets home. Would you like to lock the front door? With this weather closing in, I doubt anyone else will shop."

After locking the door and turning on the outside light, Charlotte came back around the counter. "You will get soaked so why don't you head off and I'll finish here?"

"I might do that if you're sure." Rosie collected the bits and pieces she needed to take home. "You caught up with Esther earlier?"

"Yes. In fact, we were heading to the creative hub with a lovely platter from Italia when Trev rang." Charlotte wished she'd been able to put that particular worry to bed. "I would have liked to have met the owner."

"Esther stopped by and said she is nice. A bit reserved but quite overwhelmed at the platter and said it will save her trying to shop later because she's still unpacking boxes there."

"Oh. Anything else about her?"

Rosie wheeled around the counter, handbag over her shoulder. "Apparently she was feeling the cold and wearing a thick coat and scarf."

The familiar clutch of panic hit Charlotte.

"Comes from a warmer climate. And Esther said she was older than she thought, although I have no idea how Esther formed her original opinion."

Charlotte followed her to the door. "Older?"

"Late forties or so. Didn't get much other information but she let Esther take a look around and there are some beautiful pieces of art so I cannot wait for the grand opening! The rain stopped so I'm off."

"Let me know when you get home." Charlotte opened the door.

"Yes, Mum." Rosie grinned as she went through. "See you tomorrow. Oh, darling I forgot. There was an envelope for you under the door this morning. I think I left it under the paper in the kitchen." With a wave she was off and Charlotte locked the door again.

She isn't Alison!

Relief replaced the panic and Charlotte almost laughed aloud. It took her only a few minutes to close the registers and she turned all the lights off. Money bag in hand, she went to the kitchen to open the safe.

She'd forgotten about the envelope until she saw the folded newspaper. Money locked away, Charlotte located the envelope, which was what she'd seen last night. Her name was on it. *Dr Charlotte Dean.* Something was familiar about the handwriting. There was no other identification on the plain white envelope and she tucked it into her handbag. Time enough to open it upstairs.

As she opened the door to the apartment, her phone beeped. Rosie.

Safely home. Have a lovely evening.

And some cute cat emoticons.

The rain began in earnest and Charlotte shivered with a sudden drop in temperature. She changed into tracksuit pants and a warm jumper and let her hair out of its ponytail. Hunger gnawed at her which wasn't surprising after missing lunch. She had the ingredients for dinner from last night's shopping and would have an early meal.

Another message, this one from Trev.

Can we chat a bit later? Still at station but want to catch up if you don't mind me phoning once I get home.

Anytime.

She messaged back then headed to the kitchen to turn on the oven. After slicing potatoes, leeks, and cauliflower, she laid them in an almost orderly fashion in a dish, then made a cheesy sauce. This she poured over the vegetables and then it went into the oven. She tossed a salad and buttered a crusty roll in anticipation.

After pouring a glass of wine, she did her usual routine these days of checking each window was locked. It didn't matter that she'd done so this morning. In the third bedroom, she stood for a moment in the dark to stare out at the bushland. It was inconceivable to think this natural area might be bulldozed in the name of progress. Not without a fight though.

She turned to leave and the pile of neglected items on the bed caught her eye. Leaving them there wasn't solving her own mysteries. After being interrupted at Rosie's the other night when about to open the baby book, she'd dropped it and the envelope of paperwork here again.

Envelope.

Some of the Christmas cards had slid to one side and she picked one up. As always, the beautiful art on the card touched her. And the simple words within.

You are loved. Z.

Zoe Carter Dean.

Charlotte stared at the words. Her heart began to thud.

It wasn't possible.

Back in the living room she took the envelope from her handbag and compared the handwriting. She was no expert, but…

Holding her breath, Charlotte opened the envelope and slid out a single sheet of paper. Her hands shook as she read aloud.

Dearest Charlotte,

This isn't how I wanted to contact you. Not by mail.

I am so afraid you may not wish to see me again.

After all, I left you when in hindsight, I should have stayed.

My fault.

My mistake.

If you will let me, I'll spend my life making it up to you but I don't know how to begin. Only by being physically close to you, my sweet little sister, can I feel there is a chance to reunite.

You are loved.

Zoe.

With a soft cry, Charlotte dropped to the floor as her legs gave way. She leaned against the side of the sofa and reread the words before letting the paper slip from her fingers. Zoe had found her. Or had she always known where she was? Why had she taken so long to reach out to her and why not just come and see her? Questions raced faster than she could answer them.

Bit by bit, the shaking in her legs stopped and she climbed to her feet. Dinner was about to burn. She managed to turn the oven off then retrieved the letter.

"How are you physically close to me?" she whispered. It made no sense. Zoe didn't live in Kingfisher Falls, she lived somewhere in Queensland with her gallery of sculptures and awards nights.

Rosie's earlier words about the new trader returned. "Comes from a warmer climate."

Charlotte opened her laptop and found the website with Zoe's works displayed. Image after image of delicately carved wildlife and plants, a few people, and birds. She kept returning to one—an owl with its wings extended, a stunning moment captured in flight.

"I've seen you before."

Surely this was the same piece she'd seen through the window in the creative hub?

She sat back in her chair, arms wrapped around herself. Was Zoe the woman who'd she'd thought was Alison? Watching Charlotte from a distance before fleeing every time she got too close?

No. The woman Charlotte had seen was younger than herself, not older, as Zoe was.

"You're here."

It was the only explanation. A woman in her late forties opening a gallery with works uncannily similar to those on the website. The note. Written in a familiar hand and slid beneath the door where Charlotte worked.

Zoe was here in Kingfisher Falls and Charlotte wasn't going to let another night pass without seeing her sister.

———

Halfway along the shopping strip, Charlotte wished she'd taken her car. Although most of the shops had awnings over the footpath, the alleys and roads did not, and her hair was already plastered to her skull. Near the roundabout she paused to pull up the collar of her trench coat and check her phone and keys were still buried deep in the pockets.

Way to plan a first visit, Charlie.

She glanced in the window of the closest shop and grimaced at her reflection, but the bubble of excitement rising inside her turned it to a smile.

Action had turned her reservations into anticipation.

Headlights on the roundabout glared in the glass and she glanced over as Sid's station wagon went around and then in the direction of where he lived these days. Why was he always prowling the streets?

Charlotte turned the corner and put her head down as rain came in sideways under the remaining shops' awnings. The shops gave way to houses and she brushed water from her eyes. In the distance, the SUV approached at speed. Trev needed to track down its driver and do something because tonight the roads were slippery and going so fast was asking for an accident. It passed and Charlotte watched it follow the road Sid had taken.

Another couple of blocks and the old garden centre loomed on the left. The new signage was tasteful and one of the floor to ceilings was painted with the words 'Opening Soon'.

The carpark was empty and only one external light on. Charlotte peered through the window into darkness. The red flashing lights from the camera barely lit the vast interior. She tapped on the glass. Perhaps Zoe had moved into her house now? She checked the time on her phone. A bit after seven.

"Zoe? Zoe, it's...Charlotte. Charlie. I just read your note." Charlotte tapped again, more loudly. Nobody answered. Nothing moved inside.

The disappointment settled like a weight around her shoulders. Charlotte wasn't sure if her eyes were still wet from the rain or if tears had escaped, but the weather was perfect for her mood. Reluctant to leave, she waited for a few minutes and tapped once more. She had no idea where Zoe lived. No contact details for her. She'd have to return in the morning.

CHAPTER THIRTY-FIVE

TREV PUT DOWN THE PHONE AFTER LETTING ROSIE KNOW he'd be at least another hour and would make dinner for himself. After a long meeting with Katrina and Bryce, he'd spent the afternoon finishing reports and was only now in a position to catch up with loose ends from the past couple of days.

His stomach growled and he swallowed more water to trick it into believing it was fed. Breakfast with Charlie felt days ago, not hours.

First, he watched footage from Harpreet's cameras. She had one facing either way outside the shop and had provided an hour either side of the first call about the fire. His main interest was excluding Darcy from the scene. Not only did he not see Darcy or anyone who resembled him, but there was no sign of Sally Austin.

Liar. But why?

He jotted some notes.

Jonas implied Darcy had reason to harm Cecil
Sally claims she saw Darcy running from the fire
Darcy had suspicious funds deposited into his account
Marguerite is acting oddly (for her)

On his feet, Trev went to the whiteboard, reading over the updates from the afternoon. Bryce and Katrina had little success speaking to Sid and Marguerite. They'd refused to allow the detectives inside, insisting if there was a discussion it would happen on the driveway. Sid did most of the talking for the couple, answering yes and no to most questions. His wife, who normally would not hesitate to dominate the conversation and had an opinion about everything, said little.

Only when she was asked about the alleged conversation with Cecil did she answer. "They argue a lot. Always yelling at each other. She says she'll leave him if he doesn't pay off the debt."

Katrina had questioned her further but only got grunts. Sid wasn't much better and told them he'd phone his lawyer unless they left.

Trev returned to his notes and added a line.

Marguerite claims Forests argue over money.

He sent the downloaded video file to his friend in forensics. Another favour he owed them.

A message came through from Charlotte.

Having a long shower so don't panic if I don't answer the phone.

He grinned. She was thinking of his peace of mind…or not having to replace her door if he kicked it down believing something was wrong. Before putting his phone away, he scrolled through the gallery, stopping on the unsavoury image of Sid outside the bookshop, cigarette hanging from his lips.

Sid had followed up by going into the bookshop another day, offering dubious security services for a fee. Why? And why had the camera outside the bookshop been spray painted? Trev found an empty page and made more notes, this time about Sid. Where had he and Marguerite gone after his fall from grace with the police department?

"And why are you back?" Trev muttered.

He saw little of Marguerite but too much of Sid. Almost every time he was in town, Sid drove by in that old station wagon. Usually with cigarette smoke wafting through a window. The fact the Brownes now lived on Glenys Lane's property was bizarre. Once, they'd all been friends. Until Glenys killed Octavia. Even if Sid didn't care, it made no sense that Octavia's best friend would live in the home of her killer.

Trev's last job was checking the SUV. Bryce and Katrina had left before it got to the property so he couldn't prove that is where it was heading earlier. Charlotte remembered it picking up Marguerite from outside the bookshop so perhaps it was a relative or friend visiting. As far as he knew, there were no new residents in the road. He'd check with Darcy tomorrow.

He ran the plates of the car. A rental.

With a sigh, he turned off the computer and closed the notebook. Tomorrow he'd call the hire company. And do a search for Sally Austin. He was still kicking himself for not paying better notice of her identity.

Lights off and doors locked, he jumped into the patrol car after dashing through heavy rain. He checked his phone. Nothing from Charlie. He wanted to see her. Unwind with a drink and hear her laughter. But she'd had a long day as well and was probably having an early night. Once he got home, he'd send her a goodnight message and if she replied, he'd phone. Otherwise, he'd let her sleep and see her in the morning.

———

It took Trev longer than expected to send the message. Rosie had met him at the door with a towel and command for him to dry off and get into something warm while she reheated his dinner. There'd been no point debating with her and if anything, he welcomed the thought of eating something and being dry.

Meal in hand, he kissed Rosie's cheek and left her to the

book she was enjoying on the sofa. He opened his laptop in the study. Over dinner he browsed through local real estate. He was curious about what had sold in recent weeks but just as curious about what homes were for sale. One stood out. Set on almost an acre but within walking distance of town, the house was older but lovingly renovated with a gorgeous country kitchen.

I could cook you the best breakfasts in there.

Mind on Charlotte, he sent a text to see if she was awake. His phone rang within seconds.

"Hi sweetie, wasn't sure if you'd be getting an early night." He said.

"Too much to think about. Did you just get home?"

"Mum insisted I eat and change. And I mopped the puddles I left near the front door after failing to avoid the downpour."

Charlotte laughed and the sound warmed him more than dry clothes had.

"What are you thinking about? Our visit to Darcy?"

"That's one thing, yes. Do you know how he went at the bank?"

Trev pushed his chair back enough to allow him to stretch his legs. "He dropped into the station with some interesting information. As I thought, there is a limit of ten thousand dollars a person can deposit in cash to one account a day. Any more and it needs to be electronic or the depositor has to complete paperwork."

"To prevent money laundering?" Charlotte asked.

"Exactly. Somebody has gone to a lot of trouble to cover their tracks. There were ten deposits made of nine and a half thousand dollars each, all on the same day, and all at different banks."

Charlotte made some noise as though shocked.

"I know. It was clever because no single deposit would attract attention from the teller. The person went to three suburbs of Melbourne to do this and the sad thing? We probably can't even track down who it was."

"But why? Banks have security footage."

"We've asked for help with the local police in each suburb but whether there is footage still available from a few days ago is another thing. Time consuming foot work and lots of variables."

"If you can't find who made the deposits, how can Darcy be linked to the fire?"

Good question.

"I'm waiting for the other shoe to drop. Whoever is behind this has money to burn and I'm more inclined to believe there is more to this than framing Darcy as though he's being paid off to kill someone he already had a grudge against."

There was a long silence and Trev almost heard Charlotte's mind at work. He closed his eyes, ready to climb into bed and rest weary muscles.

"Sorry, just was writing this down to make sense of it. I've heard more than once that the Christmas Tree Farm is prime land. Wasn't Octavia going to build some elite athletics training complex in Kingfisher Falls? After her husband left, she had her sights on a property she was going to buy but it never happened."

"Hadn't heard this. Do you think she was after the Christmas Tree Farm? Perhaps as some odd revenge against the woman her husband took off with."

"Even if it was, it is history now. Unless...Trev?"

"What are you thinking?" he opened his eyes with a smile.

"Glenys Lane's place was meant to be on the market to pay for her legal fees or at least, that's what I've heard. The Brownes are renting it. Can we find out if it sold on the quiet? That piece of land and then Darcy's would make a decent sized development for someone."

"And if Darcy is discredited or worse, Abbie might have no choice but to sell and it would be easy for someone to swoop in and offer to make it a painless process. You might have something, sweetheart. This whole thing might have a history we didn't see coming."

Mayhem stalked in and jumped onto the desk. He stared at the keyboard of the laptop then lay on it. Trev laughed and the cat glared at him.

"Hang on, Charlie, need to take a photo to send you." Trev snapped a picture and messaged it across. "What is it about cats and computers?"

"Since when does Mayhem like you so much?"

"Always has. I mean, he doesn't show it, but he hangs around with me more than Mellow does. Sometimes I wake up and he's lying on my chest or else he'll tap my face to stir me." He yawned, trying to cover the sound.

"I heard that. Go to bed."

"I will soon. You've not told me about your evening."

"Not much to tell. Quiet night at home."

There was a tone in her voice he didn't recognise.

Sadness? Loneliness?

"Need some company?"

"Trevor, you have to sleep." Back to normal. "It is bucketing down outside and there's no need for either of us to be soaked through again tonight."

"Either of us?"

"Well, you said you made puddles in the hallway."

"Charlie?"

"There's nothing to worry about. I'm going to get some sleep now."

They spoke for a few more minutes and arranged to meet for breakfast at the corner café in the morning before saying goodnight.

Trev rolled his chair forward. "Dude, I need to close this now."

Mayhem growled but decided against being picked up and disappeared out of the door. Trev watched him. Whenever

Charlotte said there was nothing to worry about, it worried him. He knew her too well to believe she'd meant nothing about being soaked through.

"Where did you go, Charlie?"

As if in agreement with his concern, the rain doubled its efforts on the roof.

CHAPTER THIRTY-SIX

DAWN WASN'T MUCH BETTER. THE RAIN CONTINUED although not with the force of the previous night. Charlotte had an early cup of coffee on the balcony, wrapped in her dressing gown but enjoying the fresh morning air. She adored the smell of rain and despite the greyness, there was a hint of warmth this morning.

At least the weather would slow the destruction near the river. The ground always turned soft and giving under rain and any trucks and machinery ran the risk of bogging.

Today, Charlotte would meet Zoe. Not until lunch time most likely, but she intended to buy a beautiful bouquet of flowers and take them to the creative hub. What would it feel like, having a sister? She still couldn't summon more than snippets of memories.

A smile. But no face.

A cuddle. But no arms.

How long had Zoe known where she was? Did she know where Angelica spent her life? And what about Dad? Where was he?

Charlotte finished her coffee and stood. So many questions

burned in her mind. Not the least being why she hadn't told Trev about the note from Zoe.

Sometimes I fail to understand you, Charlie.

She closed and locked the sliding glass door. Breakfast was an hour away and she had plenty to do in that time. Plenty of thinking.

———

As it was, Charlotte was late, crossing the street carefully beneath an umbrella. Water flowed along the footpaths making them just as slippery and the sky offered no clues about its intention to ease up the rain.

She closed the umbrella and shook it outside, then slid it into the decorative metal planter Vinnie left there for the purpose. With no other umbrellas deposited, she figured Trev hadn't arrived, but he opened the door for her from inside with a flourish.

"Was about to call and see if I should bring breakfast to you." He kissed her cheek. "Good morning."

"Good morning. How are you not the least bit wet?" she said.

"Table's over here. It's called wet weather gear and the police have some of the best around. Hanging by the door." He pulled a chair out for Charlotte. "At least you have an umbrella."

"Thanks. Oh that? Found it in the bookshop and don't even know if it belongs to Rosie. Did you notice all the books on it?"

He grinned. "No. But it sounds ideal for a bookshop to have."

"True. How is Rosie?"

"Last seen drying a wet cat."

"Oh dear."

"Mayhem insisted he had to investigate a branch which had

fallen down, just a small one. Took himself out and ran right back in full of complaints as only he can make." Trev chuckled. "I should have taken a photo."

"The one on your laptop last night was cute. He gave the appearance of a nice cat."

"Deceiving appearance, as you know."

Vinnie arrived with coffees and they both ordered. "I'm having security cameras installed. Too many bad things going on in town." He dropped his head. "Might have caught whoever killed poor Cecil by now if I'd had them already. Feel bad about it."

Charlotte put her hand on his arm. "No...Vinnie, don't feel bad. Whoever did it was very sneaky. They avoided being caught on any camera as far as anyone knows, not even the bookshop which has one looking toward that corner."

"Charlie's right. Nobody expected the level of crime we've had this year but I think you've made a good decision. More security deters criminals in general."

Vinnie nodded and wandered to the kitchen, but his shoulders were slumped.

"How do we find the killer?" Helplessness wasn't a good feeling, but Charlotte had no other word for it. "There has to be a clue. Something left behind."

Trev reached over the table and took one of her hands. "*We* aren't finding anything. This is hard enough without me worrying about what Detective Charlotte is up to. You know if we need your opinion—your valuable opinion, that we'll ask."

"Hm."

"Hm, nothing. You're right though. Somewhere there's a clue. Something that will lead us to the killer and believe me, nobody wants it more than I do."

Customers began coming in and the buzz of conversation along with background took over the sound of the rain. By the time breakfast arrived, both had finished their coffees which Vinnie whisked away with the promise of a refill.

"I need to tell you something." Charlotte said between bites of her delectable eggs. How the cook got them so light and fluffy was beyond her own abilities by a mile.

Trev had stopped eating and trained an expression of concern on her. She smiled.

"This is something good, Trev. Eat and I'll talk."

Still with an air of suspicion, Trev speared some pancake.

"Last night I read a note which was left under the book-shop door the previous night. Completely forgot it was there until Rosie reminded me."

"Not from Sid again."

"Not even close." Charlotte leaned forward a little. "From Zoe. My sister."

Trev's fork dropped onto the plate with a clang. "Whoops, sorry. From Zoe? How did she know where you work? And…go on."

"You've seen her. I haven't, yet. Not in person. But you saw her the other night at the creative hub."

"The new owner is your sister?"

"So it seems."

Charlotte took another mouthful, enjoying the look of amazement on his face.

"I don't know what to say. Oh, is that why you were out in the rain last night?"

She nodded and swallowed. "Once I worked it out, I just took off. Trev, I wanted to see her so much but she'd left already. I have no idea where she lives so came back disappointed. And soaking wet. But I'm going to buy her some flowers and visit her at lunchtime."

"Sweetheart, this makes me so happy. Your face is glowing. Did you have any idea?"

"That she was in Kingfisher Falls? That she knew where I live? Not even a glimmer. And it is kind of strange how she's done this. I mean, who just buys a house and moves their business to a town they've never been to?" A thought occurred to her. "Unless she has been here. I really know nothing about her."

"Don't lose that happiness, Charlie. Hang on to the excitement because there will be answers. Give her a chance to explain it all."

"I will." She'd try. "The silly thing is, I've seen a woman around town a couple of times lately and thought she was… well, Alison."

"From Brisbane?"

"Silly, isn't it. Thin woman in a thick, long coat and big sunglasses under a hat. My imagination was working overtime."

Vinnie returned with fresh coffees. "Not hungry? Or not up to our usual standard?" He gazed at their half-eaten plates.

"Very hungry and absolutely delicious, Vin." Trev assured him. "Just talking a lot. But I'm going to finish this now." As though to prove his point, he cut a giant slice of pancake and forced too much into his mouth.

Charlotte held back her laughter until Vinnie disappeared from sight but then she couldn't help herself. Watching Trev try to chew and swallow more than he'd anticipated was hysterical. His face had changed colour a bit and he wouldn't meet her eyes. She poured a glass of water from the bottle on the table and pushed it across. "There you go."

Eventually, he finished and drank from the glass.

"Did your mother not teach you how to eat in polite society?"

"Charlotte, if we were not in public—in *polite* society—you would be finding somewhere to hide right about now."

She giggled. "Are you threatening me, Leading Senior Constable?"

"Never." His banter changed to a soft tone. "You are always safe with me. Always. Even if you give me a hard time."

Her heart beat a little faster and a sense of belonging settled around her body like a hug. She leaned across and kissed his lips. There, in the café, in front of anyone who wanted to see. "You taste of maple syrup." She whispered and kissed him again.

The buzzing of Trev's phone interrupted and Charlotte sat back, picking up her coffee cup with a smile. It was short lived.

Trev listened to the caller, a frown growing deeper by the second. "I'll go there now."

He put the phone down with a heavy sigh.

"What is it?" Charlotte's mind worked overtime. "It wasn't Rosie?"

"No. No, it was Katrina. She and Bryce are on their way down and took a call from the dispatcher. Council's garbage contractor was doing his run up the hill and he came across Darcy's bin on its side."

Charlotte's stomach knotted. This was the other shoe dropping.

"He jumped out of his truck and righted it, chucking some rubbish bags back in and one split. Something fell out." Trev ran a hand through his hair. "A phone, Charlie. A phone matching the description of Cecil's."

"Someone wants Darcy to look bad. Someone is working hard to make him look guilty. But you know he isn't."

Trev got to his feet. "Got to go, sweetie. Meeting the detectives up there. The garbo is waiting."

Charlotte stood. "Shall I come along?"

"Not this time."

"You know he isn't guilty."

"All I know is I have a job to do. I'll call you."

"You go. I'll take care of the bill today."

Face grim, Trev nodded and squeezed her arm before collecting his wet weather gear from near the door. Then, he disappeared into the rain. Not once had he said he still believed in Darcy.

Don't give up on him, Trev. He's innocent.

CHAPTER THIRTY-SEVEN

THE WINDSCREEN WIPERS WORKED OVERTIME AND TREV kept his speed low. The winding road up the hill was tricky at the best of times and despite his need to get to his destination, sliding into a ditch would be a bad look.

He knew in his heart Darcy was innocent. Some people were inherently good. The only mistake he'd done was come home to the place he grew up and take on the debts of his father. People like him didn't go around killing for money. Not even a lot of money. The multiple deposits into Darcy's bank account were still a mystery and until the person responsible was found, it put the police in a difficult position.

This police officer.

Anyone else would have had Darcy in for a formal interview already. In hindsight, he should have done so, just to put it on record.

The garbage truck was parked outside the Christmas Tree Farm. Trev pulled in behind it, relieved that the rain was slowing. The detectives drove past and U-turned before parking on the other side of the road.

Trev climbed out, still wearing his wet weather gear. He

met the detectives by their car as they slipped their own gear on. "Not the best start to a day."

"We'll speak to the driver first, Trev." Bryce said. "You'll need to go through the garbage. Got a constable heading up with bags to put everything in so you can take it to the station."

Great.

"Sorry, Trev." Katrina must have seen his expression change. "None of this is fun."

"More worried about Darcy."

She nodded. "We'll take him in to interview. I prefer your theory of a set-up but this phone is key evidence. There's the driver."

Trev was happy to stand back a bit as Katrina dealt with the man, who wasn't happy about having to wait for so long.

He handed over the phone. "Only touched it with my gloves on."

Katrina asked the usual questions and he recounted how he'd picked up the bin and tossed rubbish back into it. He pointed to the bag that broke, spilling the phone out. Katrina glanced Trev's way and he headed to the side of the road. The bin's lid was open, drenching the contents so he closed it after taking a good look inside. The one on the roadside was a common white bag and not tied up. There were no tears he could see without lifting it. He took his phone out and did his best to keep it dry as he snapped a series of photos.

A moment later the garbage truck drove away and the detectives joined him.

"Nice mess." Bryce poked at the bag with his foot.

"Different bag from those inside the bin. And not tied. The other ones are all those eco-bags and are double knotted. Reckon the phone fell out. Might not even have been inside the bin."

"We're going to drive down and see Darcy." Bryce grinned. "Let you play CSI in the rubbish."

Trev collected evidence bags from the patrol car. There was a message on his phone from Charlotte.

Stay safe out there.

He would. There was a future ahead he couldn't wait to start so he wasn't about to take unusual risks. Charlie's kiss at the café was a sweet surprise and her trust in telling him about Zoe meant the world. He messaged her back.

Will do. Enjoy meeting Zoe.

For now, he had a job ahead of him. And some help. A second patrol car headed his way and it slowed as it passed the entrance to the property next door. Trev trained his phone camera in that direction and zoomed in. Sid Browne, cigarette hanging off his bottom lip, stared back.

———

Doug wandered into the bookshop after leaving an umbrella outside. "Rain has almost stopped, thank goodness. Run off our feet with home deliveries, but next to no eat-in patrons."

"Sorry, dear, we are as bad as everyone else in that regard." Rosie and Charlotte were creating a display in the centre of the shop. "Love your food so much we can't help but order in all the time."

He shook his head. "Don't mean you. It is always a pleasure to cook for you guys, or these days, watch Neville do so."

Charlotte added a final book to a rather precarious pyramid she'd built. "So, are you and Esther going to take a holiday?" She removed the book again. All it would take is someone wanting a lower book to have the display topple over.

"We will, but not for a bit. The election isn't far away and if I get onto council, I want to make a difference."

"You will. All it takes is one good person and you are he."

"Thanks, Rosie. Anyway, there is a reason for the visit."

Charlotte gave up for the moment. She'd pull the lot down

soon and rethink the project. "After a book?" She grinned. "I have some new celebrity chef—"

"Get real, Charlie." He didn't look offended. "Esther was talking to the new owner of the creative hub yesterday. She dropped back there in the late afternoon to collect the platter and it appears she has a local connection. A long-lost sister."

Rosie glanced at Charlotte. They'd talked about Zoe this morning and arranged for Charlotte to take as long as she needed on her visit later on.

Doug continued. "Esther and I thought it might be nice if two sisters had the chance to reacquaint over a decent Italian dinner one night. On the house, of course. If you'd be interested, Charlotte?"

A curious mix of happiness and confusion filled her.

"And she didn't say it was you if you're curious. She only said her sister moved here about a year ago and it had taken her almost that long to sell her previous place and find something suitable to buy. But her name is on the door in small print. Can't be too many ladies with the last name of Dean in Kingfisher Falls? Not ones who arrived so recently."

Rosie laughed. "More sleuths! Just what the town needs. Whatever will Trev think of it?"

"I haven't seen her yet, Doug. Tried to last night, but she must have left for the evening. And thank you for such a lovely offer."

"Pleasure. Let me know when you want to book." Doug headed for the door but stopped and turned back. "You said she'd left for the evening. Maybe she had to run to the shop or something, but she told Esther she's sleeping there still. Has a camp bed set up in the office." He waved and went outside.

"I'm sure there's a logical explanation, darling. But I can see you are worried so why don't you go now? It's almost lunchtime anyway."

"Are you sure? I'd rather check. Not that I have any reason

to believe anything is wrong. Do I. I mean, she might even just have been in the office. Not heard me knock."

Why didn't I knock harder?

"But I have to undo this mess I've made here."

Rosie put a hand on Charlotte's arm. "Look at me, Charlie. I will fix this and you will go get some flowers and meet your sister. And send me a message as soon as you can so I know you found her."

"I will. Thank you."

"Take the umbrella."

Charlotte hurried to the kitchen and collected it, along with her trench coat and handbag. She tossed her phone into it from the counter and gave Rosie a kiss on her way out.

The rain was all but gone and the umbrella remained closed as sunlight made a weak attempt through the lifting clouds. The florist had some lovely arrangements to choose from and she wasted no time buying one filled with gorgeous coffee coloured roses.

Doug's kind offer touched her. And the information was a bit puzzling. Zoe had known Charlotte was here so why not a simple phone call or letter? Changing your entire life on the hope of reuniting with someone from so long ago was a gamble. Zoe must love her. Must truly want to be near her again.

Pushing all the doubts and questions aside, Charlotte sped up to a fast walk, and in a few minutes, was in the carpark. There was still no sign of a car or movement. Closer, the lights were as the previous night. One outside light and none inside.

She tapped on the window. "Zoe? Zoe, it's Charlotte." A glance through the glass showed no movement so she moved to the door.

Ready to knock, she stopped.

It's open.

She leaned the umbrella against the window and placed the

flowers on the ground. Something made her find her phone and take a video as her hand reached for the door handle.

"I've just arrived at the Kingfisher Falls Gallery and Creative Hub to see my sister, Zoe Carter Dean. Before knocking, I've noticed that the door does not appear to be completely closed." She took her time to film with a steady hand as she touched the handle. "As you can see, the door isn't properly shut. I'm going to call out for my sister." She moved the phone further from herself. "Zoe? Are you there?"

Charlotte's stomach was turning in somersaults as she pushed the door open. It creaked as it swung inwards. "I'm going to step inside and see if I can locate Zoe." From just inside the door, she rotated the phone from one end of the building to the other. Then, she stopped the video.

"Zoe...please, if you are here let me know. I'd rather not intrude."

Met by silence, surrounded by soaring birds on pillars and paintings on easels, fear took over. Fear of where her sister was. Who would go to the trouble of putting in security cameras and an alarm system and then leaving such valuable items unprotected? And why wasn't the alarm on? Charlotte tapped on her phone and uploaded the video for Trev. It would take a little longer to send and she couldn't wait.

Months ago, Charlotte visited here when it was still the garden centre and run by Veronica Wheemor. Instead of dirty floors and broken packing boxes, the space was open and spotless. Above were shuttered skylights. They would allow light to flood in when opened. A discreet desk took the place of the original counter. At the furthest corner, the door to an office was just visible behind a stack of boxes. Was Zoe in there?

Another open door. Dark inside, but Charlotte found a light switch. Desk on one side with two computers and three monitors. Empty shelves. Some more unpacked boxes. And a bed. Just a narrow camp bed, neatly made. Beside it was a clothing rack with an assortment of clothes hanging in a row.

"I'm sorry to be in here." Charlotte whispered. She left the office, closing the door behind herself as though protecting Zoe's privacy.

When the garden centre was open, there was an archway leading outdoors to the plants. Now, it was glassed in with beautiful French doors in the centre. These were locked. Through them, the remainder of the property was much the same as when Charlotte visited last. Run down and old.

She turned around to face out to the street. Cars went by and people walked past. If Trev hadn't seen Zoe himself, she'd question whether her sister was ever here.

"Where are you?"

CHAPTER THIRTY-EIGHT

THE POLICE STATION WAS BUSY. EVERYONE HAD THEIR hands full and the phone was ringing off the hook. Trev finally finished working through the garbage with the constable and had kept aside a number of items of interest. As he'd believed, most of the rubbish was from the same source with recurring themes in the eco-bags. Nothing in those bags offered any suggestion of wrong doing.

The white plastic bag though was different. The phone belonged to Cecil. Once it was plugged in and charging, the logo of his business appeared and Mrs McKenzie had confirmed it after Trev sent her a photo. She'd provided the password and Katrina had spent an hour working through the information, making notes with an occasional, "Yes," beneath her breath. Fingerprints were with a crime scene investigator who'd driven up to collect a range of evidence. There had been a strand of silver hair caught in its cover and he didn't think the garbage truck driver was grey.

At the bottom of the bag, Trev had extracted several more silver hairs, bunched up. Possibly from a comb or brush. Those were tagged, bagged, and photographed and sent back. One other item stood out. A used disposable cigarette lighter. And none of the Forests were smokers.

Everything else was of less importance, at least on the surface. Empty packets of junk food and drinks. Things belonging in recycling. And not products Trev imagined were found in Abbie's kitchen.

Darcy was home again after an intense interview. He was shaken but never once showed anything except respect and patience for the barrage of questions, mostly from Bryce. Trev had felt for the younger man but it was out of his hands.

At last there was a lull in the activity until the doorbell rang. Katrina rushed to get it and a moment later, returned with takeaway coffees and a box of pastries. Those went onto Trev's desk and they all flopped into chairs around it. "Thought we needed something better than what passes as coffee in here. Trev, you in particular have had a bad morning and thank you for getting your hands dirty."

"All part of the job. And the more I found, the more convinced I am Darcy is being set up. And likely by Sid Browne."

"Why him?" Bryce helped himself to an éclair. "Jonas is on my radar."

"Agree. And them being in cahoots is possible. Jonas wants a political career and mayor is the first step, so he won't risk losing it all. Sid is dirty and will do anything for money."

"But why is he your main suspect now?"

"Why would he move to the home of the woman who murdered his wife's best friend? Proximity to the Christmas Tree Farm is my guess. Easy to keep an eye on the family next door and take opportunities when they arrive."

Katrina peered into the box of pastries. "Sounds like you think he's doing surveillance on them."

"He is. Forgot to show you this photo." Trev looked for his phone, finding it beneath a folder Bryce had dropped onto the desk. "Noticed him watching what we were doing this morning. Darn. Battery's flat."

"Plug it in like all the other devices around the place." Bryce bit into the éclair, squirting cream over himself. He swore and grabbed a napkin, making it worse the more he wiped. Katrina laughed at him and earned a glare. "Good thing this tastes so nice. Might grab a box of them to take home."

"Where you can eat them with a towel around you?"

Katrina ducked as Bryce threw his rolled-up napkin at her.

Trev ignored them as he connected the phone and waited for it to wake up. Letting his battery go flat was unusual and testament to his distraction over this case.

"Got the photo yet?" Bryce asked.

"Just about. Um…okay." A video message came through from Charlotte. He found the image of Sid first and showed the others. "Watching in the rain. Who does that?"

"Send it to my phone, Trev." Katrina picked up her coffee.

Trev began watching Charlotte's video then put it back to the beginning and turned it so the detectives could watch. "Something's wrong. She was going to see her sister who recently arrived here. Not that she knew about her until last night."

"What?" Bryce frowned.

"Sh." Katrina leaned closer.

The worry in Charlotte's voice tore at Trev. The video ended. "I'm going to call her."

"Trev, do you know anything about this Zoe?" Bryce asked. "If Charlotte doesn't know her, is it really her sister?"

"They were separated young. Zoe apparently moved here but only reached out to Charlie in a note last night and wasn't there when she went to see her. Last night that is. So, she was going there today. And did, from the look of this." He dialled, noting the look that passed between Bryce and Katrina.

Charlotte answered, her voice quiet.

"I am so sorry, my phone went flat but I saw the video. Do you mind if I put you on speaker so Katrina and Bryce can talk to you?" He did it anyway.

"Hi Charlie." Katrina said.

"Hi everyone."

"Where are you now?" Trev asked.

"On my way to the bookshop. I couldn't find Zoe."

"We'll find her. There'll be an explanation, sweetie. Perhaps she's at her house."

"She doesn't have one yet. Doug told me she's staying at the creative hub and I found a bed and clothes there. Why would she leave her door open?"

"Charlotte, its Bryce. Are you certain it is your sister? Have you had personal contact at all?"

"She put a note under the bookshop door the other night and I only opened it yesterday. But I know I have a sister called Zoe Carter Dean who is a sculptor. When I was inside there, I saw the same works she had on her website in Queensland. And Esther has met her twice now. Do you think someone is pretending to be my sister?" Her voice wavered.

"Not necessarily. Just trying to put the pieces together. Can you tell us what happened last night when you went to see her? You said she wasn't there?" Bryce's tone had softened and Trev shot him a look. Sometimes the tough exterior of the detective made him forget there was a decent man inside the suit.

It sounded as though Charlotte took a deep breath. "It was raining really hard but I was silly enough to go on foot. I wanted to get there quickly and my car is old...anyway, doesn't matter. By the time I got there I was soaking wet and I tapped on the window. Hoped she'd not think I was a mad woman out in the rain. But nobody was in there, at least not what I could see through the windows. I went home."

"Anything else you can think of? Did you try the door?"

"No, Bryce. Just tapped the window. So, I don't know if it was open then."

"Do you want me to come to you?" Trev asked. "We can go and check the place out together."

"I have to let Rosie have lunch. And although this is all strange, what if she just went for a walk? Or moved into a motel last night? I left a note inside and turned the latch to lock the door so we couldn't go inside anyway."

Again, that look between the detectives. Trev took the phone off speaker. "Are you almost at the bookshop?"

"Yes. I'm sorry to bother you when you have so much to worry about."

"There's light at the end of the tunnel, sweetie. And I'm always here for you, so give me an hour to finish up something and I'll come and see you."

They said goodbye and he put the phone on the desk.

"You go if you need to." Katrina stood and collected the empty coffee cups. "She sounds stressed."

"She's okay for a bit. Do you think this is suspicious? Her sister?"

Bryce joined Katrina on his feet, helping himself to the last pastry. "In Kingfisher Falls, everything and everyone is suspicious at the moment. But for the first time, I think we have enough to pull Sid Browne in for questioning and I'm inclined to go and collect him."

"Soon." Katrina said. "I'd like a hand going through what I found on Cecil's phone first. Another set of eyes to confirm a pattern I think I'm seeing, because if I'm right, we're going to be talking to more than Sid. We'll be talking to those who are really behind this."

————

While Katrina and Bryce poured over the information extracted from Cecil's phone, Trev followed up reports and results from forensics and other departments. An email came through from his friend in forensics with an enhanced image of the business broker. He printed it and dropped it onto the other desk.

"Good. Have you found out the name of the man yet?" Bryce picked up the printout.

"I've just called Mrs Munro again and asked her to please find the paperwork she signed to sell her business. She's agreed to drive home now so hope to hear from her within a couple of hours."

Trev returned to his desk and rang Mrs McKenzie. After thanking her for identifying Cecil's phone, he got to the point of the call.

"This may be an odd question, but do you recall much about the renting of Mrs Lane's property to Sid and Marguerite Browne?"

"Oh. Well, yes, because I did most of the work around the lease. But I'm not sure I should speak of it."

"If you are concerned about privacy, I can arrange a warrant. That way you aren't in a difficult position. But the information isn't about any of the legal side of the lease. I don't intend to ask about the financial details or anything which might be deemed private."

He waited to let her think. Katrina was on her phone now and Bryce was tapping on the computer keyboard, intent on the screen. They were onto something.

"I don't want to put you to the trouble of a warrant so ask what you need and I'll do my best." Mrs McKenzie finally spoke.

"Thank you. Do you recall how the Brownes came to lease the place? I was under the impression it is for sale."

"It is. But Cecil told me he'd been asked to make it available to the Brownes until it sold. He spoke with Mrs Lane's legal people and it was approved."

"Did Sid Browne come to him direct? You said he was

asked to make it available."

"It was Mr Carmichael. He knew they needed somewhere to live once they returned from Brisbane and —"

"Sorry? Apologies to interrupt, but they were in Brisbane?"

"I believe they went there after Mr Browne's...loss of employment. And then came back a little bit before Kevin Murdoch's passing. Cecil said they wanted somewhere private and away from town after all they'd been through."

All they'd been through?

"Thank you, Mrs McKenzie. This is very helpful. Just to confirm, Jonas Carmichael arranged for them to move into Mrs Lane's property?"

Katrina and Bryce stared at him.

"Yes. Is there anything else you need to ask?"

"That's all for now. Thanks again." He hung up.

"Did we hear right?" Bryce asked.

"Jonas got them the rental through Cecil. And listen to this. It was after they'd been in Brisbane after Sid left the force."

Katrina got to her feet and collected her keys and wallet. "Time to talk to Jonas and then Sid. I want to know why Sid went to Brisbane."

"Why does that matter?" Bryce stretched and stood. "Lots of people go there."

"And Charlie came from there. Sid threatened her multiple times when she arrived that he'd expose her past life, remember?" Trev clenched his hands beneath the desk. "How about I go and get him for an interview?"

Bryce patted him on the shoulder on his way past. "Not a chance, sunshine. I want him here in one piece. Carmichael first, then Browne. Go and see Charlotte and reassure yourself she's fine."

The detectives left and Trev stared at the computer monitor. The jigsaw pieces were all there but none were falling into place. He wanted to talk to Sid.

His phone rang and he grabbed it.

Why is Mum calling?

CHAPTER THIRTY-NINE

"HE'S ON HIS WAY, DARLING." ROSIE AND CHARLOTTE WERE outside the bookshop watching the intersection. Dozens of people milled around on the footpaths and road, stopping traffic, and waving placards. "I never thought I'd see a protest in our little town."

"Do you know any of them?" Charlotte tried to identify anyone she knew but so far, they were all strangers.

"Rent-a-crowd. That's what I think."

"Well, I hope Trev doesn't think this is my doing." Charlotte was only half joking. The signs used words such as 'Save the forest', 'Stop the destruction', and 'No development'.

The truck from the other night was stuck in the middle of the intersection and the driver had his head through the open window yelling at the protestors.

Lights flashing, the patrol car nosed slowly around the truck and pulled up in front of the bookshop. Trev looked far from amused as he climbed out and stared for a moment at the chaos. Then, he came around to Charlotte and Rosie.

"You weren't kidding, Mum. How long have they been here?"

"Not long. I came back from having lunch with Lewis and they were striding down the side street. Appeared from over the bridge and by the time I got here, they were like this. At least they are leaving us alone, but they are noisy."

"Know any of them?"

"As I told Charlie, this is a rent-a-crowd in my opinion. They are here to disrupt your investigation."

Trev and Charlotte turned to Rosie, who raised her eyebrows in response.

"Mum, that's a bit of a stretch. If we are correct in believing someone involved in the proposed development is responsible for Cecil's death, why would they create their own protest? Won't it just bring unwanted attention?"

With a small, knowing smile, Rosie turned the wheelchair around and headed for the door. "Distraction, dear. It got you here, didn't it?"

"I was coming here anyway. Just not for a bit."

"She has a point, Trev." Charlotte's eyes followed the truck driver as he opened his door and lowered himself to the road. "Who wants your attention?"

"I'm going to call it in and get some help to clear them off. Are you okay? Any update on Zoe?" Trev brushed a hair away from Charlotte's eyes. "I'm worrying about you."

"I'm fine. And we'll find Zoe. I'll go back over in a bit and see if she's reappeared and if not, then I might need some help. But you have your hands full right now."

He glanced both ways and dropped a kiss on her lips. "Talk to you soon."

Charlotte followed Rosie inside.

"Time for an early day. I can't imagine anyone shopping when there's a live show on outside not to mention blocked roads! And in the morning, we'll rethink the display because mine isn't as interesting as your original idea."

"I'm happy to keep the shop open if you wanted to go."

"No. No, I think its best we close for the day and you get a chance to find that sister of yours. In fact, I can come along and help."

"Thanks, but I think I will do some digging around on the computer first. Her website was still active when I last looked so there may be a contact number. If not, I might see if Mrs McKenzie has any details, considering they sold her the building. I should have thought of that first."

This was the best idea she'd had in ages. Get some facts before beginning a full-scale search and rescue operation.

"If you change your mind, you know how to find me. And if you feel inclined, drop by later. Unless you and Zoe are busy catching up of course."

Once Rosie left, crossing the road to take the opposite side home, Charlotte closed the shop and turned off the lights. Going up the steps, the chanting was louder until she closed herself into the apartment. It was only mid-afternoon but heavy clouds darkened the sky again and for once, she hoped for a downpour to test the commitment of the protestors.

Really, Charlie?

If those people actually cared about the damage being done by Jonas and his cronies, then she'd be protesting alongside them. But this was some staged event. Why though? If she wasn't so tired and worried about Zoe, she'd concentrate on this. But for now, she wanted coffee and some time to research. Kettle on, Charlotte changed into jeans and a light jumper. She was going to find Zoe and then, she would help Trev.

———

Trev wanted nothing more than a beer and shower by the time the crowd dispersed. He'd settle for a coffee and change of clothes. The situation had escalated when the truck driver began pushing protestors over and he was now cooling his heels in one of the two cells at the station. Kyneton were sending a car down to collect him and Lewis had kindly locked up his shop and moved the truck up the road. He'd quite enjoyed being behind the wheel of a heavy vehicle again, as he'd mentioned several times. Reminded him of taking tourists around the local wineries back in the day he had a tour bus.

The majority of the so-called protesters disappeared into the back streets of town when more patrol cars arrived, some throwing their placards into the very bushland they claimed to want saved from damage.

Katrina and Bryce arrived at the end of the debacle. They'd done little to assist until a middle-aged man yelled at them about the environmental impact caused by their car. Bryce moved quickly. Without laying a finger on the man, he'd got the information Trev had so-far failed to get from any of the people he'd asked. The difference was that Bryce didn't ask. He gave a quiet ultimatum and with a smile which Trev could only call satisfied, he'd told the man to leave town.

"Having fun?" Katrina had met him and Trev at the side of the petrol car. "We need one of those hybrid cars."

"He told me who paid him and all the others. No name, but a short, thin, bald man with an umbrella and briefcase. Cash and instructions for each person to round up another ten people. The business broker is not exactly what he seems. Trev, can you chase up his identity please?"

"Sure. What happened with Jonas and Sid?"

"Talking to Jonas is like talking to a brick wall. Might get more from a brick wall and not have to look at that smug face." Bryce shoved his hands in his pockets. "The only information we got was him throwing Terrance under the bus."

"Any more metaphors, Bryce?" Katrina grinned at him. "Trev, lots to discuss but Jonas alleges Terrance Murdoch hired some man from the city to obtain the shops along here. As Terrance owns the land abutting both the shops and the council land, he wanted in on future development."

"Where is Terrance?"

"Left for a long vacation with an undisclosed destination. We've requested warrants for his house and there's a KALOF out for him." Katrina found her keys. "Sid wasn't at home so we'll run past there now and see if he's back." Her phone beeped. "Scrap that. Warrant came through for Terrance's house so we'll grab the constable and take a look."

Trev glanced up at the balcony over the bookshop but there was no sign of Charlotte.

Soon. This will be over soon.

He headed to his patrol car.

———

Charlotte dialled with shaking fingers. Mrs McKenzie had been cautious about providing Zoe's number until Charlotte explained the relationship and that her sister was nowhere to be found. She'd sighed and made an odd comment about Zoe being the most popular person in town. "Even her agent lost her number and rang me for it." She provided the information and hung up before Charlotte could ask more.

As the phone rang, Charlotte went onto the balcony. The protesters were gone. Trev's patrol car was driving toward the police station.

"You have reached the number for Zoe Carter Dean. Leave a message." It was a recorded digital voice.

"Hi...um, Zoe? It's Charlie. Charlotte. I got your note. Um. I've been to the creative hub and couldn't find you. I'd like to see you if that's okay? Call me back anytime. Anytime."

Articulate. Not.

The SUV sped past, heading out of town. Leaving, perhaps? It disappeared over the hill. Charlotte glanced at the sky. Although the clouds were low and heavy, they were slow moving.

There was time for a walk down to the pool to clear her

head. Stop the insistent voices telling her Zoe had regretted the note. Was avoiding Charlotte. Her heart knew better. There was a simple explanation for her sister's absence and if all else failed, Trev would help find her.

CHAPTER FORTY

As he unlocked the door to the station, Trev had a phone message from Mrs Munro with a screenshot of the contract she'd signed. He sent it to his computer and put the kettle on, then changed his mind and took some bottled water from the fridge. The truck driver was gone and would be charged in Kyneton.

The contract from Mrs Munro was nothing more than a typed agreement for her to sell the property to a development group. He didn't recognise the name so did an internet search. It led to Terrance. The signature representing the group was indecipherable with no actual name below, just 'on behalf of'.

"Probably not even legal." He reached for his phone and dialled Katrina. After giving her the information, he followed up on the SUV hire car. The rental company asked for an email address and told him they'd look into the details.

Frustrated, Trev stalked to the empty cell. When Sid ran the station, he hadn't cleaned the cells in months, if not years. There was so little to clean that it was pure laziness to let it get into the state Trev inherited. The driver had left rubbish on the floor. A squashed juice box and empty chip packet he must have had in his pockets. There was a cigarette butt and that annoyed him more. Smoking was not permitted in here. It looked like Sid's butts which he rolled himself.

Trev sent a request through to Kyneton to ask the driver where he got the cigarette and a brief outline of why he was interested. Might be a coincidence. Or did the men know each other and shared a smoke?

When the phone rang again, he was ready to throw it across the room. One problem after another and roadblocks at every turn. It was Rosie and he took a deep breath before answering.

"Mum?"

She whispered. "Trev, Marguerite is here."

"At your house?"

"Yes. Arrived all upset. Crying. Told her I'd put the kettle on."

He rolled his eyes. What was the woman playing at now?

"Dear, I think you should come over because she's saying odd things. She said Sid is doing something terrible and she can't bear it any longer."

"Okay. Are you alright for a few minutes?"

"I think so."

"On my way."

This better not be another distraction. Marguerite had a history of dramatics and Sid might have put her up to keeping Trev busy while he committed some crime. He sent a message to Katrina and locked the station.

———

Charlotte followed the river until she reached the top of the falls. She stopped and caught her breath at the stunning view. The recent rain had turned the river into rapids, forcing the water into a mighty torrent that crashed into the churning pool below.

Spray drifted across the pool to the bottleneck, where the

banks barely coped with the volume of water fighting its way through.

A clump of branches fell over the falls only to be hurried to the re-formed river. Charlotte took her camera out to follow their progress as the water snatched at them, tossing pieces from side to the other until they disappeared around the curve.

Partway down the steps she slipped, grabbing a post in time to stop herself falling. The sound of the waterfall thundered as she glanced at her phone. She groaned. There was next to no signal here. Charlotte retraced her steps, until almost at the top again before the signal returned.

As she stared at the phone, a call came in and her heart jumped as she recognised the number.

"Zoe? Hi."

A long pause on a bad line. Then, "Charlotte...help. I'm hurt."

"Where are you? What happened?"

"Fell. Near...a...pool."

"Pool? Near the waterfall?"

"Yes. Hurts. Please come."

"Zoe, stay on the line. Zoe?" The call was disconnected. From here she could see the pool but little of the grassed area around it, let alone under the canopy of trees. The path was treacherous even when you knew it. Had her sister been out here since yesterday?

She tapped Trev's number as she started down again. It went to his voicemail. "Trev, I'm at the falls. Going to the pool. Zoe called and she's hurt. Near the pool if you can come and bring help. Please hurry."

A few more steps down and she tried ringing Zoe. The signal was intermittent and she gave up. She needed to get to her sister.

———

Marguerite slumped on the sofa in Rosie's living room, clutching a tissue pulled from a box on her lap. A pile of used tissues spilled onto the sofa. Since Trev arrived, she'd not spoken, only sobbed, and shaken her head.

"You must talk to Trevor, dear. I know you're terribly upset but you are quite safe here." Rosie pressed her lips together and glanced at Trev.

"Mrs Browne, what if I ask some questions and you answer what you want. Are you hurt at all?"

The woman hesitated then shook her head.

"That's good. Is your husband hurt?"

Her head shot up and she stared at Trev as if sizing him up. No answer but the tears dried up.

"Where is Sid?"

"He brought that woman to our house. He let her stay with us and didn't care if she was mean to me and rude. So rude."

"Which woman?"

Again, a head shake and a new tissue to dab her eyes.

Trev's phone beeped. An email from the rental company. *Later.*

"I told him to send her away before we got in more trouble. I told him to leave Darcy alone. It wasn't the boy's fault his mother ran off with Octavia's husband all those years ago but the man had promised Sid he'd get him started as a land owner with a gift of a block from his next development but then he left and we had nothing. Again."

Trev blinked. Rosie's mouth had dropped open.

The floodgates must have opened because Marguerite pushed the tissues aside and straightened her back. "Yes, all because of a handshake arrangement with a corrupt land developer, Sid has let himself get involved in even worse affairs. And they are all corrupt. Jonas is the worst of them. I told Sid to let things be but no, he'd just roll another cigarette and tell me the sins of the mother would come back to haunt Darcy Forest."

"Did you phone Darcy recently and use that term? Sins of the mother?"

"Of course not. I don't even have a phone anymore or access to the car which is why I walked all the way here. I had to leave after I begged Sid to stop his vendetta against Charlotte and he laughed at me."

An icy shard pierced Trev's heart.

Rosie gasped. "Marguerite, what do you mean?"

Trev opened the email and almost dropped his phone when he read the information. "Who is the woman staying with you? What is her name and where is she from?"

"She calls herself Sally. After Charlotte destroyed Sid's career, he insisted we go to find a woman who used to know her. And then she just fronts up the other week and Sid is making friends with her and ignoring me."

On his feet, Trev dialled a number. "Her name isn't Sally, is it? Her name is Alison."

A strangled sound came from Rosie's throat and Trev reached down and squeezed her shoulder. "I'll get someone over here and go find our girl."

He headed for the door as Bryce answered with "What now?"

"We've got a problem. Charlotte's in danger."

CHAPTER FORTY-ONE

ALL THE WAY TO THE BOTTOM OF THE STEPS SOMETHING nagged at Charlotte. Zoe's voice was familiar. Was it possible she would have some deep memory of her voice tucked away when so much else was missing? It didn't add up because after so many years, her voice would change. Mature with age.

The other thing was the phone signal. How had Zoe got enough signal to return her call? If she'd been here overnight, presumably she'd have tried to call for help, for an emergency service if she'd had no other numbers. Would a battery last so long? More importantly, how did she get signal from the pool when Charlotte couldn't get it even halfway down there? There were times she'd got enough signal to get messages at the pool but not under heavy cloud cover.

Something was wrong.

There was a short cut through the trees, away from the main path, and Charlotte took it. Her senses were on high alert and she jumped when a bird flew close to her.

A narrow, worn track wound through dense undergrowth. She imagined it was the one the kangaroos used to reach the pool. Here, it was quieter and colder. The trees blocked out the sky.

There was a glimmer of water through the bushes and she slowed, taking care of where she stepped to avoid making a sound. The pool was overflowing, water reaching over the grassy surrounds almost all the way to the trees.

Was any of this real—these panicked thoughts of danger? Imagination ran wild. The same all those times thinking she'd seen...Alison.

The breath left her body.

That was the voice on the phone. Alison called her from Zoe's number.

Alison was here.

Alison has Zoe.

She stifled a scream. Her hands clenched into fists and she fought the need to run.

A slight movement caught her attention. A figure leaned against a tree trunk.

It wasn't Alison.

The person's arms were extended up. Were they trying to climb the tree? That was the only way Charlotte's mind could frame what her eyes saw. Because it made no sense that the person's wrists were bound and attached to a rope thrown over a branch. But something made the person look at Charlotte.

The terrified expression on Zoe's face broke Charlotte's heart.

CHAPTER FORTY-TWO

TREV DIALLED CHARLOTTE OVER AND OVER, EACH TIME going to voicemail. He slammed the car to a stop outside the bookshop and was up the stairs in seconds. Pounding on the door and calling for her did nothing, so he let himself in with the key Rosie gave him as he left.

She wasn't there. But nor was there any sign of a struggle. Her laptop was open and beside it, a notepad with Zoe's name and a mobile number.

He dialled.

"Hello?" A woman answered.

"Is this Zoe Dean?"

Let it be.

"Sure. Sure, this is she."

"Can I ask your whereabouts please?"

The silence was long. In the background was a rushing sound, relentless and familiar. She finally answered. "Who is asking?"

"I'm looking for Charlotte."

Laughter. "Aren't we all."

Bile rose in Trev's throat and he fought it down. "Alison,

we've met. You called yourself Sally Austin and claimed you'd seen Darcy Forest near a fire. Remember?"

"No. I said I saw a young man with freckles wearing a hoodie with a pine tree on the back. Accuracy is important."

"Why did you try to harm Darcy?"

"I was returning a favour to a friend. You see, mister policeman, when someone does something good for me, I am loyal. But when people are evil, they get what they deserve. And your girlfriend is evil."

"Alison, where is Charlotte?"

"I hope you gave her a nice kiss goodbye."

"Alison!"

The line was disconnected. He redialled and it went to voicemail. Without bothering with a message, Trev hurtled out of the apartment and down the steps.

CHAPTER FORTY-THREE

"I'M HERE." CHARLOTTE THREW HER ARMS AROUND ZOE and immediately released her to inspect the ropes. "Are you alright?"

"Shh…she's waiting for you." Zoe whispered. "I can't free myself." She rattled the branch which was too high for her to reach.

Charlotte went to the end of the branch and jumped, grabbing its end. It wasn't thick and as soon as she put weight on it, it groaned. She worked her way along, pulling it lower.

With the branch at a steep angle, Zoe managed to slide the rope closer to Charlotte.

"Watch for it falling."

"Rather be free."

Both women went dead weight, straining to break the branch and with a loud crack, it snapped and fell, narrowly missing Zoe. Pain replaced the fear in her eyes and she moaned as the rope dragged her arms downward.

"I have nothing to cut the rope but we can slide it to the broken end. Then we have to run."

Zoe's face was pale by the time Charlotte manipulated the

rope until it was free. "This way." She pointed to where she'd come from and Zoe stumbled through low bushes.

Charlotte checked the pool area but there was no sign of anyone. Wherever Alison was, she had no way of knowing the area as well as Charlotte. She caught up with Zoe, reaching an arm around her waist. "I know somewhere safe."

Problem solving pushed aside the fear, bringing a sense of clarity to Charlotte's mind. She had Zoe. Nobody was going to harm her and nobody would ever separate them again. Charlotte directed them both through thick bushland, stopping and retracting their steps a couple of times. The waterfall grew louder until Charlotte decided they had to take a chance.

She put her mouth closer to Zoe's ear. "So loud here! Are you okay to climb a few steps if I help?"

Zoe nodded but her shoulders were slumped and exhaustion etched her face. Her hands were still bound and her wrists bleeding. But there was a fire in her eyes and Charlotte felt the same. Together they'd get through this.

"Stay put for a sec. I need to see if the way is clear." Charlotte helped Zoe lean against a tree and slipped between some bushes close to the path to the top of the falls. There was no sign of anyone. Not even Trev, who she most wanted to see heading her way. She checked her phone which flicked between no signal and one bar. After typing a message, she hit send and just hoped at some point it would find its way to his phone.

Back with Zoe, she guided her to the path.

At the steps, Zoe hesitated, her eyes wide at the steepness of the ascent.

"Only a few steps. I have somewhere for us to hide for a while."

Those few steps were difficult. Zoe stumbled over the terrain and Charlotte supported her. Without the free use of her hands, Zoe struggled to grip what railings were intact.

Behind, in the distance, a woman shouted. The words were swallowed by the falls.

"She wants to kill you." Zoe said. "She went up the other path to phone you with my phone."

"I know. But help is coming, okay?" Charlotte looked behind. Still no sign of Alison. "Here. See that ledge." She pointed. "It will take a big step to reach but I'll go first and help you."

The logistics of this hadn't occurred to Charlotte. They picked their way across from the steps over rocks until there was a gap between them and the ledge. The waterfall was almost close enough to touch and misty spray rained on them. Leaving Zoe on the edge of the last rock, Charlotte jumped across a deep fissure to the ledge. She turned and reached out. "Give me your hands and then step over. Lean toward me and I'll help you across."

Zoe extended her hands, the rope trailing beneath them. "I don't think I can."

"You have to." Charlotte braced her legs and took Zoe's hands in hers. "Big step and I'll do the rest."

Still hesitant, Zoe glanced over her shoulder. There was another shout, much closer, and Zoe's head swung back to Charlotte, her face set. With one motion she catapulted across the gap, almost knocking Charlotte over as she landed awkwardly. "Whoops."

Charlotte steadied them both and slid along the ledge behind the falls. There was only enough space for them to walk one at a time and as the roar overhead intensified, Charlotte questioned her decision. Rosie had said it opened up but where? It was almost dark behind the wall of water and Charlotte slowed to make sure of every step before she took it. Zoe gripped her hand and all she knew was she had to keep her sister safe.

Please, phone. Send the message.

If it didn't, how would Trev find them?

CHAPTER FORTY-FOUR

"WE'VE GOT MAYBE AN HOUR OF LIGHT. LESS ONCE WE GET down the pool. You'll need flashlights and ropes and—"

"Trev, we've got this." Katrina cut him off. "AirPol is under half an hour away. If nothing else, their floodlights from above will give us as much light as we need but I intend to find them before then. Okay?"

Trev, Katrina, and Bryce had met at the carpark. The SUV was parked there, locked and with no sign of its driver. Trev checked his phone every minute, it seemed. When a message came through, he opened it with fingers that barely worked. Rosie.

Have you found her?

Not yet, Mum. We're at the falls now.

Look for the ledge. She listens.

That was debatable. How many times had he asked her to avoid danger? To tell him where she was and what was happening.

Bryce took the phone from his hand and sent a message before giving it back to Trev. "What are you doing?"

"Rosie needs the truth, dude."

Trev read the message.

Bryce here. Nobody leaves until we find Detective Dean. Rest assured.

"Thanks, mate."

"Not letting anyone hurt her or her sister. Put the phone away and help us plan."

A few minutes later, Trev was back in the patrol car, sirens, and lights on as he sped through town. Or at least to the turn-off after the bookshop. He'd driven along the river in the past and knew it better than anyone. A four-wheel drive would have been helpful, but at least he could get himself close to the top of the falls.

Katrina and Bryce had dropped everything when he'd called. They'd left the constable at Terrance's house but called for assistance from the local towns. In a few minutes, every exit from Kingfisher Falls would be covered.

He climbed out of the patrol car at the fenced area. Using bolt cutters from the boot, he made short work of the fence and carefully drove over the dropped mesh. The cleared section made for easier driving but soon he was on the narrow fire track and avoiding potholes and rocks.

At the end of the track he abandoned the patrol car after emptying it of everything he could carry.

Before getting a dozen paces along the river, the messages came. A voicemail from Charlotte sent over an hour ago.

"Trev, I'm at the falls. Going to the pool. Zoe called and she's hurt. Near the pool if you can come and bring help. Please hurry."

He doubled back and collected the first aid kit, reading a text message that followed. This was sent later.

Alison somewhere around falls. Have Zoe. Going behind waterfall. Be careful of Alison.

After the rare use of an expletive, Trev sent messages to Bryce and Katrina with the new information. Then, he ran.

CHAPTER FORTY-FIVE

"STOP FOR A SEC, I'M GOING TO USE THE FLASHLIGHT ON MY phone." Charlotte had to raise her voice to be heard over the water.

She'd avoided using the flashlight, conscious of keeping as much battery charge in case they were there a while. But the few seconds she turned it on were worth it. The cavern Rosie had mentioned was right here.

"Here, let's go a bit inside and sit."

The cavern wasn't deep so she helped Zoe onto the stone ground at the back. "I'll find something to free you."

"My pocket. There's a box cutter in my keys." Zoe moved to give Charlotte access to her jean pocket. "Those idiots didn't even bother checking I had anything once they took the phone."

Charlotte opened the tiny box cutter then placed her phone on the floor to give enough light. "I'll be careful."

"Just get this rope off. Any way you have to."

"You said those idiots. Not just Alison?" Charlotte sliced a thread at a time.

"She rang my phone pretending to be your friend. Said you were up at her place and had fallen and could she come and get me. Someone was staying with you waiting for an ambulance."

This was a carefully laid plan. Alison was exactly the person Charlotte had believed.

"I was in such a hurry I didn't even lock the door when she arrived. But when we arrived at this horrible little place in the pouring rain, I rushed inside and found a gun pointed at me."

"Oh, Zoe. I can't imagine how frightening that was."

"Not as frightening as not knowing where you were. They laughed when I asked. I thought they'd hurt you."

Charlotte stopped cutting to look at Zoe. Her sister's eyes were filled with tears. Careful to put the cutter aside, she wrapped her arms around her, alarmed at how cold she was. For a moment she just held Zoe, then released her and slid her own coat off. "This is a bit wet on the outside but will help you warm up."

"You need it."

"Nope. And no arguing." Charlotte forced a smile and put the coat around Zoe's shoulders before going back to cutting the rope.

"Who are these people, Charlie?"

"The woman is Alison Sharnie Tomkins."

"Oh. Her."

"How do you even know...never mind. We have a lot to talk about." Had Zoe always known where Charlotte was and never once reached out? She pushed aside the negative thoughts. "Where she took you? Was there an obnoxious man with no dress sense and a woman who most likely ignored you?"

Zoe chuckled, a deep, musical laugh that made Charlotte smile. "Got them in one. Forgot to mention he smells bad. But she didn't want me there. And she really didn't want Alison there."

Interesting. Sid and Alison in cahoots but not with Marguerite's approval.

The cutter went through the final thread and Charlotte gently removed the rope. Zoe muttered some colourful words. Her wrists were raw.

"How long were you there…at the tree?" Charlotte didn't even have a tissue to wet and tend to the skin.

"A couple of hours. Not sure. She had a gun and that Sid person had tied my wrists at the cabin. He pushed me into the car and then they had an argument. His wife had vanished earlier. He was going to look for her." Zoe leaned back against the wall of the cavern. "There's a clean handkerchief in my top pocket."

"Sorry, feel like I'm getting a bit personal rummaging around here." Worry flooded Charlotte at how grey Zoe suddenly looked. "Got it. Give me a minute and I'll get some water on it. Waterfall special."

Charlotte turned the flashlight off and handed Zoe the phone. "Be right back."

For a moment she stood behind the immense power of the waterfall, unable to see through to the world outside, spell-bound by its majesty. When the weather warmed up and the river settled, she'd make a picnic and invite Trev to lunch here.

Under better circumstances.

She held Zoe's handkerchief out, careful not to let it into the actual cascade but allowing the mist to soak it. This might ease the pain of her wrists a bit.

"Not one more step, Doctor."

Charlotte froze. Alison had found her.

CHAPTER FORTY-SIX

TREV WAS ALMOST AT THE BOTTOM OF THE STEPS WHEN HE saw Sid. Somehow, he'd never considered the man would be here, not with the difficult terrain and Sid's renowned hatred for exerting himself, yet here he was.

Realising he'd not been seen, Trev squatted and messaged the others with his location and who he could see.

Sid was exactly where Trev needed to be. He was off the steps across some rocks near the waterfall. From a hazy memory of having explored the area as a kid, Trev remembered a gap between there and the ledge. Not wide, but the rocks were wet and it wouldn't take much to misjudge and fall. Sid was staring at the gap as if working out if it was worth the risk.

Which meant what? Did he suspect Charlotte might be behind the waterfall? Was Alison already there? Before he lost control of his emotions, Trev acted.

Gun unholstered, he stood and took the rest of the steps to the rocks.

"Sid Browne, you are under arrest—"

"Bull." Sid glared at him over his shoulder. "Where'd you come from?"

"Hands behind your head and face me."

"Gonna shoot me? Then shoot me. Might as well." Sid turned, one of his hands concealed at his side. "Lost everything."

"I told you to raise your hands. I want to see your hands."

"Nothing to see. Marguerite's left me. Every bad thing that's happened to me is thanks to Darcy Forest's mother and Charlotte and you."

"Stop blaming people for your choices, Sid. Last chance to show me your hands."

"You don't have the guts to shoot me, whelp."

"But I do." Bryce appeared from further down the steps, gun pointed at Sid. "Where is Alison Tomkins?"

Sid smirked. "She's a real piece of work, that one. Makes Jonas and Terrance look like angels. And she won't mess around getting what she wants."

"What do you mean?" Trev took another step.

"What do you think I mean? I hope your precious Charlotte knows how to pray, 'cos she's gonna need to."

He raised his concealed hand.

CHAPTER FORTY-SEVEN

THERE WAS SILENCE IN THE CAVERN, APART FROM THE relentless pounding of the water.

Charlotte stared at Alison, surprised she wasn't feeling anything. No terror, despite the gun pointing at her from a few feet away. Not even pity for the woman who'd gone to such lengths to prove Charlotte's diagnosis wrong, only to show herself anyway.

"Why the games? Why follow me around town and refuse to talk to me?"

"Talk about what? Old friends, catching up to reminisce about the time one of them destroyed the other person's life?"

"Sure. Why don't we do that?" It was interesting to see uncertainty flicker into Alison's eyes as Charlotte slipped into her Doctor Dean voice. "I think you intended to kill your husband. In order to protect yourself, you came to me, wanting some form of insanity diagnosis before you committed the crime...just in case something went wrong, I imagine. Instead, I diagnosed the real Alison and that ruined everything. How am I doing so far?"

"Sounds like a lot of effort."

"So does this." Charlotte gestured around. "Weeks of planning. Stalking me. Luring my sister to you. Kidnapping her. And getting me here. I think you are expert at planning, but I was onto you and foiled your plans about your husband."

Alison took a step forward. "You know nothing. And where is your sister?"

"She went up the steps. By now she'll be safe and the police will arrive soon."

"I don't believe you."

Charlotte shrugged. From the corner of her eye she saw a light flicker on then off again. Her phone must have got a message and Zoe had covered it.

Stay still, Zoe.

"She wasn't on the steps. I looked. Ran halfway up before Sid told me about this little hidey-hole. He'll be here any second and you are going to be sorry, Charlotte. You and your sister."

"How did you know about her?" Keep her talking.

"I know everything about you. Been to the house you grew up more than once. Inside it. Found all kinds of interesting information about you, and her, and your crazy mother. Tried to visit your mother but they wouldn't let me in. And then the lovely Sid Browne came calling and how could I resist the chance to come to this excuse for a town and give you what you deserve?"

"Leave my sister alone!" Zoe was somewhere in the darkness, on her feet from the shuffling sound. "I have a weapon."

Alison burst into laughter and turned her gun in the direction of Zoe's voice.

"Zoe get down!"

The crack of a gunshot rang through the cavern but it was from outside. A man bellowed in pain.

Alison spun toward the sound.

Charlotte rushed at her, crashing into her side-on.

They both hit the ground hard.

The gun flew from Alison's hand and slid across the stone

toward the waterfall. Charlotte scrambled after it on her hands and knees and reached for it as Alison grabbed her ankle screaming "Mine, mine, mine!"

If Charlotte had to push it over the side, she would but Alison was clawing her way along Charlotte's legs as if driven by mania.

Charlotte got her fingertips on the handle but Alison was on top of her, hands around her throat, knees in her back.

And then the squeezing stopped. The hands fell away.

"I told you I have a weapon."

Somehow, Charlotte squirmed from under Alison.

Zoe was behind her holding a handful of her short hair in one hand and the point of the box cutter at her neck with the other. Charlotte retrieved the gun and held it on Alison. "Don't even move an eyelid, Alison. Nobody hurts my sister."

The screams outside subsided.

A light flashed around along the ledge and footsteps approached. "Charlie! Charlotte."

"We're here. Hurry."

Trev burst out of the darkness, gun drawn. His eyes found Charlotte's. She had thought she had no feelings but the fear and concern on his face sent a jolt of relief through her so strong that her hands were shaking and her legs were on the verge of collapsing. In a second, he was at her side.

"Gun, Charlie. I've got it." He took it from her, put the safety on and it disappeared into his holster. "Zoe, hello, can you step back for me?" His own gun was trained on Alison, whose eyes darted from side to side.

Zoe straightened slowly, grimacing. She needed help and Charlotte didn't even think of what she was doing as she ducked between Alison and Trev to reach her sister.

In that couple of seconds, Alison rolled away from Zoe toward the cascade.

"Alison, stop now!" Trev yelled.

She jumped into the torrent and disappeared.

CHAPTER FORTY-EIGHT

"ARE YOU WARM ENOUGH?" ROSIE ASKED FOR THE twentieth time, tucking a blanket a bit more over Charlotte's lap. "I'll make more tea."

"Rosie, I'm fine, I promise. Stay here." Charlotte was curled up on an armchair in Rosie's living room where Trev insisted she stay until he arrived. For once she was happy to do what he said.

"I can't wait to meet Zoe. She saved your life, darling!"

Charlotte smiled. "She is amazing and you will love her."

"I already do. Didn't think when Trev brought you to meet me last year, I'd end up with two daughters!"

Mayhem jumped onto the arm of the chair and stared at Charlotte. She knew better than to extend her hand, so ignored him. "I let Trev down."

"No, you didn't."

"I let Alison get...away." Tears welled in her eyes. Through this whole thing she'd held it together but now in the safety of the house and in the care of someone who loved her, it was all too much. "Zoe was in so much pain and all I wanted...was to...reach her. Trev couldn't stop Alison in time."

Rosie patted her hand. "You do know this is all just a

response to being in such danger? Trev isn't cross with you and Zoe will be just fine. A night in hospital will get her back on her feet and then we're all going to have dinner together."

She was right. And Zoe was dehydrated and exhausted and needed her wrists tending. Tomorrow, she would go and bring her home and she would stay at the apartment for as long as she wanted. They had a lifetime of catching up to do.

"You've only told me bits of what happened after that dreadful Alison threw herself off the ledge. What is it with people and that waterfall lately? Anyway, what was the story with Sid?"

Charlotte wiped her eyes. "He had a gun and was trying to take a shot at Trev but fell down the gap between the rocks instead."

Rosie covered her hand with her mouth but her eyes gave away her mirth.

"Don't laugh or I will too. It isn't funny, at least not for him. And he could have shot someone but instead he has broken bones and will be in even more trouble with the police. Where is Marguerite?"

"Arrested. Yes, it has been quite a day. The young constable popped by earlier and took her off, something about assisting Sid and Alison in holding Zoe and other things. She'll blab no doubt and get out of too much trouble. Did I tell you I had a text message from Detective Bryce? Here, I'll send it to you."

When Charlotte saw the message, the tears threatened again. To stop them, she found the photo Trev sent her the other night from the study. "Look at this. Mayhem is like a normal cat."

Rosie zoomed in. "He's very cute but what is that on Trev's computer behind him?"

Charlotte hadn't noticed. "Nice house."

"Nice house, for sale."

"Oh. I guess sooner or later he has to move out. Not long until your wedding."

"Don't change the subject. It is a nice *family* house for sale."

"Mum, stop teasing Charlie." Trev wandered in, exhaustion lining his face.

"How did you get in so quietly?" Rosie asked. "I'm putting the kettle on." She headed to the kitchen.

Trev took off his police belt and left it on the other armchair before kneeling next to Charlie. Mayhem hissed at him and stalked away.

"Are you doing okay?" Trev touched Charlotte's face so gently she thought she'd imagined it. "Sorry it took so long to get back."

She captured his hand in hers and kissed his fingers. "You are so cold."

"You are nice and warm now. Have you heard from Zoe?"

"She called before using the hospital's phone seeing as the detectives have hers. I think she's more annoyed she can't come home tonight than anything."

"Zoe is very brave. And so are you."

For the third time the tears returned. They poured down her cheeks as she struggled for words. "I messed...up. Alison...my fault."

"Stop it." Trev reached for the tissue box Marguerite had earlier. "Only a couple left but take them. For a start, none of this is your fault. You did everything right, sweetheart. Having no phone signal made it harder but we got there in the end. And as for Alison, much to his disgust, Bryce spotted her floundering about downstream and went for a swim."

"She's alive?"

"She is. And this time she won't be avoiding what's been coming to her for a long time. I would imagine you'd have no trouble getting the board's decision reversed and go back into practice, assuming you want to."

The thought helped Charlotte manage her emotions and

she dried her face. "Sorry to overreact. Adrenaline. And I'm happy in the bookshop but I would like my reputation back."

"You faced your past, Charlie. I respect you so much." He leaned forward. "And love you even more."

"Don't mind me, just bringing some tea." Rosie put a tray onto the coffee table. "Although I'm wondering if a gin might be better."

"Tea sounds good, Mum. Then a shower. Then a gin." Trev got to his feet and kissed Rosie. "Thanks for looking after Charlie."

Charlotte glanced from one to the other. This was her family but now she had Zoe as well. There was a lot to discover but at long last there was time and opportunity.

What is in that envelope, Rosie?

Later. This wasn't the time and if the news was bad, her emotions couldn't deal with it. Did Trev know what was in there? He'd suggested going back into practice. She knew he loved her. But what if Rosie regretted her offer to sell the bookshop?

"Okay, Charlie?" Trev brought a cup of tea to her. "You look so tired."

"I might forego the gin and sleep instead."

Rosie's eyebrows raised. "Never thought I'd hear such a thing."

It was out of character, but all of a sudden Charlotte longed to lie down and have a quiet place to sob until there were no silly tears left.

CHAPTER FORTY-NINE

ZOE AND CHARLOTTE STOOD BY THE WINDOW OF THE BACK bedroom as night fell. This was Zoe's third night in the apartment. The wounds were healing and her strength returning after plenty of sleep and good food.

"We're so lucky." Charlotte sighed. "Finding that lonely grave out there and discovering the truth behind it gave me a lot to think about. And when Harmony told me I had a sister..."

"Did you ever find out how she knew?"

"Nope. And the last thing she said to me was that my future had changed and all she saw was happiness for me."

Zoe put an arm around her shoulders. "I'm so proud of you. Always have been."

Over one of many conversations going late into the night, Zoe had let Charlotte into her life a little. There was much unsaid but at last Charlotte understood some of the reasons for Zoe's absence.

As an only child, Zoe had adored her adopted sister but Angelica was jealous and pushed her away. It was part of her mental illness but Zoe as a teenager had no way to understand it. Angelica told Zoe she had to send Charlotte away because there wasn't enough money for both daughters. So, Zoe left.

Charlotte's heart broke for the young woman sacrificing so much and for no reason. Zoe spent years wandering the world alone and came home to Brisbane to open her studio, intending to see her sister. It was when Angelica and Charlotte had moved away from the city and by the time they returned, she was busy in her own life and unwilling to allow her mother to ruin what she'd worked so hard to build.

"Hey. I can feel your heart racing, Charlie. Isn't it time to get ready for dinner?"

"Yes, it is. And I cannot wait for you to meet Rosie and see Trevor in a better light."

"Better than rescuing us? Better than appearing in uniform at an appropriate moment?"

With a grin, Charlotte closed the window and locked it. "Do you fancy a man in uniform?"

"I didn't mean —"

"Teasing. One thing you will learn about me is my strange sense of humour."

"And I'm often too serious. Makes for a good cover story as an artist."

"Starving artist?"

"Now you mention it, I am rather hungry!"

Laughter was becoming a common sound in the apartment and Charlotte loved it.

———

Doug sent not one, but two bottles of French Champagne to the table, both on the house. Lewis had joined them for dinner and the restaurant was full, music and laughter creating a joyful backdrop as everyone got to know Zoe.

The conversation turned to the case and Trev updated them.

Sid was recovering from surgery and had a long list of charges to answer. Terrance was stopped trying to leave the country and might well share a cell with Sid.

"But what about Jonas?" Rosie asked.

"Can't pin anything on him. Not yet. The so-called business broker looks good for Cecil's murder but we haven't found him yet. Sid set the fire. Marguerite says so, anyway."

Lewis leaned forward. "I believe Darcy is exonerated."

"He is. Alison was found on surveillance at two banks depositing funds into his account. It was all part of a set up by Terrance to obtain his land. Instead of selling up cheaply when he had the chance, Darcy began making inroads of repaying the rates debt. Sid offered a way to get him off the land which also suited his need for revenge against the family."

Zoe looked from one to the other. "I've been here for a very short time but from the sound of it, there are crimes here which span some months."

Charlotte made a sad face. "Ever since I got here. If you are wise, Zoe, you'll leave before I corrupt you."

"Too late. Not going anywhere."

Rosie glanced at Lewis and he nodded.

What are you up to?

"Speaking of not going anywhere. Zoe, you don't have a home yet?" Rosie had the strangest look on her face.

"Unfortunately, the place I was going to buy fell through but I'll be looking again tomorrow, much as I love staying with my sister." She smiled at Charlotte. "I'm sure she'd like her place back."

"I'm sure Charlie loves having you there and there's plenty of room."

"Mum?"

"Hush, dear. Now, I know in my heart there will be more than one wedding in the Sibbritt family in the future—"

"Rosie!"

"You hush as well, darling. No point denying what all of us

can see which is the love between my son," she grabbed Trev's hand, "and you." Her other hand took Charlotte's. "I've thought a lot about this and I know you love the apartment, but you also love a garden so I see a house in your future."

Where is this heading?

Rosie released both hands and dug about in her handbag.

When she pulled out the envelope, Charlotte's heart dropped.

Rosie thinks I'll marry Trev and leave.

"What you do with it is your choice. If you want to live there forever then do so, but if you move, you'll be free to let someone else live there. Like Zoe." She held the envelope out to Charlotte. "This is for you. I meant what I said about the bookshop and the apartment and the building not being for sale."

Charlotte opened the envelope and read a brief note.

She shot a look at Rosie, knowing her mouth was open but unable to do anything about it.

Rosie giggled.

"For goodness sake, would someone explain what's going on?"

"I can't. I'll cry and I've done too much of that." Charlotte handed the note to Trev.

"You know, it never occurred to me that you might think this should be your inheritance, son."

Trev read the note, folded it, and handed it to Charlotte. Then, he kissed Rosie's cheek. "You are without doubt the most amazing mother in the world. And you know I care nothing about inheritance. I want you here for a long time." He kissed her again. "Lewis, I imagine you know what just happened, so for Zoe's benefit...last year I drove here with Charlotte to see if she and Mum got on. Charlie needed a change of scenery and Mum needed someone to help with the bookshop with the view of selling it to them."

"I know some of this." Zoe said.

"Mum retracted the offer to sell. But she has given Charlie the building—including the apartment and the bookshop—as a gift."

Zoe tilted her head at Rosie. "Why?"

"Why not? Charlie breathed new life into me. Taught me how to be a sleuth."

Trev groaned.

"Made me happy. And makes my son happy. But the truth is, even if she didn't love Trevor, I'd still give her all of this because I love her as if she's my own child."

Doug arrived at the table. "Not sure if we are all happy here or sad, but it might be time to refill those glasses."

Once he left, and they toasted each other several times, Rosie winked at Charlotte. "Now that all the book club ladies have gone, we might have to get something started ourselves. Imagine all the mysteries we can solve under the guise of a book club!"

———

Trev and Charlotte sat on the back step of the apartment. Zoe was upstairs. The evening was late but for Trev, he'd never felt so alive. If only his father was alive, his life would be complete.

"What are you thinking?"

"Do you remember at Christie and Martin's wedding we sat on a bench and talked? You told me you were coming to live here. And you kissed me."

Charlotte leaned against him. "Of course, I remember."

"I thought I'd made the worst mistake of my life. And yet, it was the right thing to do. My Dad had a saying and it stayed with me when I thought of you coming here."

"What is the saying?"

"Plant a seed, let it grow into whatever it will be. Nurture it, because one day you'll want its shade and shelter."

"Hm." Charlotte moved so she could look at him. "You

planted the seed in my head about moving here so I could follow my own path. You put me in the way of a woman you knew would give me the love I'd never had."

"I guess so."

"And now you want me to feed and house you?"

She was teasing.

"Actually, I was hoping I could feed and house you."

There. He'd said it.

Charlotte's eyes were deep pools of emotion. A man could get lost in them.

A man is lost in them.

"Yes."

His heart jumped.

"Yes?"

"Yes, I think you can consider the idea of feeding and housing me...but Rosie and Lewis deserve their special time and I would like it very much if you didn't make a formal... suggestion until after their wedding. If you get my drift."

"I've waited this long, sweetheart. I can wait longer."

Her smile was beautiful. She was beautiful. Charlotte leaned against him again. "Shall we watch the stars for a bit?"

———

She might have fallen asleep for a little while, but with Trev she was safe to do so, even outside on a cold night.

Charlotte didn't open her eyes. She just listened to the steady beat of his heart and snuggled more into the strength of his arm around her. His father was a wise man, but Trev was just as wise for he had given Charlotte the greatest gift.

A chance to experience a mother's true love. The opportunity to heal. And his unwavering belief in her that was, after all, the reason she'd learned to believe in herself.

Kingfisher Falls was the place she lived, but Trev was her home.

EPILOGUE

"WHAT IF WE'RE LATE?"

"We won't be late."

"But I can't get my hair right and-."

Zoe took Charlotte's hands in hers and levelled a calm gaze which had fast become familiar to Charlotte. "Trust your big sister. We won't be late. And your hair is perfect."

Charlotte took a deep breath. "Fine. I'm calm."

With a laugh, Zoe headed for the fridge and took out a bottle of sparkling wine. "I'm pouring you half a glass while you collect what you need to take to Rosie's house. Then you can drink it and we'll go. Anyone would think this is your wedding!"

She was right. Charlotte was so worried about making Rosie's day perfect she might have been the bride.

But you are not! So sort yourself out.

A few minutes later, with the warmth of the bubbly in her stomach settling her nerves, Charlotte carried a clothes bag downstairs while Zoe locked the door. They climbed into Zoe's car – which was a much nicer and more reliable one than Charlotte's – and headed to Rosie's. The weather was perfect and with a small smile, Charlotte relaxed. Everything would be fine.

"Much as I miss the warmth of Brisbane, I admit to loving this little town of yours, Charlie."

"Doesn't it look pretty with all the trees back in leaf? And the spring flowers through the bushland are amazing. I love that Rosie's bouquet is made of flowers from there and her own garden."

When they parked further up the road to allow the bridal car space, Zoe stopped the motor and turned to Charlotte with a smile. "You look lovely. I'll be around if you need a hand with anything but really, honey, you've got this. And Rosie is lucky to have you there for her."

"I'm the lucky one. Not only for having Rosie in my life, but now," Charlotte reached for Zoe's hand and clasped it. "for having you again."

It was true. Zoe made everything complete. In the past couple of months they'd laughed and cried, talked through night after night, walked for miles around the falls, and got to know each other as sisters. And friends. The news that the only father Charlotte ever knew had passed away a number of years ago was sad. It took a little piece of Charlotte's heart because her memories of him were better than those of Angelica. One day they'd both go to visit his grave and Charlotte could say a proper goodbye.

"Why so solemn?"

"Thinking. But now I'm going to stop thinking and go find the bride and get her to her groom on time!"

———

"When our hearts discover true love it is as though we are home."

In a gorgeous ivory dress, flowers in her hair and eyes shining with tears, Rosie gazed at Lewis as the beautiful words of the wedding ceremony filled the air. Charlotte couldn't take her eyes off her and Lewis, who knelt at Rosie's side, his hands grasping hers.

"A home filled with joy and happiness."

The garden beside the old barn at the Christmas Tree Farm was at capacity with guests, all standing except for the couple. When Rosie had arrived, Lachie beaming as he pushed her wheelchair along the narrow path, Lewis had kissed her forehead and then lowered himself so he was at eye level with his bride.

"Where understanding and respect make it easy to trust each other. And where laughter always conquers tears."

A small sigh rippled through the observers as Daphne Jones, the celebrant, paused to smile at Rosie and Lewis. Charlotte glanced at Trev and their eyes met. Pride and love was what she saw in his face. How wonderful to know your parent was happy again and be there to share their special day.

"Rosie and Lewis, we celebrate this day with you. The love you share overflows from this little garden and becomes a mighty river leading to a long and wonderful life together. And it reminds us to believe in the power of happy endings." Daphne caught Charlotte's eye.

Did you just wink at me?

Trev's lips curled up. He'd seen it.

Maybe recommending their mutual friend from River's End as celebrant was a mistake.

Except Daphne had the guests spellbound as she finished the ceremony and declared Rosie and Lewis a married couple. Applause began as they kissed and then flower petals showered them both as they were surrounded by well-wishers.

———

Music and laughter filled the old barn. The reception was casual, with a long buffet table set one side. Rosie hadn't stopped smiling, at least not anytime Charlotte looked her way, and Lewis never left her side.

"I've never seen Mum so happy." Trev brought two glasses of something bubbly to where Charlotte stood near the door to the garden. "Such a beautiful wedding."

"Darcy and Abbie outdid themselves."

"The whole town outdid itself."

Trev was right. In the weeks since Darcy was exonerated there'd been nothing but support for the family, including a couple of working bees from local residents armed with paint, tools, and goodwill. With Doug now on council, some processes were working more efficiently and approval for the site to be used for events came through just in time.

"Look at you two!" Daphne, arm in arm with her husband John, appeared through the crowd. "Rosie and Lewis were so sweet to invite us to celebrate with them but we're going to head off soon, aren't we, doll?"

"Promised Daph we'd visit the Victorian Alps so it is an early start in the morning."

"I wish you were staying longer. I long to hear all the news from River's End, more than the snippets I get now and then from Christie."

Daphne's eyes widened and she reached into the huge handbag she carried. "I forgot! She sent you one of her signature candles." She handed over a white box with a drawing of the yacht on one side. "Martin does all the artwork of course and Christie's now selling these in her salon and online. Smell it!"

The heady scent of the ocean mingled with the sweetness of jasmine and Charlotte smiled. "Jasmine Sea. Perfect."

A few minutes later, Daphne and John left with a final wave. Trev took Charlotte's hand and led her into the garden. Stars filled the velvet sky and white flower blossoms covered the grass. In the distance, the lights of Kingfisher Falls sparkled across the valley.

"Did you see Zoe and Bryce?" Trev asked.

Charlotte's eyes shot to his. "No, why?"

"Dancing. Quite a nice looking couple."

"Stop match-making, thank you. They are complete opposites and Zoe isn't interested in a relationship. Mind you, she told me she thinks she's too old now but she's not even fifty. But stop, anyway."

Trev laughed and put his arm around her, turning them both to look back at the party. Through the open doors, people danced and talked and celebrated. "Those two will head off to their honeymoon tomorrow and once they get back, I'll move into Lew's house until it sells."

"And when it does?"

"I'll need my own place. And I'll need some help finding it if you'd be willing to do that." Something changed. The tone of his voice, the way his body stilled as if holding his breath in. "Last time we were at a wedding together, you left town."

Charlotte leaned her head on his shoulder. "Nowhere to go. I've got used to Kingfisher Falls and grown attached to certain people."

"Like?"

"Rosie. Lewis. Harpreet of course. Doug, because he cooks the best Italian food. Esther. I quite adore Zoe as well." She smiled to herself. "Yup. Quite attached to them."

"I see."

"Do you?" Tired of teasing him, Charlotte moved so she could lift herself up and kiss Trev. That done, she leaned back against him. "I'm attached to them. But I'm in love with you."

His whole body relaxed and his arms went around her.

"Good."

"Good?" she asked.

"Keeping you close to me means keeping you out of trouble."

"Sure." That was convincing.

He chuckled.

Inside the barn, the lights lowered and the music slowed. Soon, they'd go and find Rosie and Lewis and have a dance or two. But for now, Charlotte was content. She'd gained a family and the love of her life. And if she ever needed to help solve a crime again?

Bring it on.

Dear reader,

We hope you enjoyed reading *Deadly Past*. Please take a moment to leave a review, even if it's a short one. Your opinion is important to us.

Discover more books by Phillipa Nefri Clark at https://www.nextchapter.pub/authors/phillipa-nefri-clark

Want to know when one of our books is free or discounted? Join the newsletter at http://eepurl.com/bqqB3H

Best regards,
Phillipa Nefri Clark and the Next Chapter Team

AUTHOR BIO

Phillipa lives just outside a beautiful town in country Victoria, Australia. She also lives in the many worlds of her imagination and stockpiles stories beside her laptop.

She writes from the heart about love, dreams, secrets, discovery, the sea, the world as she knows it... or wishes it could be. She loves happy endings, heart-pounding suspense, and characters who stay with the reader long after the final page.

With a passion for music, the ocean, animals, reading, and writing, she is often found in the vegetable garden pondering a new story.

BOOKS BY PHILLIPA NEFRI CLARK

The Stationmaster's Cottage

Jasmine Sea

The Secrets of Palmerston House

The Christmas Key

Taming the Wind

Martha

Notes from the Cottage

Deadly Start

Deadly Falls

Deadly Secrets

Deadly Past

The Giving Tree

Colony

Table for Two

Wishing Well

Sculpture

Last Known Contact

Simple Words for Troubled Times (non-fiction)

Audiobooks

The Stationmaster's Cottage (bonus Taming the Wind)

Jasmine Sea (bonus Martha)

The Secrets of Palmerston House (bonus The Christmas Key)

Simple Words for Troubled Times

Deadly Past
ISBN: 978-4-86747-322-1

Published by
Next Chapter
1-60-20 Minami-Otsuka
170-0005 Toshima-Ku, Tokyo
+818035793528

15th May 2021

CPSIA information can be obtained
at www.ICGtesting.com
Printed in the USA
LVHW092109310521
688999LV00001B/82

9 784867 473221